EVIE

JULIA STONEHAM

ISIS
LARGE PRINT
Oxford

First published in Great Britain 2014
by
Allison & Busby

Published in Large Print 2015 by ISIS Publishing Ltd.,
7 Centremead, Osney Mead, Oxford OX2 0ES
by arrangement with
Allison & Busby Limited

CIP data is available for this title from the British Library

ISBN 978–1–4450–9958–3 (hb)
ISBN 978–1–4450–9959–0 (pb)

Printed and bound in Great Britain by
T. J. International Ltd., Padstow, Cornwall

To W.H.S. "a man for all seasons"
Robert Whittington 1480–1535

Prologue

Lower Post Stone Farm
Summer 1957

Under a narrow, humpbacked bridge two children in gumboots are wading in a shallow stream. The girl, nicknamed Kiwi when she was born in New Zealand, is Kathryn Bayliss, a lanky ten-year old. Her hair swings, sleek and dark, onto her shoulders. The boy, known as Pom because he was born soon after his parents arrived back in the Post Stone valley, is younger and solidly built, his blond hair darkening as he grows.

The eighteenth-century bridge, built at the same time as the nearby farmhouse, clumsily incorporates the stones of an ancient clapper crossing. Within its steep arch a lip of limestone protrudes, creating a high shelf about sixteen inches wide, well clear of the water and close to the top of the curved space. The boy has hauled himself up onto this and with his legs swinging over its edge and his head bent forward by the curve of the arch, is examining a bundle of something that he has found there.

"What is it?" the girl asks, craning upwards into shadow. "Is it treasure?"

"Shouldn't think so," the boy says. "Yuck! It's all mouldy and slimy." From a distance they hear their mother's voice, calling them in for their lunch.

In the farmhouse kitchen Georgina Bayliss sets a platter of cheese and pickle sandwiches on the pine table where her husband is sitting, leafing through the farming section of the *Western Morning News*.

"Boots!" he shouts as the children approach the open door.

"Hands!" their mother adds and then, "Look at the state of you two! Where on earth have you been?"

"Under the bridge," the boy says, drying his hands, sidling onto a chair, reaching for a sandwich and biting into it.

"We found something creepy," the girl says. The father lowers his newspaper.

"What d'you mean, 'creepy'?"

"Well it was all rotten and yucky," the boy says with his mouth full. "Old clothes and stuff. As if rats had lived in it."

"And died in it!" the girl giggles.

"Everything was sort of chewed." the boy says. "Looked like it might have been a kind of rucksack but it came to bits and fell into the river."

"And floated downstream. Glug, glug, glug!" the girl says, pouring milk from a pitcher into a glass tumbler.

"There was a zippered bit inside," the boy tells them, "and inside that, tucked into a kind of wallet thing . . . I found this."

"This" is a square of damp card. Whatever had been written on one side is illegible but on the other is a photographic print, the once glossy surface so damaged by damp and degeneration that it proves impossible to make out what is represented by the blurred image. Georgina lays it carefully on the coolest part of the Aga and it isn't until late evening, when the children have gone to bed, that she remembers it. By now it is dry and showing more tonal contrast than when she had examined it earlier.

She is able to make out two figures. A young girl and an older woman. They stand facing the camera, their expressions unreadable. Their clothes and those of the people around them suggest the late thirties. In the background the outline of the familiar tower sets the scene on the Blackpool seafront. Georgina studies the picture for some time and then carries it across the kitchen to where her husband is sitting under a reading lamp, poring over a seed catalogue. Standing behind him she puts her arms round him and leans over him, holding the warped, sepia photograph directly under the light, and after a moment says, "Don't you recognise her, Christo?" He squints at the image.

"The woman or the girl?" he asks.

"The girl," Georgina says. Christopher takes the photo from her hand and, tilting it this way and that, scrutinises it. Slowly, as he examines the set of the girl's wide eyes, the fall of pale hair and the suggestion of uncertainty in the way the oval face is slightly turned to look at the woman beside her, he realises that she is familiar to him.

"Good grief, Georgie!" he says. "It is, isn't it! It's Evie!"

CHAPTER
ONE

Autumn 1945

It was as Hester moved forward again, picking her way back across the muddy yard, that she saw it. She stopped, scanning the face of the abandoned Land Army hostel. There it was again. An unmistakable flicker of light as though someone with a candle or a torch was moving along the upstair passage.

Hester Crocker had left her daughter safely in her playpen, her husband's dinner ready in the oven, picked up a wicker basket and crossed the deserted farmyard to the washing line. Thurza's nappies would still be damp but a mizzle, which was developing into a light rain, would prevent them getting any dryer as the September evening darkened. Hester's movements, as she reached up to unpeg the nappies and then stooped to drop them into her basket, were as lithe and youthful as they had been before she first carried and then delivered her daughter. She was, she knew, at that moment, in the gloomy yard with the warm light from her kitchen door streaming out over the cobbles towards her, totally content. Happier than she had ever been in her life. She had her Dave, her baby, her home.

She lifted the clothes basket, set it on her hip and began to make her way across the yard. To her left the outline of the empty farmhouse was a dark smudge against a darker sky, its undulating thatch held between two chimney stacks which were barely visible in the murk. Until recently, with the war over at last and the strict rules of the blackout lifted, light would have been pouring out through its small windows. The wind-up gramophone would have been wailing in the land girls' recreation room, where one or another of them might have been lustily singing, picking out a popular song on the untuned piano. Hester paused. No arguments over bathwater tonight. No clatter from the kitchen, where Alice Todd, the warden, assisted by Rose Crocker, the cowman's widow, would have been washing the dinner plates and cutting bread for the next day's sandwiches. Tonight there was just the whisper of the shallow stream that ran under the humpbacked bridge and away, along the valley floor. That was when she had seen it. That brief flicker of light, moving along the upper floor of the deserted farmhouse.

Ten minutes later, when Dave arrived home, damp, muddy and hungry after his day's work at the upper farm, Hester met him at their door. In one hand she held a torch, in the other the key to the farmhouse door.

"Afore you comes in, my lover," Hester had said, "Us must check on the farm'ouse."

"What?" Dave queried, "Now? I be soakin' wet and famished, Hes!"

"But I seen a light in there, Dave. A lamp or a candle or som'at. Come on!" She began to move away from him.

"You sure?" Dave grumbled, stumbling after her. "'Ow can there be a light?"

"Course I'm sure! And there's a shutter half open too, see? And I'm dead certain I latched 'em all when I checked 'em las' week! There be someone in there, Dave! Could be a tramp . . . Or maybe a prisoner escaped from Princeton gaol." Key in hand, she was approaching the farmhouse, Dave behind her, closing the distance between them.

The ancient door creaked open.

"Needs oil, that do," Dave murmured. The light switch in the cross-passage clicked without result and Dave swore under his breath. "'Twill be that buggerin' fuse again, most like."

They moved quietly through the building, flashing torchlight around the kitchen, scullery and recreation room, where threadbare sofas and armchairs still sagged as they had when the departing land girls had abandoned them. They climbed the narrow stairs, searched the bathroom, the torch beam probing the deep, stained bathtub, then began to move from one bedroom to the next, listening and looking.

The linen had been removed from the beds but there were still a few pillows and folded blankets on the thin, ticking-covered mattresses. Wardrobe doors stood open and the drawers in the cheap dressing tables were pulled out as though the girls had just that minute finished their packing and left the overcrowded, noisy space which, for almost three years, had housed them. But Hester and Dave had more on their minds than nostalgic contemplation. The creak of a floorboard in the next room had not escaped them.

At first the small bedroom appeared to be empty. Then they became aware of an almost indiscernible shape in the shadowed space between a wardrobe and the corner of the low-ceilinged room. Shielding its face from the stabbing torch beam, a figure stood huddled and shaking as Hester and Dave approached it. Then, with a sob, knees buckling, whoever it was, slid down the wall and cowered at their feet, dazzled by the light.

"Evie?" Hester breathed, incredulously, the torch beam wavering. Then, louder, "What you doin' back 'ere?" The girl was bruised. Her clothes filthy, her hair tangled, her face tear-stained. Barely recognisable, but Evie. Definitely Evie.

She had been Evelyn Thelma Cooper. Until, at sixteen, Norman Clark married her. Evelyn. The quiet one. Who soon became known as Evie, had arrived at the hostel six months before the end of the war, when most of the group of girls still billeted there had known one another for the best part of three years.

No one remembered being aware of Evie's arrival. Whether this was because with Christmas looming, everyone was preoccupied with their various plans for the brief break in their relentless routine of work, or because Evie herself was so quiet, so inconspicuous and so lacking in the sort of striking physical features which attract attention that she seemed to enter the small community and blend into it, causing barely a ripple of interest.

It had been mid December when she arrived. Almost at once she volunteered to be one of the few girls needed to form the skeleton workforce which would keep cows milked, eggs collected and pigs fed with swill over the few days of the Christmas break.

She was a short girl, not thin, not stout, with silky, blondish hair held back from her face by an Alice band. Her watchful eyes were wide and blue-grey under a rounded brow. Her mouth had a softness about it, almost a shy, half smile. The whole effect was self-effacing. And quiet.

During those last months of the war and the start of peacetime, the hostel would be slowly winding down. Girls and even the warden herself were going through the complicated processes of identifying new careers, finding new partners and turning their faces towards futures which, three years previously, would have seemed inconceivable to them. One was planning to run a public house in a northern town, another about to become a GI bride, two more would soon be married. The directions of all their lives had been changed by their years at the hostel in each other's company and by the wise, practical influence of their warden, Alice Todd.

It was difficult to define what Alice meant to this diverse group of young women whose backgrounds, education and experiences of life varied so hugely but as month succeeded month and each one of them fought for survival in the raw winter cold and the bleak and draughty hostel where food was limited by wartime rationing, they became united by Alice Todd's diligence, tolerance and sensitivity. Too young and too posh to be a mother-figure to them and not harsh or domineering enough to be a school marm, Alice possessed the warmth of the former and when necessary, the authority of the latter.

During her years as warden Alice too, had moved on from her own unhappy situation — she had lost both marriage and home during the course of the war — to the point where she was able to recognise and accept new relationships and opportunities for herself and her young son, Edward John. The long, slow-burning course of her association with her widowed employer, the complex Roger Bayliss, was, by that time, finding its way towards a happy resolution.

The warden had very little initial contact with Evelyn Clark — this late arrival, who was so quiet, so appreciative of the food Alice doled out each evening to her ten, hungry charges. Food which was as filling, nourishing and plentiful as wartime rationing allowed. Evie never complained, never quarrelled with the other girls and only once broke the ten-thirty curfew and then by less than half an hour.

On that occasion, assuming all the girls had arrived home together as usual, Alice had locked up and was preparing for bed when she heard someone try the latch. In hindsight she was to see the significance of that occasion. As spring arrived and the weather warmed, the land girls had resumed their habit of spending the evenings sauntering along the lanes and into Ledburton village for a shandy or a gin and orange. Evie would go with them. It wasn't until she broke the curfew that Alice discovered that although she walked with the other girls as far as the village street, once there she was in the habit of wandering off alone, rejoining the group at closing time and arriving with them, back at the hostel.

"What happened, Evie?" Alice had asked that night, more out of interest than as a remonstrance. "I thought you all went together to the pub." Evie was disconcerted. More so, Alice later realised, than the question warranted. She had hesitantly explained herself.

"I'm not that fond of the pub, to be honest, Mrs Todd. I like to walk out into the countryside, see? It's ever so pretty along by the river." The conversation had moved on to the subjects of nightingales and owls and then the warden and the land girl had wished one another goodnight. Alice withdrew into her room and Evie had gone quietly up the narrow staircase to her bed.

Having absorbed the shock of finding Evie hiding in the hostel, bruised and tearful, Hester and Dave had helped her to her feet, then down the stairs, across the yard and into their cottage where they sat her by their fire. Dave found some port, left over from Christmas, poured a little into a tumbler and persuaded her to drink it. Hester put Dave's loaded plate in front of him and while he ate, poached three new-laid eggs, toasted thick slices of bread and offered them to Evie who seemed almost too tired and too distressed to eat. Soon she sat with her eyelids drooping, a cup of warm milk between her palms; she was almost asleep by the time she'd drained the cup and Hester eased it from her fingers.

"What'll us do?" Hester whispered to her husband.

"Leave 'er to sleep, I reckon. She'll be comfy enough in that chair with a couple of blankets over 'er."

"But in the mornin', Dave? What'll us do in the mornin'? S'pose that 'usband of 'ers comes lookin' for 'er? Eh? Like 'e did afore."

Although the land girls had been barely aware of Evelyn Clark's arrival at the hostel, no one would ever forget the occasion of her removal from it. On a hot evening in late June their meal had been interrupted by heavy knocking on the farmhouse door. Burly, balding, sweating in his army uniform, Norman Clark, Evie's husband, had pushed into the cross-passage and demanded that his wife should fetch her belongings and return at once with him, to their home in Coventry. Initially Alice had resisted, on the grounds that as warden, only she could sanction Evie's departure. But it seemed that Corporal Clark had already called at the higher farm, presented himself to Roger Bayliss and, brandishing his marriage certificate, established his right to take Evie away with him. That had been almost three months ago and since then nothing had been heard of her. Until tonight, when tremulous and beaten, Dave and Hester Crocker had found her, cowering in the deserted hostel.

Next morning, when the couple crept downstairs, Evie was still sleeping, curled, like a stray cat, in their threadbare armchair. Hester repeated the whispered question she had put to her husband on the previous night.

"What if'er 'usband comes?"

"Reckon we better tell the boss. He'll know what's best. Soon as I've had me porridge I'll get off up to the higher farm and tell 'im." He was aware of his wife's anxiety "S'okay, me lover. Shan't be long. Promise."

Hester watched him go, broad shoulders hunched over the handlebars of the farm bicycle as he tackled the steep rise in the lane, turning once to wave to her as she stood, her baby on her hip, in the doorway of their cottage.

Hester and her brother Ezekiel had been deprived of a normal childhood by their father, Jonas Tucker, a lay preacher in a sect stricter and more zealous than even the local Plymouth Brethren. Jonas's religious obsessions had distorted the lives of both his children and even that of their browbeaten mother, all of them existing in an atmosphere of extreme and unnatural piety in which the world beyond their particular faith and every living soul within it was held in contempt and condemned to everlasting damnation. It had taken the war to remove both children from their father's influence and introduce them to a world which, initially, they found difficult to comprehend. The group of young women in whose company Hester was to spend her time as a land girl, at first reduced her to a tongue-tied, almost scandalised silence. The Post Stone girls, with their make-up, provocative clothes and flamboyant behaviour, would have been denounced by Jonas Tucker as scarlet women. Harlots, consigned to hell's everlasting flames. It had taken Hester several months to discover that, in fact, the girls were kind, generous, loyal, and in most cases, singularly lacking in malice. These new friends had persuaded Hester into pretty clothes and to release her spectacular blond-gold hair from the tight bun her father had always insisted on.

"You look like the girl in that picture" someone said, thinking of the foxed print of Lizzie Sidall which hung above the fireplace in the hostel's recreation room.

Dave reached the yard of the upper farm and knocked on the open door to the kitchen. Eileen, her white apron clean on that morning, was busy preparing the day's vegetables. She had known Dave Crocker "since afore you was born" as she often told him.

"What's up, Dave?" she asked him, picking up on the urgency in his voice.

"Gotta see the boss" he said "S'important."

"They'm not up yet, Dave. I've took 'er breakfast and her post up to his room . . . um . . . their room. She on'y got back from Lunnon late las' night, see."

Eileen, like everyone else in the valley, was having trouble adjusting to the fact Mrs Alice Todd, who had been warden of Mr Bayliss's Land Army hostel, had recently become his wife. Post Stone people were finding it hard to remember to call her "Mrs Bayliss". Mostly, they forgot and called her "Mrs Todd . . . um . . . sorry . . . Bayliss".

"Tell him som'at's come up an' I needs to see him, urgent." Dave hesitated. He might as well tell Eileen, she'd hear about it soon enough. Everyone would. "Tell 'im 'tis Evie" he said.

"Evie?"

"Yeah. Tell him . . . and Mrs Todd . . . um . . . Bayliss, that Evie's come back."

In her bedroom at Higher Post Stone, the new Mrs Bayliss was enjoying her breakfast in bed. Roger, still in the first flush of husbandhood, had, the evening before, met the London train at Ledburton Halt and affectionately welcomed her home. He had missed her company during the week she had been in London where, now that her duties at the hostel were over, she was to spend some of her time working as a freelance consultant for a firm of architects. Although, given the choice, Roger would have preferred her to have declined their offer, his tolerance of the arrangement had been, in part, a condition of her acceptance of his proposal of marriage. Nevertheless, his wish that she should have the satisfaction of achieving one of her ambitions was genuine enough and now he was enjoying watching her butter a slice of toast.

In her mid forties, relieved, after almost three years, of her unremittingly hard work as hostel warden, Alice's newly achieved happiness with Roger, her son's willing acceptance of his stepfather, together with her enjoyment of her status in the domestic design department of Woodrow Bradshaw & Associates, had restored to her appearance much of the charm of her

14

youth. Her thick hair was still a rich, honey-blond, her eyes wide and clear, the skin on her slender neck, shoulders and arms, creamy, against the pale silk of her pyjamas. On her breakfast tray was a small pile of envelopes.

"You've got some letters, my darling," Roger said, adding, "And a late butterfly on our windowsill". He opened the window and watched the creature flutter out into the grey morning. "It didn't seem worth sending the mail on to you. Should I have?" Alice shook her head, bit into her toast and examined the letters.

"Aha" she said. "There's one from Annie." She turned the envelope over and read the sender's details on the back. "It says 'from Mrs Hector Conway'. How sweet!" Alice used her knife to open the envelope, took another bite of toast and began to read.

Annie's registered name, when she first arrived at the hostel, had been Hannah Maria Sorokova. She was one of the original intake of land girls who had arrived at the hostel, as Alice herself had, in early 1943, and the daughter of Polish immigrants who had established a thriving garment factory in the East End of London, into which Annie had been absorbed and was being primed for management. She was intelligent and beautiful. Dark-haired, dark-eyed and with the elegance typical of her race. When a Dutch refugee, given sanctuary on the farm, committed suicide, leaving, painted on a barn door, a spectacular depiction of the fate of Jews at the hands of the Nazis, Annie had been instrumental in preserving the work. Her efforts had introduced her to Hector Conway, a bookish arts graduate working for the War Artists Advisory Commission. As well as falling in love with her, Hector had revealed a new world to Annie and eventually the two of them had quietly and happily married. Hector was now curator of a north-country museum while Annie studied to become a librarian.

"This is about Evie," Alice said, lowering her slice of toast and concentrating on the letter.

"Evie?" Roger repeated, vaguely.

"Well, Evelyn," Alice murmured, her attention on the letter, "But we called her Evie . . ."

"Wasn't she the one whose husband, Norman something — a corporal, as I remember — turned up at the hostel, and hauled her off?

"Yes . . ." Alice murmured, reading on. "My God!" she exclaimed. "When was this written?" She checked the postmark.

"Why?" Roger asked.

"I'll read it to you . . . she says, 'Dear Alice. There is something you must know. Hector had some business in Stratford-on-Avon (not far from Coventry) so we made a detour and called on Evie. What we found was very worrying. As you know we were all upset when her husband arrived at the farm and took her away but none of us could have known how bad things were going to get. Her husband opened the door to us and told us Evie was out. I thought I'd seen a movement in an upstairs window so we walked a little way along the road and watched from a distance. After a while her husband left the house. We retraced our steps and someone was waving from the attic window. It was

Evie. She called down to us that she was locked in. Hector wanted to go for the police but Evie said no. She is scared of what her husband might do. I tied some money up in my hanky and Hector managed to throw it up to her. It was about ten pounds, which was all we had. Then she made us go, in case her husband came back. What should we do? Do you think Mr Bayliss would know?' The letter is signed Annie and Hector," Alice finished.

There was a tap on the bedroom door. Their housekeeper begged pardon but Dave Crocker was downstairs asking to see Mr Bayliss or Mrs Todd — she quickly corrected herself, "Um . . . I mean . . . Mrs Bayliss . . ."

"Yes," Roger smiled, "We do know what you mean, Eileen!" Eileen blushed. The sight of Alice Bayliss, as she now was, in Mr Bayliss's bed was enough to bring the colour to her ageing cheeks.

"And he won't take no," Eileen finished, breathlessly.

"I'll see to him," Roger said to his wife. "You enjoy your breakfast, darling."

"But . . . This letter!" Alice began.

"One thing at a time," he told her, reverting to along-established air of authority.

"Where is she now?" Roger asked, when Dave concluded a confused account of the discovery of Evie Clark, hiding in the lower farmhouse.

"I've took 'er over to me mother's," Dave said. Rose Crocker had set up home above her tea shop in Ledburton village some months previously, leaving the tied cottage at the lower farm to her son and his new wife. "We ain't got no room for 'er, see," Dave said, straightening his broad back and meeting his boss's eyes. "An' anyroad, sir," he said, slightly more firmly than Roger was expecting, "I bain't riskin' that bastard turnin' up at Lower Post Stone, lookin' for 'is missus and findin' mine! Lord on'y knows what 'e might do if he thought we was hidin Evie! He's beaten 'er, you know! Black and blue she be!"

"Understood, Dave," Roger said, evenly. "You did absolutely the right thing. Probably a good idea if you work close to the lower farm until we get things sorted. Use the time to repair the wall round the slurry pit. Been meaning to get that seen to for a while. One of those things that gets put off, eh!" He brought a hand down in a paternal way onto his cowman's massive shoulder. "Better get on your way now, just in case."

Dave acknowledged his orders, threw a leg over the crossbar of the mud-spattered bicycle and freewheeled down the steep lane that ended at the lower farmhouse. Although unaware of it, he was feeling the benefit of Alice's steadying influence on her new husband, a man whose darker side had, in the past, made him unpopular with his workforce. He was a fair boss but well established as moody or cold.

Rose Crocker had lit her boiler, filled her bath tub, found a pair of slacks, a blouse, a jumper and some underwear for Evie and left her in the steamy little washroom to let the hot water ease her bruises and remove the stains and traces of her prolonged journey

18

and the days she had spent hiding in the deserted hostel.

Clean and rested, Evie had joined Rose in her kitchen where she was loading into her oven a batch of pasties, which were doing better at this time of the year than the cream teas she sold to holidaymakers in high summer.

Evie was aware that Rose was avoiding eye contact and that her lips were pursed in a way which, experience had taught her, was a sign of disapproval.

"It's ever so good of you, Mrs Crocker," Evie ventured, timidly. "Taking me in and everything."

"I'm doing it for my Dave, Evie. I don't want that husband of yours turnin' up at Lower Post Stone and upsetting Hester and the baby. I knows 'e done wrong, strikin' you. But I daresay there's some as would say you had it comin'." Rose closed her oven door rather more noisily than was necessary.

After Norman Clark, home from his long internment in a German POW camp, had arrived at the hostel that summer evening and demanded that his wife return with him at once to Coventry, word had got around that Evie's evening walks had not been as solitary or as innocent as had been supposed, taken, not alone, but with Giorgio Zingaretti, one of a local group of Italian prisoners of war. Distressed by her sudden departure, Giorgio had appeared at the hostel, where one of the girls — nobody was sure who — had given him Evie's address. When he tracked her down in Coventry, her husband had clouted him with a length of lead piping, knocking him senseless. It had only been the thickness of his shaggy hair that limited the head injury to a gory, five-inch gash. He had made his way, groggily, back to Devon, put his throbbing head under a yard pump and washed away the dried blood.

"You might say," Rose had continued, piously, "that 'tis none of my business, but the fact is that while your man was fighting for his country, you was misbehavin' yourself with an enemy soldier!"

"The Italians hadn't been our enemies for ages, Mrs Crocker! They'd surrendered! And Norman wasn't fighting them nor anyone else, 'cos he got captured in '43 and he was in a POW camp himself after that!"

"That's as maybe," Rose conceded, bowed but far from beaten. "But that's no excuse for your be'aviour, young lady. Not in my book it's not!" Evie stood, pale-faced, grey-blue eyes brimming.

"If only you knew, Mrs Crocker . . . If only you —" She was interrupted by Alice's arrival. Roger Bayliss's car had pulled up outside Rose's door.

"We want you to come to Higher Post Stone with us," Alice smiled. "Alright with you, Rose? We need to have a talk with Evie. To sort things out and make a plan. Mm?"

At the higher farm Evie was led along the wide hall and into the dining room. Higher Post Stone was not a grand residence. It was simply the comfortable home of a well-established and successful farming family and looked now very much as it had over all the years that Roger Bayliss, its present incumbent, had known it, first as a child, then as a young man who, at barely twenty and due to his father's ill health, had taken over the running of both the farms. Following his first wife's early death, Roger had found himself single-handedly raising Christopher, his only child. The growing boy's life had revolved round his schooling while the father's followed the routine of each farming year. They treated one another with respect rather than affection, while Eileen cooked and cleaned for them, taking the place of the missing mother when Christopher went through the usual childhood illnesses.

Evie was intimidated by the Bayliss dining room. The long, narrow table was the largest she had ever seen and the most highly polished. Alice led the way to one end of it where the three of them sat down. Alice placed Annie's letter, in its envelope, on the table in front of her and smiled encouragingly at Evie. Eileen approached the table with a laden tray from which she dispensed coffee.

"Milk?" Alice asked Evie, and when the girl nodded, indicated to Eileen that she should add milk to Evie's cup. Sensing that Eileen's reaction to the unfolding situation would be similar to Rose's, Evie sat with her eyes downcast, staring at her coffee cup, afraid to lift it in case her hand shook so much that she spilt its contents into her saucer. When Eileen had left the room she declined the biscuit that Alice offered her and sat, wiping her eyes with a damp handkerchief and glancing briefly at Roger and then at Alice.

"I'm ever so sorry," she began, "for being such a nuisance and everything. It's all my fault, causing all this!" Alice leant across the table and patted Evie's hand.

"You're not a nuisance," she said reassuringly. "And it's not your fault. We just want to help." Roger's approach was more practical.

"Shall we not start apportioning blame until we have all the facts, my dear? Now . . . Evie, in your own good time . . ." Evie stared at him. If she understood what was expected of her there was little evidence of it. Alice suggested that she should try to relax, collect her thoughts and when she was ready, tell them what had brought her to this difficult point in her life.

Although Alice knew some of Evelyn Clark's history, that her parents had separated and her marriage an unhappy one, she had not, she soon realised, involved herself any more than was necessary in her role as hostel warden in the details of the girl's situation and was quite unprepared for what followed.

"But I dunno . . ." Evie whispered. "I dunno what to . . . Where do I start . . .?" She twisted the handkerchief into a damp ball and bit her lip.

"At the beginning?" Alice suggested quietly. "Right at the beginning. When things began to get . . . well . . . complicated." There was a pause while Evie sat, her eyes fixed on Alice's, the three of them becoming aware of the measured ticking of the grandfather clock.

"I weren't much more'n a kid," Evie began, surprisingly. "Ten years old when me Dad left us and then he died." Slowly the facts began to emerge, one leading on to the next. Her father's insurance policy had paid off the mortgage on the two-bedroom "back-to-back" in a Coventry suburb but there was no money coming in and Enid, her mother, took work on the assembly line of a local factory where she met an unskilled labourer, fifteen years her junior. There had been no physical attraction between them but Enid was an insecure woman who had been overdependent on her late husband. With him gone she had needed someone to fix the gutters, mend the gate, lay new lino in the kitchen and contribute to the household budget. Norman Clark was to fulfil these requirements in return for cheap lodgings.

Before long the heavily built man, with his florid face, thick neck and belligerent expression, had established himself in the dingy little house, placed his razor, strop and shaving brush on the bathroom shelf and unpacked his few possessions in what had been Evie's bedroom while she moved in with her mother.

"At first I didn't like him being there," Evie told them, her eyes moving from Alice's to Roger's, "'cos he made the place smell of cigarettes, and on Friday nights of his dirty overalls and his beer. But it suited Mum. He bought a little car and he took us for outings in it. Sometimes there was trips to the pictures, or to a cafe for tea and cakes. Mum liked that."

"Just your mother?" Alice asked, "Or . . .?"

"Both of us, Mrs Todd . . . I mean, Bayliss. He always took both of us. We went to the seaside one year. Blackpool. Stayed in a boarding house. He was kind, then. Gave me presents and painted the house for Mum and bought a new carpet for the front room . . . When I turned sixteen Mum told me I was to marry him. Looking back, I was daft to agree. I didn't much like him — except in a grateful kind of way for what he done for us over the years. I told Mum I didn't want to marry him 'cos I didn't fancy him but she said life wasn't about fancying people and all that rubbish I watched down the picture palace, and that you should marry a man as would look after you proper and not some good-looking ne'er-do-well. She said the house was too small for the three of us and that if I refused to marry Norman I knew what I could do." Evie's voice faltered and stopped. Both Alice and Roger were regarding her in barely concealed astonishment. Alice composed her face and began topping up Roger's coffee cup while he got to his feet, and with the poker, adjusted the position of a log in the hearth.

"I don't think I ever said yes to him," Evie continued. "Like I said, I was barely more than a kid and I'd always done as Mum told me, see. She'd get angry, Mum, if I didn't do as she said. They bought a second-hand bed and we went to the registry office and I signed my name on a form. After that I had to sleep with him. I didn't like what he done to me but Mum said I was a big girl now and it was something women have to put up with. I didn't know any different. Not in real life. Not then."

She carefully lifted her cup and sipped the coffee. "That's nice, that is." She smiled briefly, looked from Alice to Roger and asked, hesitantly, "D'you want me to go on? Or have you had enough?"

"Go on," Alice said quietly. Evie seemed to be gaining in assurance. Perhaps putting her strange

24

history into words distanced it slightly from the harsh experience of it and gave her a new perspective on events that had for so long overwhelmed her. She sat up straighter in her chair and put her cup carefully back onto its saucer before continuing.

"I fell pregnant straight off," she told them. "It was a dear little boy but he was stillborn. I was ever so poorly and the nurse said I'd lost my womb. Norman got angry. He'd wanted a son, see. When they told him I couldn't 'ave no more kids he wouldn't speak to me. Neither of 'em would. They made me sleep downstairs on a camp bed. I got sent out to work, soon as I was well enough and Mum took all me wages for me keep. That's how it went on till the war started and Norman got called up. When I turned eighteen I had to do war service and Mum wanted me to work in a munition factory near where we lived. But I'd grown up a bit by then," she said. "I'd seen the posters for the Land Army and it seemed like a good chance to . . ." she hesitated ". . . to get away."

"So you came to Lower Post Stone," Alice said, amazed that this girl, of whose history she knew so little, after having had such a bad experience of life, had been absorbed so successfully into the community at the hostel. But there had to be more, and there was.

Now we come to the difficult part, Roger realised, silently. *The part when this girl, against the advice of her warden, and against Land Army regulations, fraternised with an Eyetie POW.* Unpleasant as her husband undoubtedly was, Roger found it difficult to condone Evie's behaviour. A man fighting for his country should be able to count on the fidelity of the girl he'd left behind him.

"Did he write to you, while he was away, fighting?" Roger asked, in a tone that Alice considered slightly confrontational.

"No," Evie said. "He never did. After VE Day he wrote to Mum to tell her he'd be comin' home soon. I was a land girl by then." There was a slight pause before she continued. "I know I shouldn't of, but I'd hoped Norman wouldn't come back from the war. That he'd get killed like so many of 'em did. But he'd got took prisoner a coupla months after he was called up, see, and after that 'is letters had come from a camp somewhere. I didn't hear nothing from him 'til that night he come to the farm and took me away." She paused. "I couldn't never work out why he did that. It wasn't as though he wanted me. But I was his wife. So I suppose it was like he owned me. It wasn't as if he loved me or nothing. Not Norman." Suddenly her throat closed. She dropped her face into her hands and wept silently, shoulders shaking, tears running from between her fingers. "Not like Giorgio," she whispered, eventually. "Not like my Giorgio loves me! He got my address, you know. One of the Post Stone girls give it him and he came to find me. He broke his parole, doin' that. He risked being sent to jail, 'cos it was against the rules of some convention or other. He could even of got shot! But he come looking for me. And he found me. And then Norman half killed him! Giorgio wants to stay in England, see. Farmer Lucas is keen to keep him on at his place. All we want is to be together!" She was speaking directly to Alice and Roger now. Both of them were affected by the simple intensity of her words. "I need to see him! I really do! Please can I see him?"

"You shall, Evie," Alice said, "You shall. I promise you."

"But we need to clarify a few things first," Roger stated, flatly, picking up Annie's letter.

"It's from Annie and Hector," Alice told Evie. "They wrote to us because they were concerned about you."

"We know they visited you and tried to help you. What happened after that?" Roger's question hung in the air, unanswered while Evie seemed to struggle to know how to answer him.

"Evie?" Alice prompted, gently.

"After Norman got 'ome that day Annie and Hector come . . ." Evie began, hesitantly, "he was ages before he brought me supper . . . I was locked up, see, in the attic . . . He asked if anyone had come while he was out and I pretended no one had."

"So he didn't know Annie and Hector saw you?" Alice asked, Evie shook her head.

"I told him I wanted to see to Mum. She was ill, see. Coughin' and coughin', she was. But he wouldn't let me. She'd been bad for days and Norman wouldn't send for the doctor. I told him if he didn't let me see her I'd break a window and shout for help, so he said he'd send for the doctor next day. But he never and no one came. I couldn't hear Mum coughin' no more. Next time he brought me food I shoved past him. He came after me, down the stairs. I got to Mum's bedroom before he grabbed me. I could see Mum were

27

real bad. Strugglin' to breathe, she was, and there was blood all down her nightie. I don't think she even knew who I was. Norman grabbed me and dragged me back to the attic. He was pretty rough. That's when I got me bruises. He locked me in again. I was that scared. For meself and for Mum. I never thought I could get out of that attic winder or down onto the ground without killin' meself — but I had no option, so I done it! Down the drainpipe, across the outhouse roof and then a drop down into the back alley. It was pouring down with rain and all I had was the clothes I was wearing and the money Hector had thrown up to me."

"So you . . .?" Roger asked, made almost speechless by a story which was becoming increasingly astonishing.

"So I ran all the way to the station, hid in the Ladies 'til a train come. Got to Birmingham and waited ages for an Exeter train. I walked all night from Ledburton Halt to the hostel. It was just startin' to get light by the time I got there. It was all locked up but I managed to get in through that little winder in the scullery, you know the one Mrs Todd . . . Bayliss. I dunno how many days I hid there. There was water, of course, but nothing to eat except I did find a tin of spam at the back of the pantry cupboard. And one night, after Hester and Dave had put their light out, I went across to the barn and took a couple of swedes. It was the next night, yesterday, that is, that Hester must of saw the light from the candle I was using." She paused, miserably. "You know the rest and I'm ever so sorry. Can I see Giorgio now? I'm scared for 'im, see! Scared that Norman'll guess where I am and come lookin' for him!" She turned desperately from Alice to Roger. "And then there's me mother! It's true she weren't good to me but she were that sick and I left her with no one to care for her!"

CHAPTER
TWO

The Italian surrender in 1943 had resulted, as time passed, in a considerable laxity in security at the POW camp near Ledburton. As time passed, trusted inmates were to be seen working without guards on the various farms in Post Stone valley.

On one April morning and only weeks from VE Day, Giorgio Zingaretti, who had proved himself to be an excellent worker, was fixing a drinking trough. The sun was warm on his broad back. Under the shock of dark hair, perspiration glistened on his forehead. His olive skin which, even after the long, English winter, had not lost its Mediterranean glow, was already acquiring a deeper tan.

A girl, wearing khaki dungarees and wellington boots was striding uphill towards him. He smiled at the Englishness of her blue eyes, creamy complexion and the pale hair, braided into a thick plait. He wiped the back of his hand across his brow. As she drew level with him he said, "*Buongiorno, bella signorina!* Why you so much in a hurry, eh?"

Like most of his fellows, Giorgio, through his contact with the camp guards, the local farmers who availed themselves of his labours, and to a more limited extent, the civilians whom the prisoners encountered when, on Sundays, a farm lorry ferried them to and from the Catholic church in Exeter, had acquired a limited use of the English language. More recently — and always under surveillance — the trusted prisoners were allowed to shop in the village store.

The girl had stopped to catch her breath after the steep climb. She held up a hoe, the shaft of which was in two pieces.

"'Cos I've broke me hoe!" she told him, "An' I gotta take it up to the farm and get Mr Jack to fix it." When he appeared to be having trouble understanding her she repeated, slowly and clearly, "Mister Jack? Fix?"

"Ah!" Giorgio smiled. His teeth were even and white "Si! Mr-Jack-fix-hoe!" In the warm air the girl was conscious of the heat coming from him. And of the sweet smell of his sweat. It was not like any sweat she had smelt before. It was not how the land girls smelt at the end of a day of summer heat, hoisting hay onto the carts. And it was not how her husband Norman had smelt.

"*Che?*" Giorgio queried, reacting to her changing expression and the soft blush which had washed across her face.

"I best go," she said, moving off up the lane, "or I'll be in dead trouble!" He watched her go. The heavy plait bouncing on her shoulders.

April became May. During the VE Day celebrations there was an evening of dancing in Ledburton square where an amplified gramophone belted out Glen Miller.

To begin with the village girls and the Post Stone land girls were slow to respond to the group of smiling Italians who, scrubbed up and in basic fatigues rather than their usual, mud-encrusted dungarees, were almost unrecognisable. But after a while, when the girls had first smiled and then giggled and the men shuffled their feet, ranks were broken and partners decided upon. It was as the couples gathered, hands were taken and arms placed round waists, that Giorgio caught sight of a figure in a floral dress. Her hair was held back by a ribbon at the nape of her neck. With a slight sense of shock he recognised the girl with the broken hoe.

They danced together until the gramophone finally fell silent and Alice Todd began shooing her land girls towards the farm lorry which would unceremoniously deliver them back to the hostel.

Giorgio had held her gently and protectively. Their bodies, as they danced, soon felt as familiar to one another as long-established lovers. They did not speak. Not he in Italian nor she in English. They did not need to. When the music stopped he led her towards the lorry, discretely releasing her before they reached the gaggle of girls jostling to climb up into it and anxious not to show their camiknickers or ladder their precious nylons.

"Come on, our Evie!" someone shouted as arms reached down to haul her into the truck.

"Evie." Giorgio had said aloud and in his uncertain English. "So. She call Evie."

In 1940, the year in which Mussolini committed Italy to the war, Giorgio had been employed, like his father

32

before him, as an episcopal carpenter, responsible for maintenance work in several Neapolitan churches. He was newly married and his wife pregnant, when shrapnel from an Allied bomb struck and killed her and the unborn child she was carrying. In an inconsolable response to the tragedy, Giorgio enlisted in the navy, only to be taken prisoner following the routing of the Italian fleet at Cape Matapan, after which he and a small group of survivors had been transported to rural England where they were interned for the duration of the war. During this time the men had been reasonably well fed and provided with weatherproof clothing but the barn in which they were housed had bars on its windows, barbed wire around its perimeter fence and guards who were armed.

Many of Giorgio's fellow prisoners had histories as tragic as his own. Although they were simple men they were intelligent enough to despise the leader who had inflicted first humiliation and then defeat on the country they loved. They celebrated when, after his surrender to the Allies, Mussolini was punished by his own people. Hanged, ignominiously by his feet, he had swung, together with his mistress, above the heads of jeering crowds.

During the first years of his internment Giorgio lost track of time. He worked, ate and slept. He shivered through the brutal English winters, while the summers only served to remind him of the blissful warmth of the Italian sun. He occasionally received letters from his brother, who was married now and the father of two small children. When one of Giorgio's fellow prisoners, injured by a collapsing barn, was repatriated ahead of the rest of the group, he, like the other men, had been jealous, until the thought of resuming his life in Naples without the girl who had always been at its heart plunged him into a deeper depression.

Most of the prisoners vented at least some of their pent-up frustrations by shouting obscene comments at the local women they glimpsed from the truck that took them to and from the various farms where they worked. When they caught sight of the land girls, driving stock, stooking wheat sheafs, lifting potatoes and swedes or innocently hoeing their way down the long lines of brassicas, the air turned blue. Fortunately no one who heard them was aware of the level of crude abuse that poured from them. They transposed lewd words into well-known Italian songs, and smiling, bawled them in the general direction of any women within earshot.

After his first encounter with Evie, in the lane where he was repairing the gate, Giorgio no longer joined in these ribald choruses. Although he knew she did not understand the words, it seemed to him inappropriate that they should be polluting the air she breathed.

When, as early summer had given way to harvest time, the war in Europe was over at last and Japan's surrender only a matter of weeks away, the sense of impending change became as palpable in the Post Stone valley as the stench of smoking oil from the clattering reapers, blundering their way through the ripe cornfields and the juddering, dust-caked threshing machines. It was the time when the girls cut the legs off their dungarees, rolled down their heavy, regulation socks, exposing their legs from thigh to ankle. Hair became bleached, foreheads, forearms and shins tanned and sometimes reddened by the hot July sun.

At the hostel that summer and before matchmaking had blossomed into formal engagements and even weddings, there had been a lot of "does he, doesn't he?", "will she won't she?" "do I don't I?", questions, which all too often had been referred to the warden herself. Much of this, the confidences, the stormy tears, the misunderstandings, reconciliations and celebrations, went over the head of Alice's young son. Nevertheless Edward John had become increasingly aware of the importance in his mother's life of her employer, Roger Bayliss, and it had occurred to him that should the two of them marry, he could happily delete from his shortlist of worries the threat of a compulsory move back to London when his mother's duties as hostel warden ended.

Edward John Todd had turned twelve during that summer. He was a robust child with a touch of his mother's solemnity, her dark-blond hair and direct, grey-blue eyes. The break-up of his parents' marriage had affected him more than he had realised at the time and diminished his previously affectionate feelings for his father but, largely due to his mother's example, he had weathered the experience. On Friday evenings he arrived at the farm from his weekly boarding school in Exeter and late on Sundays caught the bus back. At the hostel he slept on one of the two divans in a ground floor room which was his mother's bedsitting room. He had become enchanted with the idea of living on a farm even while his mother hesitated before making the decision to take on the role of hostel warden. Nothing, over the past two and a half years, had disappointed him and the one cloud on his horizon, that third summer, had been the possibility that when the war was over, his mother would pursue an offer of work in London.

By the time his school broke up for the long summer holiday the hostel had been alive with romance. First there had been the wedding of Georgina, his favourite land girl, to Christopher, Roger Bayliss's son, at which he served as a pageboy and had been allowed a glass of hock during the reception at her parents' elegant home.

It was on that occasion that Edward John first encountered Pamela, the fourteen-year-old daughter of a wealthy family who farmed a large acreage adjacent to the Post Stone valley.

Pamela had by then completed her first year at an expensive boarding school. After just twelve months the change in her had astonished her parents. Yes, they intended her to become well educated, articulate and self-assured, but the young woman who had stepped neatly down from the train at Ledburton Halt at the start of her school holidays, seemed, initially, to be almost a stranger to them.

Edward John, a tidy boy in his school uniform, his hair slicked down, a white carnation in his buttonhole, his first glass of wine in his hand, had stared at the most beautiful girl he had ever seen. Pamela stood, cool and smiling, responding sociably to those wedding guests who spoke to her, her eyes appraising the women's hats as she accepted compliments from her father's middle-aged friends, who barely recognised the gawky child she had been when they had last seen her.

After that initial encounter, things had not been the same for Edward John. He was, although he did not at the time recognise the symptoms, quite simply in love. It was not the sloppy sort of love expressed by the simpering heroines of the movies he saw, with their flouncy sulks and huge, bunchy skirts. Nor was it the flirty, rowdy, bawdiness of the land girls which occasionally caused Rose Crocker to purse her lips and his mother to call her girls to order.

"Not in front of Edward John," she would murmur if her son was within earshot. No. What Edward John was experiencing that summer was, he was certain, unique, significant and unquestionably everlasting.

He made it his business to discover Pamela's habits. It was not difficult. She, like many girls of her class and her age, was devoted to horses. She rode Playboy, her piebald pony, at local gymkhanas and agricultural shows and had, over the years, accumulated an impressive collection of rosettes and even trophies. With little else to do with herself during the long school holiday, she and Playboy ranged the valley and beyond it, climbing up through the Bayliss forest, past the woodman's cottage to which, after the breakdown which had seen him ignominiously discharged from the RAF, Christopher Bayliss had withdrawn to allow his

37

shattered nerves to heal. And where he and Georgina had, eventually, become lovers.

Edward John's familiarity with the topography of the valley made it easy for him to discover where Pamela was heading on her daily rides.

She would see him approaching on a reciprocal course, or descending an opposite hill, or appearing suddenly in a stand of young beeches or rounding a curve in the path that followed the stream. He would raise the hard-hat his mother insisted on, in a way that he hoped suggested not only good manners but sophistication.

"Where are you heading today?" he'd ask her.

"Nowhere in particular," she'd shrug. "Might go over The Tops and home via the ridge track."

"Can I join you?"

"If you want to . . ." And they would ride, side by side except where the path narrowed, Playboy and Tosca, the bay mare Roger Bayliss had put at his stepson's disposal, falling into step with each other.

As the stream thrust its way down through the Post Stone valley, there were places where it narrowed significantly, restricted by outcrops of smoothed, mossy granite which created waterfalls and, below them, deep, dark pools. Sometimes the riders would stop, dismount and let the horses drink and then graze the short grass. One hot July day they pulled off their riding boots and waded into water which had the colour and clarity of cider.

"If it wasn't so cold we could swim," Pamela said, lightly.

"It's always freezing here," Edward John informed her. "It's because the headwaters are up on the moor, in the granite."

"You don't say!" Pamela said, embarrassing him. He felt himself blush, turned away and lobbed a white pebble, watching as its colour changed from silver to dark gold, before glimmering down into the jet-black depths.

"Anyhow, we haven't got our bathers" he said.

"Bathers?" Pamela echoed, adding to his embarrassment.

"Bathing costumes," he said.

"I do know what bathers are, Edward John! But who needs 'bathers'? At school we often give our sports mistress the slip and swim, stark naked, in our pool." Edward John made a fast recovery.

"I sometimes swim here, stark naked," he lied, casually.

"Thought you said it was freezing," she countered, nailing him with her beautiful eyes.

"Yes it is," he said, putting his foot in Tosca's stirrup, swinging up into her saddle and kicking her on. "I dive off that boulder," he told Pamela, indicating a smooth slab of granite which overhung deep water. "That's how I know how extremely cold it is."

And then the summer holidays had been over and Pamela left for her boarding school, returning only for the odd weekend.

Edward John had continued his rides, rehearsing imaginary conversations with the absent girl, practising being knowledgeable, fascinating and, more importantly, witty. He assiduously cultivated this apparently necessary skill until he felt confident enough to experiment with it on his classmates, and even, if he was feeling especially sharp, on some of the younger members of his school's teaching staff.

Roger Bayliss, who was genuinely fond of his stepson, encouraged serious conversation at the dinner table at Higher Post Stone.

"He has an enquiring mind, that boy," he told Alice approvingly, one evening after dinner, when Edward John, having been particularly erudite, had excused himself to check on an injured heifer and his mother and stepfather were taking a turn round their garden in the late summer half-light.

"An enquiring mind, has he?" Alice had said, vaguely, watching swifts swooping under the house eaves.

Roger was thinking of university courses and possible professions. "A mind like that could take him a long way," he said.

"I'm not sure he would want to go 'a long way'," Alice murmured, her eyes on the rolling countryside below them. "No further, in fact than this valley."

"Unlike my Christopher," Roger sighed, thinking of the son who, after his bad experience in the RAF, had opted for a two-year contract with the New Zealand Forestry Commission. "Never had much time for the farm, Christopher."

"Nonsense," Alice said, gently. "He loves the valley, and like you, he has farming in his blood. It wasn't

40

indifference that made the New Zealand job appealing."

"No." Roger sighed. "It was me. It was me. I know it was me." They were referring, as indirectly as possible, to the situation which, as Christopher matured, had resulted in an estrangement between father and son that had been painfully exacerbated by what the RAF had referred to as Christopher's "crack-up".

Because of a similar experience of his own, a deeply buried trauma from the First World War, Roger had found himself unable to respond sympathetically to his son's condition. It had been his developing relationship with Alice Todd that had eventually enabled him to confront the situation and release the deeply suppressed feelings which had haunted him most of his adult life. This eventually made it possible for him to respond not only to Alice but, to a limited extent, to his son. However the reconciliation, such as it was, had come too late to alter the newly-weds' plans to emigrate.

"It was both of you, darling," Alice said, slipping her arm through his. "You and Christo. Anyway, it's all over now."

"Well, nearly," Roger said, smiling at her.

"Yes. Very nearly." Alice stopped to pick a dead head from a rose bush. "Georgina's mother telephoned today. She's had a letter from her. The first one since they disembarked in Wellington."

"Oh? Alright are they?" Roger asked. "Madly in love with New Zealand, I suppose?"

"Not sure. She says Christopher was sent off almost immediately on some survey or other, leaving her alone in desperately dreary government lodgings with absolutely nothing to do but wait for him to come back in ten days' time."

"So the 'travelling hopefully' was more fun than the arriving, was it?"

"Much more fun, apparently! Poor old Georgie! She's not a girl who would take kindly to being left behind, twiddling her thumbs!" Alice shivered and pulled her cardigan more closely around herself. "Let's go indoors. The wind is a bit sharp this evening."

With the war in Europe ended, Evie had been anticipating news of her husband. None had come and as the weeks passed she and Giorgio had continued their clandestine evening meetings, observed only by cattle pulling at the lush grass in the valley, a stealthy fox or two and a flock of sheep who would lift their heads, stop chewing the wiry grass on the high ground and stare at the two figures walking, hand in hand, through the summer twilight. Once, when a rainstorm rolled down from the moor, the lovers had sheltered in the small byre on The Tops, lying together in the fresh straw, piled ready for the lambing season. As weeks became months with still no sign of Corporal Norman Clark, Evie and Giorgio dared to begin to hope.

"P'raps 'e got killed," Evie would whisper, "and they forgot to tell us."

"No." Giorgio, shook his shaggy head. "When a soldier die they send *un telegramma. Sempre.*"

"Well maybe he decided he didn't want me no more. He had no time for me, Giorgio, not after they told him that part of me insides is missing." They had discussed the fact that Evie was no longer able to bear children. In the context of their present situation it seemed almost irrelevant. At other times Evie was less optimistic. "He'll come for me, Giorgio! I just know he will! Mum'll tell 'im where I am and 'e'll come and fetch me home and no one can stop 'im!"

"We make plan," Giorgio soothed her. "We make plan for if he come!"

"What plan?"

"I not know yet," he confessed. "But soon I know. Soon I will have good plan!" Then, suddenly, it was too late.

"Where Evie?" Giorgio had shouted to one of the land girls as she freewheeled down the lane after evening milking was finished.

"Gone!" the girl had called over her shoulder, her front wheel bucking dangerously amongst the potholes. "Her bloke come las' night and fetched 'er 'ome!"

Edwin Lucas, whose farmland, adjacent to Roger Bayliss's, ran west, from the crest above Higher Post Stone, down into the next valley, had been impressed by one in particular of the Italians who, under the supervision of an armed guard, had worked on his farm. Over the years of Giorgio Zingaretti's internment, Edwin Lucas had come to appreciate the young prisoner's equable temperament, his physical strength and his willingness to deliver a hard day's labour. He knew Giorgio's tragic history and had suggested that if the idea appealed to him, it might be possible, when peace was finally declared, to obtain permission for him to remain in England as part of the Lucas workforce. Giorgio had accepted Edwin's offer and on the day the makeshift internment camp had finally closed and with the necessary paperwork in place, dumped his kitbag on the mud floor of a near-derelict, tied cottage that stood to one side of the Lucas farmyard.

The small building, which consisted of two rooms, one above the other, connected by a narrow flight of stone steps, was built of limestone, its interior, many years previously, coated with whitewash which was now mildewed and peeling. Its condition was considered unfit for Edwin's current labourers.

Clarissa, Edwin's wife, was to provide Giorgio with a meal each night and with sandwiches for his lunch. He soon got the measure of the rusted iron range in his dank quarters, and when he finished work, would light a fire. With the small windows open to the summer evenings, he drove the damp from the abandoned building. With Clarissa Lucas's ample food inside him and the warmth from his fire relaxing him, Giorgio began to visualise a future. He would hose the little place, whitewash its walls, replace the panes that were missing from its windows and the worm-eaten boards on the floor of the upstairs room. He would repair the pipe that had once delivered water to the granite sink. When sleep overtook him he dreamt a scene in which Evie would arrive at his door with the news that her husband was dead, a casualty of war. When he asked her to marry him she would say, "*Si*, Giorgio. *Ti amo molto*."

While Evie was telling her story, Roger Bayliss had been deciding what was to be done with her in both the long and short term. He was not unsympathetic towards her but the situation, should it involve him, was complicated by the fact that he had recently been invited to become a Justice of the Peace, a voluntary position consisting of occasional duties at local magistrates courts. He, as he had explained to Alice, apparently met all the criteria needed to fit the Lord Chancellor's requirements. He was an upright, educated and well-respected man, his family and his antecedents were very much part of the area's history. He understood the rural economy, employed local labourers and had a reputation for treating them fairly. There had been the unfortunate incident when his son, a Fighter Command pilot, had been dismissed from the RAF. But the boy had been ill, hospitalised in fact, when, after being deployed to breaking point, his nerves failed him.

Roger's concern, as Evie reached the point in her story which had resulted in her tearful presence, here, in his dining room, was that should the situation between her and her husband escalate into more serious areas, such as assault or abduction, he himself would be disadvantaged by having any connection with it.

Alice had been surprised when Roger got to his feet and announced that Evie, for the time being at any rate, must now be returned to Rose Crocker's care. As she and Roger drove back to Higher Post Stone, having promised to arrange a meeting between Evie and Giorgio, Alice queried his decision.

"I realise that we can't expect Rose to house her indefinitely," she said, as her husband nosed the car through the lanes. "So why don't we take her in? It won't be forever. She could help Eileen with the housework and she'd be safer with us than anywhere if the husband turns up."

"It's not as simple as that," Roger told her and explained his concerns about the legal complications of his own involvement.

"So. What do we do?" Alice wanted to know.

"The fact is that I can't pay Rose for Evie's keep," Roger told her, "because that could legally be seen as an involvement on my part, but —"

"Is this all about the magistrate thing?" Alice demanded, "Because if it means you're not allowed help out one of our land girls when she needs us, I'm not sure I approve of it!"

"But there are ways round it, my dear one," Roger said, changing gear as he negotiated the narrow bridge from which point the lane rose steeply towards the higher farmhouse. "Rose's tea shop needs an outside lavatory — something to do with the new planning regulations. As the building is part of the Post Stone estate the cost of any building work on it is met by the maintenance funds, not personally by me. D'you see what I'm getting at?"

"So Rose gains a new lavatory and you keep your flawless reputation! Very neat!"

"And Evie is safely taken care of, for the time being at any rate."

Roger's next move had been to put the entire situation into the hands of the police. Statements were taken regarding Norman Clark's conduct since he had almost forcibly removed his wife from the Land Army. Hester and Dave Crocker verified her injuries when they had discovered her hiding in the empty hostel. Annie and Hector had been asked to present themselves at their local police station in order to sign statements regarding Evie's imprisonment in her mother's attic in Coventry, where the police already had witnesses to his attack on a man who was yet to be identified as Giorgio.

Some days later the police arrived at Rose's door to break the news to Evie that her mother's body had been found by a Norman Clark, who claimed to be her son-in-law. The cause of death had been confirmed by a coroner as heart failure following double pneumonia. They did not tell Evie that the death had taken place approximately two weeks previously, or that the body was already decomposing in the horribly soiled bed in which it had been discovered.

On the following day, Evie and Giorgio were briefly reunited. Alice and Roger drove her to the Lucas farm and watched her approach the door of the cottage where Giorgio was waiting for her.

"Better keep an eye on things," Roger said. A light rain was falling, so he and Alice stood in the shelter of the farmhouse porch from which Giorgio's cottage was visible. Clarissa withdrew into her kitchen and while she brewed a pot of tea and decided whether or not to use her best china, her husband, ignoring the rain, sat on a low wall, and with one eye on the door to Giorgio's cottage, began to fill his pipe.

Inside the cottage the lovers embraced, then, holding her at arm's length, Giorgio reacted to the sight of her bruised face and forearms, cursing himself in his native language for leaving her to face her husband's violence. Even without translation Evie understood his words.

"But stayin' would of done no good, Giorgio! He would of killed you! And if the coppers had come they would of jailed you for breaking your parole! You were brave, Giorgio! Brave! And you made me brave! I never would of had the guts to get away from him but for knowing you was 'ere, waiting for me!"

In the porch Roger and Alice sipped their tea. The rain had stopped and the farm chickens strutted and scratched, a cat stalked silently along a wall. There was no sound from within the cottage. Alice and Roger replaced their cups in the saucers of Clarissa Lucas's porcelain tea set.

"I wonder what they said to one another," Alice murmured, almost to herself, as, having returned Evie to Rose's care, they drove back to the higher farm.

Whatever it was that had passed between the lovers during the half-hour they had been alone together, it seemed to have had a positive effect on both of them. Evie, getting into the back seat of Roger's car, had been calmly composed. She sat, her eyes on Giorgio as he

48

stood at the doorway of his cottage, looking steadily across the yard at her.

"What happens next?" Alice asked her husband.

"With any luck the police will arrest Corporal Clark and charge him with GBH. That's grievous bodily —"

"Harm," Alice finished for him. "Yes, I do know what GBH is, darling!"

"Forgive me," Roger said, "I'm still not used to living with an educated woman!"

"Poor Roger!" she teased him. "I keep forgetting it's been milkmaids and cowman's wives since you were widowed, hasn't it!" They exchanged wry smiles. "So you think Norman will be arrested?" Alice asked, more seriously.

"I'm sure of it. It can only be a matter of time before they find him. There were witnesses to his attack on Giorgio in Coventry and plenty of evidence of Evie's injuries, plus the mystery of the mother's death."

"Evie said she was ill and obviously needed medical attention . . ."

"He has a lot to answer for, that bastard."

Days passed without incident. The repairs to the wall round the slurry pit were almost complete. On the fourth day Dave had taken the tractor up to the higher farm to fetch a load of coping stones, while Ferdinand Vallance sat contentedly munching his way through the sandwiches his wife had cut for him that morning. Orphaned at nine, crippled by a rolling tractor at fourteen, Ferdie had surprised the world by finding his life's partner in Mabel Hodges, who, overweight and under-washed, had been one of Alice's girls, arriving at the hostel the day it opened its doors to the first intake of ill-assorted young women. Instantly drawn to one another, their shared disregard for personal hygiene adding to their mutual attraction, two happy events had eventually taken place in the form of twins, Scarlet O'Hara and Winston Ferdinand, who, added to Mabel's son, "little Arthur" — the result of an undisclosed, previous impregnation — completed, for the time being at any rate, the Vallance family.

Stuffing the last of his sandwich into his mouth, Ferdie smiled at Hester who was approaching the slurry pit with a mug in her hand.

"A cuppa with your elevenses, Ferdie?" she asked him.

"Ta, but this be me twelvses," he confessed, with his mouth full. "A bit on the early side I daresay, on'y I were feeling peckish". For a while the two of them sat on the low wall, he munching and sipping and both catching up on the latest news concerning Evie, whose story was proving excellent material for gossip and speculation.

"Reckon she be a bit sly, that one," Ferdie said. "All those months, creepin' round the countryside with an Eyetie." Ferdie had lowered his mug and was squinting into the sharp sunlight. "Who be that then . . .?" he said.

Making its way down the lane towards Lower Post Stone, the figure of a man could be glimpsed through the thinning autumn foliage. He was heavily built and had a light knapsack over one solid shoulder and

Hester, who knew Norman only by reputation, guessed at once who he was. She clutched Ferdie's arm.

"Its him!" she whispered, pulling Ferdie down beside her until only their two heads, their outlines broken by a tangle of old man's beard, were visible. "Evie's fella! See? That's an army kitbag over 'is shoulder! 'E's come for her! Get down, Ferdie! Don't let 'im see us!"

Norman Clark moved silently towards the empty hostel and stood, listening and looking, his eyes moving over the face of the building, at the closed shutters and drawn curtains. His back was to Hester and Ferdie and the only sound was the mallards on the farm pond and the stream as it funnelled under the humpbacked bridge.

Hester froze. Across the yard, inside the open door to her cottage, she had left Thurza in her playpen, amusing herself with her toys. It would be no good expecting Ferdie to run for help, his maimed leg prevented any movement beyond a rolling hobble which, though fast enough for herding stock and sound enough for driving horse and cart or tractor, would be no use to him on this occasion.

"Stay there, Ferdie," Hester told him. He gaped at her, struggling to comprehend the situation and focus his mind on devising a plan to deal with it. In the meantime he would do as Hester told him. "I'm gunna try to get round the back of the barn to the yard phone!" she said. "Make sure you keep your 'ead down, Ferdie!"

Using the cover provided by a collection of old carts, made redundant by the increasing use of tractors,

Hester reached the rear of the barn and began making her way round it towards the yard. The telephone, the farm's only communication with the outside world, was attached to a wall just inside the large opening to the barn's interior. Historically, the telephone had only ever been used in emergencies during the Land Army's occupation. Now that Dave, Hester and Thurza were the lone occupants of the lower farm, it remained, for that reason, connected.

Ferdie raised his head just high enough for him to peer carefully over the low wall. He saw Norman Clark approach the farmhouse door. After beating on it with his closed fist he rattled the latch without effect and stepping back and lowering a massive shoulder, charged it. His heavy frame juddered with each impact but the solid oak resisted him once, twice and a third time. In that moment Ferdie had seen Hester slip round the corner of the barn and vanish into its shadowy interior. By now, he calculated, the loud telephone bell in the yard of the upper farm would be demanding attention. Someone would hear it, cross the yard, lift it from its hook and answer it. Mabel, his missus perhaps. Winnie, or possibly Gwennan. Or Mr Jack or even Roger Bayliss himself.

The ringing continued. Roger Bayliss heard it from the farm office. Mabel Vallance, pegging her washing on the line at the side of her cottage, heard it. Eileen, in the Bayliss kitchen, filling jam jars with bramble jelly, heard it, Winnie, sorting eggs, heard it but everyone thought that someone else would answer it. Dave Crocker, his cartload of copping stones loaded and ready for the descent to the lower farm, heard it as he flicked the reins across Prince's glossy shoulder, turned the animal's head towards the entrance to the lane and gee'd him forward. On the far side of the yard Mr Jack was checking the water in the idling engine of the tractor while the strident sound of the unanswered bell continued to bounce off the farmyard walls. Dave hesitated. Then he leapt off the cart and sprinted back, across the yard, reached the phone, grabbed it off its hook and then was gaping at the news his wife was giving him. Crossing the yard he shouldered Mr Jack aside, hauled himself onto the idling tractor, slammed it into gear and shouted to his boss, who had just emerged from the farm office.

"'E be there, Mr Bayliss, sir," he bellowed. "Norman Clark! 'E be down to the Lower Farm with Hes and the baby . . . an' on'y Ferdie to help 'em!"

Mabel, once Hodges and now Vallance, blanched at this news.

"Keep an eye on my babies!" she yelled at Eileen, who had appeared at the Bayliss's kitchen door. "That Norman fella's got my Ferdie!" She hauled up her skirt, swung a short, plump leg over the crossbar of the farm bicycle and wobbled off to the head of the steep lane.

CHAPTER
THREE

Norman Clark stepped back from the farmhouse door. He stood, slightly breathless from the exertion of his assault on it, swearing under his breath, rubbing his shoulder and searching the empty yard. Then, from the open door of Hester's cottage came the whimper of a young child. Thurza, bored with her golliwog, wanted her mother. As her cries grew more demanding and Norman turned towards the sound, Hester broke cover and ran from the barn, across the yard towards her cottage, knowing Norman would have seen her and would pursue her. Without looking back she reached her door, slammed it behind her, locked it and shot the bolts. She knew she was not safe. Neither her door nor her windows were robust enough to withstand Norman Clark. Calculating that it could not be many more minutes before her husband arrived back at the lower farm, she lifted Thurza from her playpen and stood, waiting tensely in the middle of her kitchen. If Norman attacked her locked front door she would escape through her scullery into the yard behind the cottage. What she would do then she did not know, nor did she have time to consider, because Norman's heavy shoulder was already making her front door creak.

Ferdie Vallance, hearing Thurza cry, had known what Hester would do. Disregarding her own safety she would go to her child. Grabbing the pickaxe he had been using on the construction of the wall, Ferdie hauled himself from his hiding place near the slurry pit, arriving in the yard behind Hester's cottage just as she emerged from it. They heard the hinge on the front door give way and by the time Norman had pushed through the cottage, lurched out of the dim scullery and was standing, blinking into the sharp sunlight, casting about him and breathing like an inflamed bull, Ferdie had placed himself defensively in front of Hester.

For a moment they stood, a small, middle-aged, lame David and a towering, enraged Goliath. Norman made short work of Ferdie. Seizing the pickaxe in both his huge hands he wrenched it upwards pulling Ferdie off his feet and then, catching him neatly under the chin with a swiftly lifted knee, sent him sprawling at Hester's feet.

Hearing the arrival of the tractor and Dave's raised voice shouting for his wife, Norman snatched up his kitbag and bolted. Had he known that Dave was alone, he might have stayed, but as his objective was a singular determination to assert his will where Evie was concerned and because being arrested for assaulting a lame farmhand did not seem likely to get him closer to this, he struck off, skirting the slurry pit, pushing through a hedge and loping away along the valley floor before veering uphill, towards The Tops and avoiding the higher farm.

Dave found his daughter crawling happily round his backyard and his wife cradling Ferdie's head.

"'E bain't, dead, be 'e?" she asked her husband, anxiously. But Ferdie was already stirring, blinking, struggling to sit up and rubbing his jaw.

"Where did the bugger go?" he asked, his head swimming.

"Down along there and then up over," Hester told him, pointing to where Norman had last been visible. Then, turning to her husband she said, "'Tis no good you chasin' 'im, Dave. He be well gone be now! And even if you caught 'im he'd most likely kill you!"

At that point Mabel had arrived in the main yard and her voice could be heard, shouting loudly for her husband. Seconds later she emerged from the cottage like a rotund and frantic dervish. Seeing Ferdie still befudddled she hurled herself onto the ground beside him and wrapping her stout arms round him, rocked him.

"What have they done to you, my lover? Just look at the state of you! Oooh! You've bit your poor tongue! There's blood all down you!" While his wife fussed over him and Hester told her how brave he had been, Ferdie began to enjoy the situation, wincing convincingly when Mabel examined his grazed jaw and modestly dismissing his heroism.

"'Twas nothun, Hester, my dear. No more'n any bloke callin' 'iself a man would do for a defenceless woman an' child like you and young Thurza was."

At this point Roger Bayliss joined them. He had suggested to Alice that she use their car to drive into

Ledburton village to warn Evie that Norman was in the valley, while he himself, and on foot, took the short cut down to the lower farm.

During the war all firearms had to be strictly accounted for. Roger Bayliss had unlocked his gun cupboard and loaded a double-barrelled shotgun. Arriving at the lower farm he found Ferdie back on his feet, supported by a tearful Mabel.

"Evie's bloke be heading Mr Lucas's way, sir," Dave told his master. "Reckon he could be lookin' for Giorgio." Roger agreed that this was a possibility and that he had already taken the precaution of telephoning Edwin Lucas and warning him that Norman Clark was in the area.

"You alright, Vallance?" he asked Ferdie.

"Me, sir? Oh, yes, sir! Reckon I give that varmint summat to think about! But he caught me a sly one, sir! Took an unfair advantage, he did! A bit below the belt, like. I'd of had 'e but for that!"

"Course you would of, lovie," Mabel purred, dabbing at a small abrasion over her husband's left eye. "Course you would of!"

Constable Twentyman arrived on his bicycle soon after Roger had left on the tractor, taking the Vallances with him back to the higher farm and leaving Dave Crocker with his family. Putting the loaded shotgun into Dave's hands, Roger had told him to use it only if he had to, to fire warning shots. Dave's experience with firearms had been limited to taking potshots at rabbits with the other village boys before the onset of the war had turned them all into soldiers. Due to a slight defect in his right eye, Dave's involvement in the hostilities had been restricted to the catering corps, consequently he had only rarely come within range of a German bullet and it had been a piece of friendly shrapnel that had wounded him. He acknowledged Roger's orders and placed the gun, well out of Thurza's reach, on the top of the kitchen dresser.

Constable Twentyman had cycled carefully into the yard, his face so flushed from his exertions in the steep lanes between the police station and this farm that he seemed in danger of rupturing a blood vessel. His bulk made the frame of the machine look worryingly fragile as he dismounted, propped it against the wall outside the Crockers' door, stooped to remove his cycle clips, stowed them in a pocket in his tunic, patted the pocket, drew his notebook and pencil from another pocket, removed his helmet, settled it in the crook of his arm, cleared his throat and loomed, breathlessly, in the Crocker doorway. Soon he was sitting at Hester's kitchen table and she was putting a cup of tea in front of him.

"And where did the alleged incident take place?" he began, his pencil poised.

One of the changes Alice had made to the daily routine at the higher farmhouse and quite soon after her permanent arrival there, had been to suggest that dinner, the main meal of the day, should be served earlier than previously. At six-thirty instead of seven-thirty. This made for a shorter working day for Eileen. Lunch was to be a lighter meal than it had been, involving soup or eggs, poached or scrambled and even, sometimes, although Eileen disapproved of this, sandwiches.

"No better nor what they land girls used to 'ave!" she muttered darkly after Alice had made clear her plan. "I suppose samwiches is what she got used to, down to the 'ostel, but the master alus liked a sit-down lunch, 'e did!" Soon, although she never admitted it, Eileen began to enjoy the fact that her workload was lighter and her hours shorter than they had been. Today she had made a thick, aromatic, artichoke soup, thickened it with cream and served it with home-baked bread which was still warm and crisp from her oven. She had smiled modestly and lowered her eyes when both the master and the new mistress had heaped praises on her and asked for second helpings.

It was as they spooned up the last of the soup that they heard the clang of the yard telephone. After a moment Eileen came breathlessly into the dining room.

"'Tis Rose Crocker!" she said. "She'm in the phone box outside her cottage! She says to tell you Evie's gone!" Alice left the table immediately and went to the yard phone.

"What's happened, Rose?" Alice asked, sharply. "You were supposed to be keeping a close eye on her! You shouldn't have let her out of your sight!"

"But I 'as me business to think of, Alice, an' I needed more skirt of beef for me pasties, so I popped along to the butcher's. I were on'y gone a coupla minutes and there were no sign of Norman Clark when I went nor when I come back."

"And no sign of Evie, either!"

"She'd gone up to 'er room, see, just afore I left. And I didn't think to check on 'er when I come back . . . but when I called to 'er that 'er lunch was on the table I got no answer and 'er room was empty."

"You mean she took her things?"

"She didn't have much in the way of things. Just a few bits and bobs of clothes as Winnie and Gwennan 'ad put together for 'er. And there was Marion's Land Army greatcoat what she give me when 'er left for America. 'Angin' on a hook behind me door, it were. And she's took me wellin'ton boots . . ."

"And you searched the village?"

"As much as I could . . . And I asked everyone I met if they'd seen 'er but no one had so I thought it best to phone you and Mr Bayliss."

"D'you think Norman could have got hold of her?"

"No, I don't!" Rose answered stoutly. "I reckon if he had, she'd of screamed the place down! The whole village would of known about it!"

It was not until early the next day, when Giorgio failed to fetch in the dairy herd for the morning milking at the Lucas farm, that Edwin found the cottage empty and Giorgio's bed unslept in.

A Sergeant Fullerton, Constable Twentyman's immediate superior, arrived that morning at Higher Post Stone to give Roger Bayliss the news that Norman Clark had been seen on the previous afternoon by the stationmaster at Ledburton Halt, boarding the Birmingham train. He had been alone. Of Evie there was no news nor had there been any sightings of her.

The hostel was searched, as it was thought that there was a possibility that she might have returned there, but there was no trace of her.

After a few anxious nights and watchful days the tension in Post Stone valley began to stabilise. Dave Crocker took the precaution of teaching his wife how to discharge the shotgun.

"Keep the barrel well up, Hes. So the shot goes high. You're not aiming for anyone, see. This would on'y be a warnin' shot. Then brace yourself, left foot forward. Tuck the barrel in real close to your shoulder. That's it. Now you'm ready for the recoil, see. Otherwise the kick will knock you clean off your feet and bruise you black and blue. That's my girl!" he said, admiring her stance and impressed with her quick response to his instructions. "That's my clever, brave girl!" Hester laughed and swung the gun to the left and then the right. Closing one eye and squinting down the barrel as she'd seen girls do in the cowboy films she'd watched in Exeter with her fellow land girls.

"Pow! Pow!" she shouted. "Git your 'ands where I can see 'em and kip 'em thar!"

"Steady on, Hes!" Dave told her. "This be on'y a precaution, Mr Bayliss says!"

Various speculations regarding the whereabouts of the missing lovers were voiced each evening in the bar of the Maltster's Arms.

"Reckon they've took off together. Could be anywhere be now."

"What would they be doin' for money, though? 'E can't of bin earning much up at the Lucas farm. Ole Edwin's a bit on the tight side where wages is concerned." There was indulgent laughter and general agreement with this statement.

"And what with Giorgio getting lodgings and food thrown in, reckon his pay packet would of been a slim one!"

"And she had nothin' with 'er but some small change left over from the tenner Annie's Hector give 'er."

"Maybe they've gone fruit picking," the young barmaid suggested, optimistically.

"What? Fruit pickin' be mostly over be now, duck."

"Not the cider crop, over Taunton way," the girl countered. "They'm still takin' on pickers there."

"True . . . Yeah . . . They could be over Taunton way . . ."

Weeks passed. The days grew shorter and colder. The land absorbed the autumn rains. Winnie and Gwennan, the only remaining land girls from the original intake who were still employed on the Bayliss farms, had, since the closure of the hostel, been enjoying the comparative comfort of digs above the bar of the village pub. Both girls were impatient to begin their post-war careers, Gwennan in Wales, managing her uncle's funeral parlour and Winnie as landlady in the public house she was to run in a northern town. In the meantime they relished the plentiful supply of hot water, the pub food and the social life the saloon bar provided.

Marion, Winnie's childhood friend, who had become a GI bride when she married Sergeant Marvin Kinski, sent her friend glowing reports of life as an army wife in the US.

"Ever wish you'd married a GI and gone to live over there?" Gwennan asked, her Welsh accent as strong as it had been on the day she arrived in Post Stone valley two and a half years previously.

"If I'd met a bloke like Marvin I might of," Winnie said, blowing on her varnished nails. "But there was only one Marvin and Marion got him!"

"She pregnant yet?" Gwennan asked, eyeing her unremarkable reflection in the dressing table mirror.

"Come off it, Gwennan!" Winnie scoffed. "She on'y got wed a couple of months ago!"

"How time flies. As far as I know none of our brides is pregnant. Not Annie. Not Marion. Not Georgina."

"What about Mabel's twins, though, and Hester's Thurza!" Winnie laughed.

"Oh, yes indeed. Forgot about them!" Gwennan applied crimson lipstick and worked her thin lips together. "Georgie was married in June. She could be in the club by now"!

"Shouldn't think so."

"Why not?"

"Well, it wouldn't be much fun, would it, having a baby out there, thousands of miles from your mum and everything . . ." The noise from the bar reached them through the uneven floorboards of their room. "Sounds like there's a good crowd in tonight."

"Not like when them Yanks was here, though, is it!"

Gwennan sighed.

"Them was the days, eh!"

"Guess we'll always remember them days . . ."

"Yep. Guess we will. But you was never as keen on kickin' your heels with the GIs as some of us was, Gwennan."

"No. But looking back . . ."

"Wish you'd let your hair down a bit more, do you?"

"Not really." Gwennan's expression tightened into its more familiar cast of faint disapproval. "Not when I remember where it landed you, Winnie!" Gwennan was referring to the unwanted pregnancy and the narrowly avoided disaster that followed it.

"Thought we'd agreed not to talk about that no more?" she said, sharply.

"Yeah, we did," Gwennan conceded. "Always sayin' the wrong thing, me! Famous for it!" Screwing the top onto her bottle of varnish, Winnie smiled magnanimously.

"Get movin', girl!" she said. "There's a gin and orange on the bar what's got my name on it!"

Edward John selected a robust young beech tree in the Bayliss hardwood plantation. He carefully incised the outline of a heart into the smooth bark, pierced it with an arrow and added the relevant initials. He was slightly ashamed of defacing the tree but such was the level of his passion for Pamela that, on balance, and because it was absolutely necessary for him to express it in some way, he felt justified.

A small cloud on Edward John's horizon was the fact that his father, James Todd, now remarried and with a young daughter by his second wife, insisted that he should abide by a clause in his parents' divorce settlement and spend each half-term holiday with his father and his new family.

Edward John still nursed strong feelings of disapproval of the way his father, after moving him and his mother out of London when the family home was bombed, had abandoned them in rented rooms in Exeter with so little financial support. Alice had been forced to take the only work she could find which provided a home for herself and for the small boy who had then watched his mother struggle with her excessive workload in the primitive hostel, in an environment and amongst people who were mostly alien to her previous experience of life. He had seen her attempt to win the confidence of the land girls, of the acerbic, critical Rose Crocker and of Roger Bayliss, her detached and cold employer, and he had seen her gain the respect and finally the affection of all of them.

Edward John had always understood that to resist this half-term visiting arrangement only added to his mother's problems so, apart from the first chaotic occasion, when he gave his father the slip at Paddington Station and made his way back to the Post Stone farms, he had dutifully complied with it.

There were boys at his school who had lost their fathers in the war. The form was that you were fetched from your classroom and taken to the headmaster's study. After ten minutes or so you were handed over to the matron who led you to the sickbay where you were given tea and biscuits and allowed to remain, sometimes until the next day but more often for just a few hours, after which you were released, red-eyed, back into the routine of the school day.

In Edward John's case the impact of the news of his family's break up had been more protracted. His father, a middle-ranking civil servant, based at the Air Ministry but deployed near Cambridge, made several visits to the rented rooms in Exeter. On each occasion Edward John had been sent on errands, to feed the pigeons in the cathedral square or to buy himself a comic, while his mother was given more details of the uncompromising news that his father, having formed an alliance with the young WRAF officer who was acting as his assistant, now wished to marry her.

"How do you feel about all this, Edward John?" his uncle had asked him, while visiting his boarding school and making arrangements to pay his fees.

"I don't really know," the boy had answered, vaguely. It was true. It was possibly the conviction that whatever he might feel would have little or no effect on what was about to happen to him that produced an impression of indifference. Maybe he was more affected than he realised by his father's behaviour and was in a state of passive denial. His main emotion was an undefined sense of shame that his father, this man, whom he had loved and been proud of and who, he had assumed, loved him, clearly did not and had betrayed both son and wife. From being their protector he had become indifferent to them and was now deserting them. Edward John had watched his mother absorb this situation. He saw her draw on her courage, muster her skills — which, after an early and apparently happy marriage, were limited to domestic ones — and set about providing for the two of them. Had she been childless, Alice's high-school education would have equipped her for some form of skilled work in one of the armed services, but with a small boy in tow, who needed to be well and safely educated where no bombs would fall, Alice soon found that her work opportunities were limited.

At first, Edward John, barely nine years old when his life was so drastically changed by the war, was understandably anxious about how these changes would affect him. Although his mother did her best to conceal how much her husband's desertion had damaged her, Edward John was aware of her unhappiness. His reaction to the news that she was considering working as warden in a Land Army hostel had immediately intrigued him. "What's a hostel? What does a warden have to do? Will there be animals and can I come too?" had been his first list of questions. To which Alice had responded, "It's where land girls live when they work on the farms. A warden has to supervise the hostel, cook the meals and take care of the girls. Yes, there will be animals and yes, you can come every weekend. You will be a weekly boarder at your prep school." There were further enquiries regarding what, exactly, land girls were. What did supervising mean and what sort of animals would there be and wasn't there a village school he could go to instead of being a boarder in Exeter? The inquisition had continued, concluding with Alice informing him firmly that, yes, there was a village school but no, he would not be attending it.

It had been largely Edward John's overwhelming enthusiasm that had influenced Alice to cast aside her doubts about accepting the wardenship. She had already seen the near primitive condition of the ancient, Devon longhouse that was to accommodate ten girls. She had been informed that the only assistance she would receive would be from Rose, the cowman's widow, who made clear her disapproval of the choice of Alice as warden. While Edward John's enthusiasm had not been solely responsible for her decision, it was true that his happiness was high on her agenda and with no other employment on offer, enough for her to find herself in the office of the Land Army Regional Officer, signing a contract committing her to at least twelve months as warden of the hostel at Lower Post Stone Farm.

Edward John found the land girls surprising. He was unfamiliar with the way they spoke and the way they behaved. Nevertheless he took to them and they took to him. In fact, he saw very little of them, because except for milking and at harvest time, the general farmwork ceased at midday on Saturdays, giving most of the girls that afternoon and all day Sunday off. This meant that on the two days when Edward John was at the farm, the girls were mostly absent from it.

During the run-up to the D-Day landings the South West had been overrun by troops, many of them American GIs, and all of them in the final stages of training for the invasion of northern France. The Post

Stone girls had been in great demand for barrack room hops and for trips to Exeter to the cinemas, dance halls and pubs. There had even been a cricket match at a nearby camp — land girls versus GIs — followed by high tea in the mess and dancing to a regimental band from a nearby Fleet Air Arm establishment. It was on that occasion that Hester Tucker had met Private Reuben Westerfeldt, a relationship which resulted in marriage, followed, tragically, by Reuben's death on Omaha Beach and, later and more happily, by the birth of his daughter, Thurza.

Most of the girls' conversation either went over Edward John's head, or, being mainly concerned with boyfriends, clothing coupons and the procurement of nylon stockings, failed to interest him. Sometimes, if the subject under discussion became inappropriate for her son's ears, Alice would raise a warning finger to her lips. On one occasion, just before Edward John's tenth birthday, he had inadvertently silenced the supper table by asking what a "period" was. He had been baffled when, after a brief silence, his mother explained that it was "a portion of time". He had been unable to satisfactorily discover why Marion was given an aspirin because she was having a bad "portion of time".

He enjoyed the rowdy, clamorous, turbulence of the hostel when, soon after his own arrival for the weekend, the laird girls got back from the fields and fought noisily over the limited hot water in the one, peeling bathroom. In the summer there would be the sweet smell of female perspiration and then, after their shared ablutions, the scent of cheap perfume, face powder and nail varnish as they prepared themselves for whatever social life was on offer that evening. He liked the raucous choruses round the out-of-tune piano and the howl of the wind-up gramophone with its limited selection of records, the words and tunes of which would remain with him all his life. "Some day I'll find you, Moonlight behind you . . ."

After two years Edward John's fascination with the farmland which rose from the valley floor and up towards The Tops was undiminished by familiarity. He loved the Bayliss's shadowy woodland, with its smell of mouldering leaves and fungi. He loved the steep tracks that wound across the heathland and on up onto the moor itself, where bumble bees lumbered clumsily over the warm, golden, butter-smelling gorse. Most of all he loved the freedom he was allowed, which developed in him not only an infallible sense of direction but wider instincts of self-preservation and common sense.

Roger Bayliss had been quick to see these qualities in Edward John. The boy was observant where the stock was concerned and on more than one occasion had spotted an ailing or injured animal and been instrumental in saving its life. When "little Arthur", Mabel Hodges' small son, had crawled into the bull's pen it had been Edward John who had distracted the inflamed animal and pulled the little boy to safety through the framework of the stall.

Although he was unaware of it, Roger's relationship with Edward John was much easier than that between him and his own son. The relationship between them had been complex. Perhaps they were too alike. Both had been unable to articulate their feelings about the loss of Frances, the boy's mother and Roger's wife. And when Christopher had become a flier and was under huge pressure, as were all the young Fighter Command pilots involved in the Battle of Britain, Roger's fears for his son had not been confined to the regular hazards of aerial combat but that he would crack up, as he himself had done when, as an underage volunteer in World War One, overwhelmed by the horrors of trench warfare, he had, for some considerable time, lost his reason.

In 1943, when history had repeated itself, Roger had failed to respond to his son's need for sympathy and support, leaving this to Georgina, whose feelings were also in a state of confusion as she herself was caught between her family's pacifist ideals and her own increasing intolerance of the Nazi regime.

Half-term approached and to Edward John's enormous relief, his compulsory visit to his father was cancelled on account of a mumps epidemic at his half-sister's kindergarten.

Pamela was due home for a weekend, which coincided neatly with a Young Farmers dinner dance, held at the Rougemont Hotel in Exeter, to celebrate the start of the fox-hunting season.

Edward John had realised, as he made his way through the guests gathering in the hotel foyer, that he was one of the youngest of them. There was an animated contingent from Seale Hayne Agricultural College, some of whom were self-consciously sporting dinner jackets and black ties, probably for the first time in their lives. Others were wearing what looked like sixth-form blazers with the insignias of their various public schools on their pockets.

In his final year at his prep school, Edward John had been required to wear his first pair of long trousers together with a new blazer, the sleeves of his old one having become noticeably too short. He was a tallish boy for his twelve and a bit years, so that with his height, his long trousers and his new blazer there was very little evidence of the fact that he was several years younger than most of the other boys there, who already considered themselves to be young men.

He positioned himself in the ballroom, directly opposite the entrance, so that he would see Pamela the moment she arrived.

He barely recognised her. She was taller than he remembered and more woman than girl now. With the freedom of her dress-allowance she had bought herself a gown of such sophistication that her mother had almost forbidden her to wear it. But Pamela's will had prevailed and there she stood, slender in midnight-blue chiffon, shoulders bare except for narrow velvet straps. Her hair was up, revealing her long neck and she was smiling her cool smile. As if it had been waiting for her appearance — and perhaps it had been — the small orchestra began to play. Instantly surrounded, Pamela surveyed the available partners, and choosing the best-looking of the Seale Hayne boys, allowed herself to be led onto the dance floor.

Quite what Edward John had expected that evening, he did not know. Certainly not this. He had some vague idea that he would be there and she would be there and that would somehow be enough. Had he intended to ask her to dance? No. Because he didn't know how to. There had been no dancing classes at his prep school. Next year, at his public school there would be. Tonight he and she would have sat, he had supposed, side by side on the small gilt, brocade-covered chairs that fringed the dance floor and talked. About ...? Probably their horses? Or whether they would ride next day? Or go into Exeter to the cinema? Another of the Seale Hayne boys was dancing with her now. When the dance ended and she had been escorted back to the table where her parents had settled themselves, Edward John crossed the floor.

"Hullo," he said.

"Oh, hello, Edward John."

"Would you like a ... can I get you a ...?"

But Mr Seale Hayne was back. In his hands two glasses of champagne in which bubbles were rising exactly as one would hope. As he handed a glass to Pamela, her father indicated the only empty chair at their table and said, "Won't you join us ... um ...?"

"Philip." Pamela smiled. "His name is Philip, Father."

Edward John chose not to remember the details of the rest of that evening. At one point his mother had tried to persuade him onto the dance floor.

"It's a waltz, darling! Ever so easy. Anyone can waltz. Just one two three, one two three, one two three ..."

Next day, hoping to encounter Pamela, Edward John rode out into the familiar landscape, scanning the places where experience had taught him she was most likely to appear. And suddenly there she was, emerging from a plantation of softwood saplings, turning Playboy's head uphill, towards The Tops. Then, immediately behind her, another horse appeared. The animal was a mature bay. Edward John recognised the rider. Philip sat his horse well. With practised skill he turned the animal's head round, drawing level with Playboy and blocking his path. He reached across and taking Pamela's reins, brought both horses to a perfectly controlled stop. Then he leant across and kissed her. And she let him. She could have stopped him, kicked Playboy on, turned her head away. But no, she let him, leaning towards him, then allowing her head to fall back so that he could more easily reach her lips with his.

"I expect you're tired, darling," Alice said when, that evening, Edward John declined a second helping of Eileen's famous chocolate sponge pudding. "We didn't get to bed 'til almost one and you were off riding at cockcrow this morning. Have a nice hot bath and an early night."

"I don't think he enjoyed last night very much, do you?" Alice asked Roger as the two of them finished off the pudding. "Very few people of his own age. D'you think that was it?" Roger shook his head.

"No, no" he said. "It was that Pamela girl. The one he met at Georgina and Christo's wedding. Completely smitten, as I remember."

"Was he?" Alice asked. "I wasn't aware of it."

"No? Ah, well. It takes a man to recognise a heartbreaker when he sees one."

74

"A heartbreaker? You mean Pamela what's-it is a heartbreaker?"

"Undoubtedly, my darling."

"But . . . How dare she! Oh, Poor Edward John!"

Roger was laughing.

"He'll survive. We chaps all fall for women out of our league from time to time. I thought I had with you."

"Did you? When?"

"When you were being heavily pursued by that ghastly fellow from the Fleet Air Arm. The adjutant fellow. Maynard, was it? Oliver Maynard?"

"Oh, him!"

"Yes 'him'. Gave me a few sleepless nights, I can tell you!"

"Roger! How sweet. And I never knew!"

"Young Pamela probably doesn't know, either. Bloody women!"

Winnie and Gwennan were sitting at the kitchen table in the pub, making short work of the meal their landlady had placed in front of them only minutes before. They had been hungry. They were always hungry. Today's work had been even tougher, wetter and muddier than usual. It had involved more mangels than could be imagined, all of which had to be unloaded from the carts, put into piles and covered with straw ready for when they would be needed as cattle fodder. The girls' meal consisted of one rasher of bacon each, a spoonful of baked beans, a generous helping of mashed swede and another even more generous pile of mashed potato. All of this swamped with thick, brown gravy.

"Well," Gwennan murmured, conspiratorially, "what I reckon is this. Norman Clark come back next day in 'is car and —"

"'E 'asn't got a car, Gwennan!"

"Yes 'e has. Evie said so." Gwennan, between mouthfuls, expanded on her theory regarding the now legendary disappearance of Evie Clark and Giorgio Zingaretti, both of whom had been missing for almost three weeks.

"I reckon 'e found her hiding at Rose Crocker's place and strangled her, shoved her in the boot of his car and drove off with her!"

"Never!"

"Why not? They say he half-killed Giorgio when 'e caught him sniffin' round their place in Coventry!"

"But stranglin' 'er? Our Evie? 'Is own wife?"

"Yeah! Well, look what Crippin did to *his* own wife!" Gwennan went on to suggest that having disposed of Evie, Norman had sought and found Giorgio and told him he had Evie locked in the woodman's hut. He then drove up into the forest, killed Giorgio, dragged the pair of them away from the track and dumped them in thick undergrowth. "That's where they'll find 'em, Winnie, you mark my words." Then Gwennan asked their landlady for a second helping of potato and gravy. When this was refused she muttered darkly about how, at the hostel, Mrs Todd had always cooked enough for seconds.

CHAPTER
FOUR

For Georgina and Christopher the month it took the *SS Oronsay* to cover the thirteen thousand nautical miles between Tilbury and the docks in Wellington on New Zealand's north island had been an idyllic, extended honeymoon.

A trail of picture postcards, most of them written by Georgina, had arrived at her parents' home and at Higher Post Stone. Roger and Alice, John and Isabel had telephoned one another to compare notes as the newly-weds' voyage progressed.

"We had a card from Gibralter last week," Isabel announced. "They saw the apes!"

"We had one this morning!" Alice replied. "All about Pompeii. Some of the murals are so saucy that women are not allowed to see them! Georgie was furious!" At Port Said they had ridden camels. The Suez Canal had been "amazing", at Aden they walked through the old town and at Colombo Christopher had bought Georgina a moonstone ring and they had swum in the Indian Ocean at Mount Lavinia. The ship had called briefly at Perth, Adelaide and at Melbourne on "cup day", when everything and everyone was focused on the world famous horse race and Georgina and

Christopher had the city centre almost to themselves. Many of the public houses only allowed women into their saloon bars. "A bit prehistoric don't you think" Christopher wrote to his father "for a progressive country?" While in Sydney they boarded the "the Manly boat" and were impressed by the extent and beauty of the harbour: "blue silk surrounded by green hills," Georgina wrote, waxing lyrical to her mother. "And a rocky foreshore broken by sandy coves."

"It's no wonder Australians brag about this place," Christopher told his father and step-mother, "It's truly amazing, 'bonza' as they call it. Only another week before we arrive in Wellington."

"What will it feel like?" Georgina wrote to Alice, "coming down to earth again after this brilliant voyage? I could go on forever! Up through the Indonesian islands, 'dipping through the tropics by the palm green shores', across to Panama, through the canal and down to South Africa! Why stop now? Why stop ever? What's going on at Post Stone in my absence? Anything I should know about? Love to everyone. Georgie. XXX."

Alice wrote back, addressing her envelope c/o The New Zealand Forestry Commission. There was very little news other than the unfolding of the as yet unresolved saga of Evie and Giorgio, so her letter was all about that, finishing, disturbingly with the news that "We don't know where they are or what is happening to them. Edwin Lucas is keeping Giorgio on his payroll for the time being, which is good of him, otherwise he would be in serious trouble for breaking his contract with the War Office."

The government apartment which had been put at Christopher's disposal until a more permanent posting was decided upon, was in a civil service office block in the business district of Wellington. Its mean windows looked out onto the back of a similar building, its three rooms were small and beige. Immediately after their arrival, while Christopher was sent on a series of surveys, which took him on extensive tours of both islands, Georgina found herself alone in the beige apartment with their unpacked trunks. Twice Christopher had returned for a brief weekend but there had been times when she had been alone for almost three weeks. It was true that the wife of one of Christopher's colleagues had invited her to "baked tea".

Georgina had been unsure what to expect at five o'clock on a Sunday afternoon and had been surprised when a plate piled with overcooked lamb, roasted pumpkin and baked potatoes was put before her.

Noeline was a kind-hearted girl with two small children. Her husband was a forest ranger who worked for weeks at a time in remote areas, spending only a few days a month at home with his family.

"No, we don't see that much of each other," she told Georgina, equably, "but you get used to it!"

Georgina was not, nor had she ever been, a snob. Nevertheless, the life experiences of these two young women were so totally different that each was as conscious as the other of the effort they were both making to communicate. Georgina told her hostess that she was hoping to get a job in order to usefully fill her time while Christopher was away.

"That'd be a good trick," Noeline enthused, smilingly spooning mashed pumpkin into her two-year-old. "What sort of job d'you fancy?"

"I don't know," Georgina said "It would depend what's on offer."

"What was your last job?" Noeline enquired, helpfully.

"Flying," Georgina told her.

"Flying? Flying what?" Noeline had paused, mid spoonful. Her baby, fascinated, fixed its huge, blue eyes on the dripping spoon.

"Planes," Georgina said, conversationally. "We were what they called 'ferry pilots' for the ATA. That's short for Air Transport Auxiliary. It was part of the RAF." If Neoline was astonished, Georgina was unaware of it. "Before that I was a land girl," she added. "Because I was a conscientious objector, you see. All my family are."

"What . . . pacifists you mean?"

"Yes. I had to do war work but didn't want to fight. So the Land Army fitted the bill. My parents farm, you see."

"Oh." Noeline was confused. "But . . . you said you were in the RAF."

"No. Just affiliated to it," Georgina corrected. "Not in it. No combative ops. We just moved planes around. From workshops to airfields."

"Oh. But . . . if you were a pacifist, why did you leave the Land Army?" Noeline wanted to know.

"Long story," Georgina told her, hoping that Noeline would transfer her attention back to her young child. The baby was drowsy. His mother laid him in the crook of her arm and rocked him. The second child was playing happily on the floor at her feet.

"Go on, then," Noeline said. So Georgina told her how, just weeks before he cracked up as a result of his experiences during the aftermath of the Battle of Britain, she had met the man who was now her husband, an RAF pilot in Fighter Command and seen him go to pieces. "This brave person, not much older than a schoolboy, was reduced to a shambling ruin. It was awful. He was out of his mind for months. In a loony bin, basically. And it changed my views on pacifism. I wanted someone to be punished for what they'd done to him. Stupid, really!" Despite herself the old feelings almost overwhelmed her.

"No," Noeline said, cradling her youngest. "I think it's nice. Really nice. You must have loved him ever so much."

"I did," Georgina said, then she laughed and added lightly, "I do."

"Dear Alice" Georgina wrote, a few days after her visit to Noeline.

If I'd known it was going to be like this I wouldn't have come! I'm in a dreary rented flat with absolutely nothing to do. Chris is away week after week and although it's lovely when he's here, most of the time he isn't. I've tried to get a job to fill in the time but my only experience is in agriculture

81

and flying. Not much of either in this dreary city! I've done all the sights. Museum. Art gallery. Oh Alice, I do wish we hadn't come out here! I wish we were back in the Post Stone valley making our home in the lower farm. Hester and Dave and little Thurza across the yard. You, Edward John and Father-in-Law just up the hill, Rose in her tea shop and "all right with the world". I suppose two years is not forever, but today it feels like it.

She reread the letter. Then she sighed, screwed it up and tossed it into the beige waste-paper basket where it lay with two other discarded letters, one to her mother and one to Christopher.

It had been weeks since Norman Clark's appearance at Lower Post Stone and the simultaneous disappearance of Giorgio and Evie. Ferdie Vallance's bruises had faded, work on the wall round the slurry pit was completed, the mangels were harvested and were ready to be fed to the cattle when the grass failed, the nights were drawing in and woodsmoke hung about the village chimneys.

Alice spent a couple of days in London working on the early planning stages of a new kitchen for a north London hospital before returning home to complete her design plans in the comfort of the room at Higher Post Stone that was now her studio. Edward John, in his last year of prep school, had become a vigorous and enthusiastic rugby player. Because of his height and his powerful build he was selected to play as a right-winger for his house team.

As usual at the weekends, Rose did not use her big ovens for the pasties she sold during the week. Often the Crocker family would arrive on Sunday mornings to find a large piece of roasted meat reaching perfection and lying, its juices flowing, surrounded by crisply baked potatoes. While Rose thickened the gravy, Dave slid the carving knife through the succulent flesh, laid the thick slices on his mother's willow-patterned dinner plates and set them on the white tablecloth in front of his wife, his mother and himself. Hester watched as Rose cut two slices of the meat into small pieces and put them into a dish from which, twenty-seven years ago, Dave himself had taken his first solid food.

"That be too much for Thurzie, Mother-in-law," Hester said, removing half the helping from her daughter's plate.

"Well then, give it to Dave," Rose muttered, adding something about daughters-in-law always knowing best. "'E won't say no, will you, son!"

"'S a great piece of pork, Mum. Yeah, I'll 'ave Baby's."

They ate with gusto. The easy family silence only broken by Rose enquiring if everything was all right with the potatoes, carrots, Brussels sprouts and gravy and Hester and Dave repeatedly assuring her that it was. Knives and forks clattered and Dave mopped up his gravy with a thick slice of his mother's home-made bread.

"Well, it's discourteous, to my way of thinking," Rose announced suddenly.

"What is?" Dave asked her with his mouth full.

"Those two. Evie and what's 'is name. Buggering off like that, without so much as a thank you to Mr Bayliss and Alice — or Edwin Lucas, come to that. They'd all been good to 'em, one way and another — but off they goes without a bloomin' word." This was Rose Crocker's method of opening a discussion which she intended to use in order to procure information. She waited patiently through the short silence which followed.

"Mr Bayliss wrote a letter to Annie las' week," Hester told her, "for to ask if they'd turned up at 'er place by any chance. Annie wrote back straight off and said she and Hector hadn't seen or heard a dickie bird."

"They could be dead," Dave said, helping himself to more pork.

"Dead? Why would they be dead?" Hester wanted to know.

"Norman might of tracked 'em down and done 'em in."

"Done 'em in?"

"Yeah. Taken an axe to 'em. Hacked 'em up and chucked the bits in the Exe where they would of bin carried out to sea."

"Don't say that, Dave, that's terrible!" Hester looked at the half-eaten pork flesh in front of her, and then, when her mother-in-law's eyes were not on her, slid it onto her husband's plate.

"Beats me where they could be to," Rose said, thoughtfully. "It's not as if either of 'em's got any family to help 'em out, and there's precious little work about this time of year, specially when they've got no ration books nor nothin'."

"Evie might have hers," Hester said. "She must of 'ad one in Coventry — Mrs Todd would of give it 'er when Norman come to fetch 'er 'ome that night."

"Well, she didn't have it when she come to me," Rose told her, and Dave's opinion was that she'd have hardly waited to pick it up when she was giving her old man the slip by climbing out of his bedroom window. By the time they had finished Rose's apple pie and clotted cream it had been agreed that neither Evie nor Giorgio had ration books and consequently were most probably both dead.

It was Sunday night in Wellington. It had been a good weekend. Christopher had arrived at the beige apartment on the Friday night. On the Saturday they had hired a car and headed out of town along the coast road, found a ramshackle cafe overlooking a wide beach and eaten baked lobster. By midday Sunday, faced with another fortnight alone, Georgina, when Christopher asked her why she was so quiet, had told him.

"You can't imagine how boring it is!" she began. "What am I supposed to do all day? And this place!" she glared around the beige room, warming to her subject. "Look at it! It's enough to drive anyone insane!"

"I think you got a bit spoilt on the voyage, Georgie," he told her. "We both knew it would be down to earth with a bump once we got here!"

"But that's the point, don't you see? You have your work! I have nothing! Nothing to do but sit here, waiting for you to come back!"

"It's only for a few weeks. Once I get posted —"

"It's been six weeks already, Chris! And now it's going to be another two . . . Have you any idea what it's like?" Christopher shrugged his shoulders, which was unwise of him. Georgina's eyes narrowed. "You have no idea how I feel! You might at least try to understand! You think I'm behaving like a spoilt brat, don't you!" He smiled. This too, was unwise.

"Well . . . You are a bit, darling, don't you think?" he asked her gently, but, arguably, not gently enough.

It was not often that Georgina lost her temper. She had done so once when Roger Bayliss had refused to go to visit Christopher when he was locked in a psychiatric ward at the start of his breakdown. She did so now for basically the same reason. Just as his father had done, Christopher was proving himself incapable of seeing past his own feelings when someone else needed, even demanded, indulgence and understanding. While it was true that Georgina was being unreasonable and that these early weeks of his contract were demanding a lot of Christopher, leaving him focused on more immediate and pressing things than his wife's moodiness, he was proving to be curiously inept when it came to a simple demonstration of sympathy. Much as his father had done when he himself had most needed him, Christopher was focusing on his own situation and was blind to Georgina's. Just as Roger had done when faced with Christopher's breakdown and ignominious dismissal from the RAF, Christopher was sidestepping his responsibility to Georgina, slamming down the portcullis and hauling up the drawbridge, leaving himself in an isolated state of self-defence. It was how both he and his father had reacted when his mother had died and they had carried on with their lives almost as though it had never happened. "Life must go on, my boy," Roger Bayliss had said to the nine-year-old Christopher on the day after earth had thudded down on his mother's coffin lid. "So we won't dwell, overmuch, on our loss of your mother."

Although mortified by the distress he had caused Georgina, instead of taking her in his arms, Christopher seemed to her to be almost embarrassed by her outburst. So she suppressed her feelings and they spent the rest of that evening behaving like well-brought-up strangers. At one point she had smiled at him.

"What?" he said. She shook her head.

"I had never realised until now how amazingly alike you and your papa are."

"Chip off the old block, am I?" he said, finishing their bottle of wine and trying to make a joke of her unexpected remark. Georgina blinked hard in order to prevent tears forming in her eyes.

The next morning she went with him down to the ferry where he and his colleagues were to embark for the south island to carry out a feasibility study involving the selection of a particular type of spruce for a specific site. Georgina stood on the dock and waved until, as the boat slipped away from the quay, she lost sight of him.

The morning was sunny. The southern hemisphere seemed to have moved suddenly into full summer. Unable to bear the thought of the beige apartment, Georgina walked aimlessly, eventually finding herself in a small, shady park. Office workers on their lunch breaks sprawled on the grass or sat on benches, eating sandwiches.

She found a cafe, and sitting at a table outside it, drank a delicious glass of iced ginger beer. Her spirits rose slightly. Someone had left a local newspaper on her table. She picked it up and read about a pod of dolphins that had become stranded on a nearby beach. A man had severed his thumb in a sawmill. A woman had given birth to triplets only one of which had survived. She ran her finger down the small ads. A department store was advertising for assistants in its soft-furnishings department. There were vacancies for waitresses and cleaners. It was as she refolded the paper that she noticed a small news item that immediately caught her attention.

Speculation on the whereabouts of Evie and Giorgio continued at the higher farm where Alice, Roger and Edward John exchanged theories at the dinner table when all three of them were together at the weekends.

"Strictly speaking," Roger began, one Friday evening, using his napkin after finishing his helping of a particularly succulent mutton casserole, "we should not be referring to them as 'runaways'. We are assuming they are together but we have no hard evidence of that. The police have been checking the property in Coventry in case either of them — or both — have returned there —"

"She might have been taken there," Edward John interrupted with his mouth full. "Against her will. By Norman."

"There was no sign of either of them when the police searched the place. They've dug up quite a bit of information about Norman's history, incidentally. No existing birth certificate but evidence that an aunt and uncle took him out of a foundlings hospital in Birmingham. But it seems the aunt died when he was about six and the uncle was deemed 'unfit', so Norman ended up in an orphanage."

"You're not suggesting that excuses him, are you?" Edward John had been scandalised by Norman's attacks on both Evie and Ferdie Vallance. "He beat a woman and knocked down a cripple!"

"Better not let Ferdie hear you describe him as a cripple, old man!" Roger laughed. "But you're right, there is no excuse."

"But it doesn't mean there isn't an explanation," Alice ventured. "No parents. No siblings. No relatives other than an 'unfit' uncle. Shoved from pillar to post. As a young man he possibly saw Evie's mama as a sort of 'mother figure'. There's a whole tragic story here."

"And unfortunately it's not over yet," Roger said, acknowledging the bowl of stewed gooseberries and junket that Eileen had just placed in front of him. "It's a possibility that Giorgio has already been repatriated to Italy along with the thousands of his compatriots who were over here."

"What? And left Evie behind?" Alice exclaimed. "I don't think so! He adores her, Roger! Remember how devastated he was when Norman took her away from the hostel!"

"Maybe she's gone to Italy with him?" Edward John suggested.

"That would be more difficult than its sounds," Roger told him. "The POWs are being transported in Royal Naval vessels. No civilians. If the pair of them were married she could get shipped out to join him but she's still legally married to Norman and he'd scupper any idea of divorce. Absolutely not what he has in mind! Enquiries are being made as we speak concerning Giorgio's whereabouts, both in the POW HQ and at the Italian embassy. No news from either so far, and you can imagine the bureaucratic pandemonium going on in those offices at the moment. Thousands of men to be accounted for. As for Evie, I'll wager she doesn't have a passport and she'd need a lot of documentation — birth certificate, medical certificate, marriage certificate, application for Italian citizenship and heaven knows what else, if she wants to enter Italy on a permanent basis . . . Can you imagine Evie being capable of organising all of that, because I can't!"

Roger sank his spoon into his junket. Edward John was silent.

"I expect we'd have to help her out if it came to that," Alice said, wondering exactly what, how, when and where such assistance might be required. There was a pause. "But if he has gone home to Italy, where on earth is *she?*"

"I keep thinking she might head back to the hostel and take refuge there," Roger said. "For that reason I've asked Hester and Dave to pay particular attention to the place."

"Hester's checking it." Alice assured him. "I think she's rather enjoying it. She ties threads of cotton across a different doorway each day so that she'd know if anyone had been moving about inside. And she leaves the curtains and shutters open so she and Dave would see any lights at night." They smiled at the idea of Hester Crocker — super-sleuth.

"And what are you getting up to this weekend?" Roger asked his stepson. The boy had been kicking his heels rather aimlessly lately. Edward John shrugged and stared into space.

"Might go for a ride tomorrow," he said eventually and without much enthusiasm.

"Good idea," Roger said. "Tosca could do with a bit of exercise. You've been neglecting her." Edward John continued to stare, then excused himself from the table and left them. Alice and Roger exchanged glances, Roger pulling a "down in the mouth" face.

"D'you think it's that blessed girl?" Alice asked him. "Pamela thingamy?"

"Shouldn't be surprised," Roger said. He left the table and lifted the tray of coffee things that Eileen had left for them on the sideboard. "Let's take this in the other room. It's warmer there."

West Coast Air Services Inc., Georgina discovered, was a small, international aviation company specialising in internal flights and used, mainly on a contract basis, by commercial organisations and government departments who needed to fly their VIPs between sites, installations or conference centres, and, occasionally, by journalists accessing trouble spots. The company, registered in Canada, was expanding fast, riding the wave of post-war recovery across Europe, through Africa, the Far East and into Australasia. It was about to open its New Zealand offices in Wellington. "WCAS flies off in Windy Wellington" was the headline Georgina had seen in the local paper. Georgina called the newspaper office, was given WCAS's number and after half an hour of hard talking and on the basis of her flying qualifications, was grudgingly given an interview.

The staff Georgina initially encountered gave her a hard time. They were all young New Zealanders. To them she was an interloper, a "stuck-up pom" trying to impress them with her flying experience. When it became clear that they had never heard of the ATA, Georgina had to explain to them what it was. It's affiliation to the RAF was a card Georgina played reluctantly but with instant effect. She heard someone in the inner office say, "Who? Who did you say? Where is she?" And then there he was, standing in the

92

doorway, smiling his memorable smile, holding his arms out to her. "Good grief! It can't be! It bloody is! Georgie!"

"Fitzie!" They hugged. He held her at arm's length, looked her over, threw back his head, laughed and hugged her again. She stood, smiling, as he introduced her to his colleagues in his usual, larger-than-life, colonial way.

"Pilot Officer Georgina Webster!" he announced. "ATA. And one of the best women fliers who ever resisted my not inconsiderable charms!"

"Bayliss," she corrected him, laughing. "Georgina Bayliss. I married Christopher."

"So you did! How could I forget?"

"And you married your Lucinda."

"Ah, but I didn't you see! Lu saw the error of her ways and withdrew her hand before the wedding day. We parted good friends, though. So? Where is your Christopher?" He pretended to scan the room for a sight of her missing husband.

"He's here. Well, not exactly here. He's near Dunedin this week. At least I think it's Dunedin. He's working. A two-year contract with the Forestry Commission."

"And you?"

"I came too," Georgina told him, aware, suddenly, of how lame this sounded and how unlike the Georgina Webster whom Fitzie had known two years ago — a competent aircraft pilot who was capable of flying any RAF planes that needed ferrying from factory to airbase, landing strip or repair workshops.

Neil Fitzsimmonds, a member of a powerful manufacturing family, whose various enterprises were situated on the west coast of Canada, had been completing an engineering degree in London when the Second World War was declared. He was due to return to Vancouver to take up the executive position for which he was being groomed but, like many young Canadians, he became drawn to the defence of the England he saw being blitzed on a nightly basis by the Luftwaffe.

Despite several years of civilian flying, Fitzsimmonds' qualifications were unacceptable to the RAF. His options were to return to Canada, enlist in the Royal Canadian Air Force and then apply for a foreign posting, or remain in Britain and join the ATA as a ferry pilot. He chose the latter, soon distinguished himself, and was promoted to instructor.

Some of the ATA pilots took their flying very seriously, for others, mainly well-educated young women, flying had been, prior to the war, little more than an expensive hobby. At White Waltham Airbase it was Neil Fitzsimmonds who honed their various skills until they were considered fit to deliver the Hurricanes, Spitfires, Mosquitos and even Lancasters to and from whichever airfield needed them. Georgina herself fell somewhere between these two extremes and while her attitude to flying was a responsible one — she soon became one of the most proficient and respected pilots in the group — she also enjoyed the camaraderie and enthusiastically embraced the often over-exuberant social life. While some of her co-fliers confined their passions to the planes they flew, others pursued the pleasures they had been enjoying before the outbreak of the war and for which there were plenty of opportunities.

Georgina, whose licence to fly had been the result of a course of lessons given to her on her eighteenth birthday, proved to be both keen and quick. Such had been the shortage of ferry pilots that she was soon allowed to take her place amongst them.

From the beginning, Fitzsimmonds was attracted to the fact that Georgina stood out from amongst the other young women at the base. She had a quality about her that he found intriguing and perhaps challenging. He was fascinated by her unselfconscious elegance which distinguished her from the group even when she entered into the noisy fun everyone was having. She was slender but not gaunt and while most women at that time wore their, often bleached, hair in elaborate, frizzy curls, Georgina's was sleek and dark, cut in a short, fringed bob which, together with her solemn eyes and high cheekbones made her look faintly French.

"It won't curl," she told Lucinda, with whom she shared a room in various ATA quarters and who was urging her to try a "perm". "It simply won't!"

Neil Fitzsimmonds — whom everyone on the base called Fitzie, became intrigued by Georgina's history. Eldest child of an affluent family of pacifist farmers, the Land Army was an obvious choice when she was conscripted for war service. Despite some initial hostility from one or two of the Land Girls, Georgina was soon accepted as the warm, level-headed person she was. Although her close friendship with the warden was, to begin with, based on the fact that both of them were from middle-class backgrounds, there was no room at the hostel for the class system and any references to it were almost always in the form of jokes or teasings.

"So, why did you leave the Land Army and join this caper?" Fitzsimmonds had wanted to know over a pint of bitter in a pub near White Waltham Airfield one cold night. So she he told him about the young pilot she had met during her early days in the Land Army.

"He was a bit of a pain," she began. "Good-looking, very gung-ho RAF. You know the type." Fitzsimmonds did. "His father owns the farm I was working on. He took me out a couple of times when he was home on leave. He wasn't much fun. The thing was, although no one spotted it, he was cracking up. He'd flown Hurricanes during the Battle of Britain, you see. Then, when the big raids on Germany started, Fighter Command was, of course, used to escort the bombers. He was shot down once and crash-landed twice. Lost a heap of friends. One incinerated in front of him. He got his hands burnt trying to pull him out of the wreckage of a Spit. Anyway the next thing was I found him, quite by accident, hiding in the sheep byre on the farm. He was filthy and starving and, well, raving. Fact was, he'd been AWOL for three weeks. His father knew this but for some reason, didn't tell anyone. The MPs came and arrested him. I tried to stop them. Physically. It was disgusting. Someone who'd done all that, being man-handled as if . . . well . . . as if he was a coward. I visited him in hospital. He had to be drugged to begin with. But the thing was, Fitzie, it completely changed my mind about pacifism. That was why I joined the ATA. I just felt someone should have to pay for what they'd done to him. To all of them. The ones who died and got burnt, shot up or driven mad like he was. But when he began to recover and I told him I was going to fly for the ATA he was furious! It turned out that I'd rejected pacifism at the same time that he embraced it! He wanted me to stop flying and when I refused he didn't want to see me any more. When they let him out of hospital he went off alone and lived like a hermit in a woodman's cottage in his father's forest. I didn't see him for ages. Last time I did he said I knew where he was if I wanted him. But it would have to be on his terms. And I . . . well, on those terms . . . I didn't want him." She paused, smiling uncertainly at Fitzsimmonds, her grey eyes searching for his reaction.

"So here you are," he said, trying to lighten the mood. "Miss Ferry Pilot 1944! 'Nother beer?" Georgina shook her head.

"Can't," she said. "Got an early flight. A Mosquito to Brize Norton."

Fitzsimmonds had walked her back to her quarters, putting an arm round her when she shivered in the easterly wind. At the door of the hut which housed the female pilots he kissed her, finding her mouth warmer and more responsive than he had dared hope.

The relationship had progressed very slowly, due not to any reluctance on either side but to the pressure of work under which the ATA operated. Fitzsimmonds' skills as a manipulator of women were considerable. But he realised that the conquest of Georgina required careful thought. Anything flashy, shallow or hasty would be immediately perceived as precisely that. While he was considering his options it was she who took the initiative, making it clear that what she wanted was not the one night in a cheap hotel with the noise of planes landing and taking off from a nearby airstrip, which was all that seemed available to them, but a week of leave, together, at a borrowed cottage near Porlock Weir.

Everything had been arranged and then, forty-eight hours before their seven precious days were due to begin, Fitzsimmonds received a telegram.

"Can't make it Fitzie. Stop. Sorry. Stop. Will explain one day. Stop. It's to do with Dresden. Stop. Chris is right. Stop. Am resigning ATA commission. Stop. Love Georgina. Stop."

The reunion in Wellington was to be a brief one. Fitzsimmonds was flying out on the following morning. He was unable to give Georgina the job she was hoping for but it was agreed that if a vacancy occurred the company would consider her formal application.

He took her to lunch. They found a Greek taverna close to the quay, sat at a rickety table under a cloudless sky, ate dolmades, drank ouzo and reminisced about the war.

"Great flying day," Fitzie said, squinting into the bright sky. Then he was on his feet, throwing some notes onto the table, taking her by the arm and hailing a cab.

They took off over the city and were soon clear of the surrounding suburbia. Fitzsimmonds banked to the north and followed the coastline. Georgina was as astonished and as delighted as he had intended her to be.

"Okay?" he asked her.

"Beyond okay!" she laughed. "Way beyond!"

"You take her," he said, hauling himself out of the pilot's seat as she slid into it. He watched her find her way round the unfamiliar controls and felt the little craft respond and steady in her skilled hands. For a long time neither spoke. For Georgina the experience lifted her mood, releasing her from the feelings that had been depressing her since she and Christopher had arrived in Wellington. The physical sensation of flying again, of doing something she was good at and being valued for it, washed, disarmingly over her. She became increasingly aware of Fitzsimmonds beside her, the unconsummated familiarity of him came disconcertingly back to her. The warm arm against hers. His jawline. The way his hair grew. The remembered way he lit two cigarettes and passed one to her. All the elements of the strong attraction they had once felt for one another began to exert their various influences over both of them as the small plane slipped smoothly on, through the blue afternoon. When he leant across and kissed her she responded.

Because his hotel served "the best fillet steak in Wellington" they ate there, on a roof terrace onto which his suite opened. Looking back on that day and the night which followed, Georgina realised she had been intoxicated. Not with wine, although that would have played its part, but by Fitzie himself. By the way he regarded her, amused her, appreciated her, studied her and made her feel significant. When, eventually, he led her to bed he turned her to face him as though seeking affirmation that her feelings, regarding this turn of events, matched his.

"Unfinished business, Georgie," he said with a small inflection that didn't quite turn the words into a question but made it open to that interpretation.

As they parted next morning, he into the hotel car that was to take him to the airport and she into the cab he had called for her, they both knew that it was over. That the coincidence which had reunited them was unlikely to recur by chance and that neither of them would deliberately seek it.

"As unfinished business goes," he had said, smiling sweetly, "that was the very best!"

"Beyond the very best," Georgina had told him.

As he reached the car he turned, smiling and executed an exaggerated RAF salute to which Georgina responded in kind.

There were two letters in her pigeonhole when she arrived back at the beige apartment. One was a thick blue airmail envelope, addressed in Alice's handwriting to Mrs Christopher Bayliss. The other was from Christopher and postmarked Dunedin. This, Georgina feared, was going to give her the news that his return to Wellington had been delayed, since he would have been unlikely to write, had he been arriving, as planned, next day. Because of this Georgina decided to read Alice's letter first and she was halfway through a detailed account of events, exclusively relating to the ongoing complications involving Evie and Giorgio, when footsteps approached the apartment door and Christopher burst through it. She gaped at him, speechless with surprise.

Chris dumped his overnight bag on the floor, crossed the room to her, pulled her to her feet and into his arms. Nuzzling her ear, he began to pour out apologies for the way they had parted two weeks earlier.

"I was a bastard, Georgie, an absolute bastard. I just wasn't thinking about what it's been like for you, stuck here, on your tod with nothing to do and no one to do it with!" he searched her face which expressed a mix of shock, surprise and, although Christopher was unaware of it, or of its cause, guilt. "Anyway, anyway, anyway," he murmured happily, "everything is alright now! We've got our posting! No more beige! From now on we'll be together! You've read the letter, of course, so you know . . ." His letter lay unopened on the table. He picked it up, stared at it and then at her. The letter had arrived on the previous day but lain, since then, in the pigeonhole from which, only half an hour before, she had collected it together with today's mail.

"I only just this minute got it," she said, carefully not lying. "Yours and this one from Alice!"

"Don't read it now," he said, taking his letter, unopened, from her hand. "I'll tell you what it says. Come on! Let's go out and celebrate!" With their arms around one another they dawdled through the streets. He gave her his news and the details of his posting. They were to be based on a softwood project near Milford Sound on the South Island. Their house, a wooden bungalow, overlooked a beach. There were horses, a sailing dinghy they could borrow and skiing on the Southern Alps. There was a lively community of farming and forestry people, many of whom he had already met. The posting would be his for at least twelve months.

Christopher led her to the same small Greek restaurant where she and Fitzsimmonds had eaten on the previous day. If the waiter recognised her he was too discreet to give any sign of it.

CHAPTER
FIVE

It seemed unfair to Edward John that by separating their birthdays by three years and making Pamela the older of the two of them, fate had played a cruel and fatal trick on him, placing her, for ever, just beyond his reach. He had depressing visions of Pamela and Mr Seale Hayne walking hand in hand into adulthood and then, arm in arm down the aisle of the village church or possibly Exeter Cathedral, moving side by side into the blissful future which should have been his, while he rode, alone and inconsolable, about the Post Stone valley. "Why?" people would ask, when by middle age, Edward John remained a solitary bachelor. "Why don't 'e wed?" "'Tis 'cos 'is heart were broke when he were a young lad," they would reply.

It was autumn now and the days were shorter. Edward John had left the higher farm after lunch, saddled Tosca and ridden up through the rising ground onto the eastern extremity of The Tops. Here the land levelled and formed a plateau, perfect grazing for the Bayliss sheep which ranged for miles, cropping the wiry, resilient grass. On the western side the steep lane, which climbed from the higher farm, ended in a gate. Near it stood the byre used in the lambing season and well stocked at this time of year with straw bedding ready for the ewes and their offspring.

Precisely when the area first got its name no one knew. The older inhabitants of the valley declared that their grandparents had always referred to it as The Tops and that was good enough for them. Over the generations the name had also proved good enough for many land sale documents and for various leases and legacies.

Reaching level ground, Edward John had encouraged Tosca into a canter and then a full gallop. He avoided the burrows of the rabbit warren on his far right and brought the mare round in a wide curve, eventually slowing her to a canter, then a trot, as he approached the byre.

The light was fading. He would need to let Tosca have her head in the lane so that she could safely pick her way down the stony decline. He reined her in and sat for a moment watching the valley below him dissolve into one huge, soft, familiar shadow. Suddenly Tosca's head swung in the direction of the byre. Her ears were pricked, her nostrils flared, her attention fixed on the dark shape of the old building. It was then that Edward John caught the unmistakable redolence of chicken cooking.

He dismounted, slipped the reins over the gatepost and warily approached the byre. On its southern side there was a wide opening, where once a pair of stout doors had hung. Through the opening Edward John became aware of the steady glow of a dim light.

Since the end of the war the number of vagrants discovered living rough in the countryside had grown significantly. Many were regular tramps and relatively guiltless. For them the nomadic existence was a chosen lifestyle. Others were demobbed soldiers; for them, five years in the armed services had resulted in an aimless detachment from civilian life and in some cases from family relationships which had not survived the war. This situation was thought to be the cause of a number of incidents involving violence and vandalism in the Ledburton neighbourhood. There had been brawls in local pubs. Gates and sheds had been demolished and the timber used to fuel campfires. Because of this Edward John's approach to the byre was cautious.

Evie and Giorgio were sitting, side by side on a makeshift bench, balancing bowls of stewed chicken on their knees. He was wearing an ex-army greatcoat and she the Land Army overcoat she had taken from a hook in Rose Crocker's cottage. His beard was thick and dark, her pale hair, dull and tangled. Even in that low light, her skin looked smudged and her eyes hollow. The fire on which they had cooked their meal was no more now than a scatter of glowing ashes. The flame in a rusted oil lamp was turned low.

For a long moment the three of them stared at one another and the only sound was the wind moving round the old building.

"Don't tell!" Evie whispered at last. "Oh, please, Edward John, don't tell." She began gathering up the tin plates and enamel mugs. "We'll be gone by mornin', honest. You won't hardly know we was ever 'ere!"

"But where will you go?" Edward John wanted to know and Giorgio raised his hands in a gesture of defeat and rolled his great, dark eyes.

"Not know," he sighed. "We have nowhere. No one. But we go. We go."

"No!" Edward John insisted "You mustn't go!" He spoke urgently, keeping his voice low, as though this might prevent their discovery. "I won't tell a soul you're here, I swear on my life! As long as you promise not to go! Do you promise? Do you?" They stared at him and then nodded. "How long have you been here?" Edward John asked and then, seating himself on an upturned bucket, slowly drew their story from them.

On the occasion when they had been allowed to meet for a precious half-hour in Giorgio's cottage in the Lucas farmyard, with Roger, Alice and Edwin Lucas keeping vigil in the drizzling rain, Evie and Giorgio had wasted no time in making their plan.

Evie was already familiar with the lambing byre on The Tops and she gave Giorgio directions on how to find it. At the first sign of Norman's reappearance in the valley they would independently make their way there. Giorgio had subsequently made several furtive trips to the byre, taking with him old blankets, cooking pots, a frying pan, tins of beans, matches, candles and an oil lamp. He discovered the piles of straw that were fresh and dry and behind the byre, a brimming cattle trough, fed by rainwater from the slate roof.

On the day that Alice had arrived at Rose's tea shop with the news that Norman was at Lower Post Stone, Evie used Rose's brief absence — "just popping out for some shin of beef" she had said — to grab a few last-minute things, including half a dozen of Rose's pasties, a Land Army top coat and a pair of Wellington boots that she found in Rose's hallway. Then, leaving the little building through its backyard, she struck uphill towards The Tops to find Giorgio, who had heeded Edwin Lucas's warning and made his own way to the byre, already waiting there for her.

The high ground on which the old building stood made it invisible from the valley below it and from either of the Post Stone farmhouses. There was always enough wind on The Tops to disperse any telltale smoke from Evie and Giorgio's low fire.

That first night and most of the following day they did little more than relish the fact that they were, at last, together. By the second day their supply of food was gone. Cautiously, Giorgio made his way downhill towards the higher farm and into some tangled scrub where he knew that Ferdie Vallance set his rabbit traps. He heard a commotion amongst the farm hens ranging in the nearby cider orchard and saw a dog fox approaching him with a dying hen in its jaws. Moving forward he found another two birds, one dead and the other maimed, amongst a scatter of gory feathers. These, together with some mangels that had fallen off a cart and lay in a ditch, mouldering, fed the pair of them for two more days. He stole one of Ferdie's snares and set it up near the rabbit warren. Once, at night, he ventured down to the farm and into the henhouse where he pocketed the only three eggs that Winnie had failed to collect at the end of that day. But they had no bread and only water from the trough to drink.

They had not known, until Edward John told them, that Norman had left the valley, that nothing, since then, had been heard of him nor that the police had issued a warrant concerning his assault on Ferdie Vallance but that, so far, he had not been apprehended.

"So he's still somewhere," Evie said heavily, the weary tears that ran from her eyes making trades through the grime on her cheeks. "We've thought and thought about what to do," she told Edward John, miserably. "Giorgio's broke his parole so if he was to give himself up he'd be arrested and most likely sent to jail."

It was now almost totally dark. Tosca's whinny reminded Edward John of the long, steep decent down the potholed lane to the higher farm. He got to his feet.

"I've got to go," he said, looking into two pairs of anxious eyes. "You must stay here. I swear I won't tell anyone where you are. Cross my heart and hope to die. I'll bring some food tomorrow, I promise!" They watched him turn and leave the byre. Once in Tosca's saddle he swung her head towards the entrance of the lane, loosened her reins and let her carry him safely home.

When he arrived at Higher Post Stone, Alice and Roger had given up waiting for him and had begun their dinner. He apologised as he took his place at the table and his mother spooned shepherd's pie onto his plate.

"We were on the point of sending out a search party!" Roger smiled and then catching a suggestion of embarrassment on his stepson's face, changed the subject by waving a blue airmail envelope in the air. "Splendid news from the Antipodes!" he announced "The lovebirds have their posting at last and are thrilled to bits with it!"

"You can read all about it when you've eaten," Alice told him. It was obvious to her that her son was concerned about something. She recognised the small signs which had become familiar to her as he had emerged from infant into little boy and then on, to become the adolescent he was now. A slight clouding of his eyes. A faint drawing together of his brows, and an almost imperceptible compression of his lips indicated to his mother that all was not well with him. With each year it was becoming more difficult for her to read him. Soon, she realised, she would cease to know where his thoughts lay or how to soothe him. Whatever it was that was worrying him tonight did not affect his appetite. She piled a second helping onto his plate.

It was still dark when Edward John woke next morning. Since the onset of the war and possibly in response to the various tensions it created, he had developed an unexplained ability to wake whenever he wanted to. He dressed and moved silently down through the house, into the kitchen and then the pantry. Hanging behind the door was a selection of capacious canvas bags from which Eileen selected one or another to use on her weekly shopping trip into Exeter. Edward John took a loaf, four large potatoes, half a fruit cake, a tin of corned beef, two packets of biscuits and a small piece of cheese and stowed them in the bag.

Although the war was over there had been no lessening in the acute shortage of food, the distribution of which was still rigidly controlled by the use of ration books. Aware of this and the fact that Eileen's sharp eye would detect any significant changes in her stock of foodstuffs, Edward John was careful not to take too much of anything. No more, in fact, than could be accounted for by the family's use of the pantry during the hours since Eileen left the farm on Saturday evening and arrived back on Monday morning, Sunday being her day off.

An hour later, with the bag of groceries balanced on the pommel of his saddle, Edward John arrived at the byre just as Evie emerged from behind it. Draped in a Hessian sack, she was shivering and water was dripping from her wet hair.

"I've had a wash in the trough," she said through chattering teeth as she rounded the byre and ran through the gap in the wall where Giorgio met her, wrapped her in the Land Army top coat and led her close to the low fire.

Edward John wished he had thought to include a bar of soap and a bath towel from the farmhouse airing cupboard but food was the first necessity, toiletries could follow. The problem was that he had to return to his boarding school that night and would not be able to bring more supplies until the following Saturday.

"We're going to have to tell people where you are," he told them.

"But you promised," Evie wailed, her grey-blue eyes heavy with accusation.

"If you do, then we must go from here," Giorgio said. "I *criminale* now for breaking my parole. If Signore Bayliss hide me on his land, then he also *criminale*!" Edward John considered the situation. He knew not only that what Giorgio said was true but that the man showed courage and even nobility in accepting the fact and taking responsibility for it.

"The police are still looking for Norman. Once they catch him you'll both feel safer and your explanation of why you went missing will be accepted, Giorgio. But in the meantime you should stay hidden and I'll get supplies to you somehow." Evie was shaking her head while Giorgio, with his limited knowledge of English, struggled to fully understand what Edward John was telling them.

"But how can you? You're away at school all week!" Evie said. The fire was warming her. She no longer shivered and her drying hair was shining in the low lamplight.

"Hester and Dave Crocker!" Edward John announced suddenly. "They'll help!" Giorgio and Evie stared uncertainly. "You know they will! I'll make them swear not to tell anyone! You can trust them! I'll go and see them today. We'll sort this out between us, I promise you! Just stay hidden. Be careful of smoke until nightfall unless the wind is blowing hard." He slung the empty bag over his shoulder. "I'll get off home now.

Don't want to have to answer too many questions about where I've been or what I'm doing! Just . . . stay put." He reached the opening in the barn wall, checked no one was about, urged them to try not to worry and left them.

Half an hour later he joined his mother and his stepfather for Sunday breakfast, clattering into the dining room as though he had just got up.

"Sleep well?" Alice asked him.

"Like the proverbial log," he told her. Well, it was half true. He had slept very heavily until, at precisely six o'clock, he had been suddenly wide awake.

It being Sunday and Dave Crocker's day off, he and Hester had risen late. While she prepared Sunday lunch, to which, this week, her mother-in-law was invited, Dave was encouraging Thurza's first attempts at walking.

"I'm doin' oxtail stew, Dave," Hester told him over her shoulder, as she sliced onions. "Shall us 'ave dumplin's with it, or do your ma like piecrust best?"

"Piecrust every time," Dave told her. She laughed at him.

"You'm on'y sayin' that 'cos it's what *you* like" she chided him. "Watch out Thurzie don't bump 'er 'ead on that table leg!"

In the desk drawer in his bedroom Edward John had two ten-shilling notes tucked between the pages of his post office savings book. There was a half-crown and a sixpence in his blazer pocket. Before he left for school

112

that evening his mother would give him the ten shillings that was his pocket money for the coming week.

With the notes and the half-crown in his trouser pocket, and a bar of Sunlight soap and a bath towel rolled up and stuffed into a paper bag, he left the higher farm, made his way on foot, down, through the fields, to Lower Post Stone, where he knocked on the door of Hester and Dave's cottage.

Having first sworn them to secrecy, he told them of his discovery of Evie and Giorgio and the dilemma that faced them. They stared at him as he laid his money, the bath towel and the bar of soap on their kitchen table and told them that Evie and Giorgio probably had enough food to get them through the next couple of days.

"If you could get supplies up to them by Wednesday, I'll go up on Saturday with some more. That's all the money I've got; if you spend any more than that I'll pay you back, I promise!"

"No need for that, Edward John. Hes and I be glad to help out, bain't we, love?" Hester nodded.

"What's Evie doing for clean clothes?" she wanted to know. "I'll put together some things and Dave can take 'em up to 'er, can't you, Dave?"

Dave pushed Edward John's money back across the table towards him.

"Us doesn't need your pocket money, lad," he said but Edward John shook his head.

"Buy food with it," he said. "Or whatever else you think they might need. But be careful not to let anyone know what you're doing. We shan't be able to keep it up for long but once the police catch Norman they'll be safe."

At midday, as Rose, Hester, Dave and Thurza settled down to eat stewed oxtail under Hester's deliciously light piecrust, the conversation turned, as conversation tended to turn at that time, to the subject of Evie and Giorgio's disappearance.

Rose Crocker's reputation as the best-informed woman in the valley was based, largely, on her ability to recall everything of any significance that had ever happened there since her earliest years, when she had sat, in a hand-me-down pram, in the village street, outside her parents cottage, watching. She watched at school. Absorbing the behaviour of the teacher, and the friendships, or not, between the other pupils. Then, as the years passed, she watched the courtships and the demeanour of the young men from whom she carefully chose William Arnold Crocker who, for as long as he lived, which, sadly, was not very long, proved to be an exemplary husband to her and father to her only child, Dave.

During the two years she had worked at the hostel, Rose had observed the land girls, knew who was "trouble" and who was not, saw romance blossom between Christopher Bayliss and Georgina Webster and Annie and her Hector and between Marion and Sergeant Marvin Kinski — which had resulted in Marion becoming the farm's one and only GI bride. She saw the relationship between Mrs Todd — the diffident warden, whose Christian name she had soon been invited to use — and Roger Bayliss, the austere

114

widower who was their boss, slowly develop, through mutual respect, into attraction, affection and finally the strong feelings that had resulted in their recent marriage.

The war had seen Rose herself emerge from overprotective widow, to competent assistant to the hostel warden, into successful proprietor of her own small bakery and tea shop.

Hester and Dave's cottage had, since the closing of the hostel, been the only inhabited building at the lower farm. Its distance from Ledburton village where Rose now lived above her tea shop, had become a problem for the Crocker family, it being too far for Hester to wheel Thurza in her pushchair and too time-consuming and tiring for Rose to walk to and fro on a regular basis, often in wind and rain. Some weeks ago she'd heard of a car, on the market for twenty pounds, and after some tense negotiations, had bought it.

"It's been in the valley for years," she told her son. "You most probably seen it heaps of times. Big old brownish thing? First off Tom French had 'un, and t'weren't new even then. When 'e got 'is next car he handed the old one down to 'is boys. Then, when the war come and they was called up, it got stood on blocks in 'is cart shed. Four years it must of bin, and it rusted terrible. Then, when the boys was demobbed, they got it going and drove 'un 'til they went off to college. Tom's men's bin usin' 'un round the farm since, but he's just got hold of some sort of ex-army truck thing and 'e don't want the car no more. You'll need to give the inside a good clean out afore you puts Hester and the baby in it, Dave, 'cos its bin used for all sorts lately. I've given Tom 'is money, so you can pick 'un up any time." It wasn't the first time his mother's unexpected decisions had left Dave gaping.

"But . . . Does it go?" was his first question.

"Course it goes! What do you take me for!"

"But . . . I bain't got a licence, Ma!"

"What d'you want a licence for, round 'ere!"

Within days Dave Crocker had been in possession of his first car. His familiarity with the internal combustion engine had developed from a long and close association with the first of the farm tractors. During his war years in the catering corps he had driven trucks and lorries and been licensed by the army to do so. The obtaining of a civilian driving licence was only a formality. Soon the car was proving its worth, transporting his family between the village and the lower farm without them becoming drenched in the autumn rains.

Apart from her watchfulness and her familiarity with almost everyone and everything that happened in the valley, Rose's perceptions had, historically, become alerted by meticulous observation which, backed by immediate scrutiny, almost always resulted in an uncanny ability to identify an irregularity. Even the smallest clues had the effect of focusing her attention and sharpening her powers of observation and deduction. And so it was that as she enjoyed her oxtail stew that Sunday and complimented her daughter-in-law on the excellence of her pastry, she picked up unexpected traces of tension in both her and Dave

116

when the subject of Evie and Giorgio's disappearance was raised.

"No fresh news of the runaways, then?" she asked innocently and knew at once, when both Hester and Dave chorused "No! Nothing new! No . . ." that they were lying. For a while the only sound was the baby, happily striking her dinner plate with her spoon.

"I notice you've made another pie, Hester, dear," Rose said, conversationally. She was referring to the smaller version of the large pie the four of them were eating, which Hester had taken from her oven and set at the back of her range. "Who be that 'un for, then?" As the colour flooded into Hester's cheeks, Dave, with his mouth full, leapt into the breach.

"'Tis for us, Mother. Hes of'en cooks two meals in the same oven and then heats one up, later in the week."

"And that little apple pie on the side there? Be that for 'later in the week' too? Mmm?" Rose looked sharply from her son's face to his wife's and back again. "You know some'at, you two! You can't fool me! It's Giorgio and Evie, bain't it! You knows where they be to! You should be ashamed, David William Crocker! Lying to the woman as brought you into this world and taught you to be a good and upstanding citizen!"

"We're not lying, Mum, honest!"

"Honest? Honest? Don't you 'honest' me, boy!" Rose looked and sounded like an angry hen. If she had feathers they would have been ruffled. She squawked, blushed and blustered and almost choked on a piece of piecrust.

If there was one thing that Rose Crocker hated more than another it was not being the first to know of a really good, significant and preferably slightly scandalous, piece of news.

"We're sworn to secrecy, Ma!" Dave said, almost pleading for her understanding, if not her forgiveness.

"We promised Edward John!" Hester announced and then covered her mouth with her hand.

"Edward John?" Rose exclaimed. "Edward John? What's he got to do with it?"

So they told her. She listened attentively, absorbing all the facts and then allowing herself to be sworn to secrecy too, because if there was one thing Rose enjoyed almost as much as being first with the news, it was a good, solid secret.

"I 'asn't touched me umbrella nor me galoshes for weeks!" Rose would inform anyone who cared to listen, since the family's acquisition of motor transport. These days, when it had been Hester's turn to cook the family Sunday dinner, and the dishes were washed and dried, a pot of tea brewed and a slice of fruit cake consumed, Dave would bring his car as close to his door as he could and Rose, replete with Hester's good food plus the latest news and well satisfied on every score, would pick her way round the puddles and arrange herself in its passenger seat.

"Bye-bye, Hester dear! Bye-bye, Thurzie."

Time passed. Between them, Edward John and Dave Crocker managed to augment the rabbits Giorgio was snaring and the eggs he was stealing, with a modest supply of available foodstuffs. Although meat, bacon, tea, sugar, butter and cheese were impossible, because they could only be purchased on the production of a ration book, the odd loaf of bread, found its way up onto The Tops together with plenty of potatoes, eggs, carrots, swedes and windfalls from the apple orchard. Rose donated pasties. Hester made extra apple pies and baked more bread than her small family needed, she raided the airing cupboard in the hostel which still contained the few towels and blankets that had been overlooked when the place was cleared. Dave invented a reason to take the small farm cart up to The Tops and delivered a significant load of appropriate supplies to Evie and Giorgio, whose first question was always the same one. "Have they caught Norman yet?"

"Not yet. But they will," Edward John or Dave would assure them. But they all knew that with the days getting shorter and the nights colder, the situation could not continue indefinitely.

Georgina's letters, both to the Bayliss family and her own parents, had become full of excited approval of Christopher's posting.

"Dearest Alice, Father-in-Law and Edward John," she would begin, the next pages full of detailed and enthusiastic descriptions of the small cottage they were to live in for the next twelve months.

It's a sort of wooden bungalow on stilts and with a wide verandah all round it. It has a tin roof which is very noisy when it rains and is practically on a

119

beach where there is almost always a surf running. The forestry commission base is a mile along the coast where there is a tiny settlement with a general store and a guest house for people on holiday, as we are not far from Milford Sound or the snowfields of the mountain range called the Southern Alps. There is still snow up there and we hope to go skiing and mountain walking soon. We are so glad we came! Christo is loving the work!

Hugs from us both . . . Georgina.

ps How awful about Giorgio and Evie! What can have become of them? Perhaps they could emigrate? There are a lot of people coming out to settle in New Zealand. Liner after liner disgorging immigrants at the Australian ports and here in Wellington and Auckland. Some are from home [I mean GB] but there are Greeks as well as "poms" here. And Italians. Just a thought.

A thought that lodged in Edward John's mind.

The daily struggle to keep themselves fed, reasonably clean and warm enough to prevent their teeth from chattering was beginning to tell on the runaways. They had to range further and further afield for firewood. When it failed to rain for a week, the cattle trough contained more slime than drinking water.

"What I'd give for a hot bath!" Evie sighed, "'nd to think I used to moan 'cos I had to share one with the other girls at the hostel! Goodness, how we used to fight over that bathroom! Fisticuffs it almost came to, many a time! Mrs Todd used to shout up to us from the kitchen to behave ourselves! Oh, Giorgio . . . Will we ever get away from 'ere? Will they ever catch Norman?" Giorgio would wrap another frayed blanket around her, hold her in his arms and rock her until she fell into a light sleep.

Alice, watching her son, was convinced that whatever it was that had been causing his preoccupation remained unresolved. He had asked for extra pocket money and given her a vague and unconvincing reason for needing it.

"Oh . . . It's just this project thing we're doing at school. I need more glue and stuff from the model shop, that's all. So can I have a fiver?"

"I might be stupid, Edward John!" Eileen told him in a hoarse whisper, catching him in the linney when, for a second weekend, he had taken food from her pantry. "But I knows as you've been takin' food and I also knows you don't go short here, nor at your school so it's not hard to guess who it's for. It's Evie and her Eyetie, bain't it? You knows where they'm to, don't you? Be they in the woodman's cottage?"

"No! No they're not!" He was relieved she had not guessed correctly.

"Where, then?" she persisted.

"I can't tell you!" Edward John whispered, desperately. "I swore I wouldn't! If I do they'll disappear again! And they've nowhere to go, except up onto the moor! And they'd die up there! Oh please, Eileen! It's only 'til the police catch Norman! They'll be safe then! Please don't tell anyone!" She looked at him for a long moment.

"Well . . . Just for now, I won't," she said at last. "But you need to tell your ma and Mr Bayliss, Edward John. They'd know what to do. They'd take charge. Somebody's gotta do some'at or the lord only knows what'll become of 'em. I'll hold my tongue for one more week. Then, either you tell your folks or I shall. It's up to you. D'you understand me?"

"Yes, Eileen" he said.

It was mid afternoon on the second Sunday since Edward John's discovery at the byre. He was in the stable, curry-combing Tosca's glossy hindquarters. He had ridden up to Hie Tops earlier in the day with a supply of groceries he'd bought in Exeter using the five pounds his mother had given him. She joined him in the stable and stood, leaning on the framing of the stall, watching him. She held an apple on her open palm. Tosca swung round, her velvet lips enveloping the apple as she crunched it.

"I get the feeling something's bothering you, darling," Alice said to her son, as casually as she could. "If it's anything I can help with, you would tell me, wouldn't you?" Edward John continued to draw the curry comb across Tosca's haunch, putting all his weight behind each stroke. "Is it school? Or something here at home? Or to do with your father, perhaps?" Edward John, relieved that she was so far from unearthing the truth, shook his head and laughed.

"Good heavens, no!" he said emphatically. This and the nature of his denial gave Alice the clue she needed. All his solitary rides — Pamela was away at school now and could neither feature in his expeditions or influence his mood. Then there had been his need for extra pocket money, plus the fact that for two weeks he hadn't asked for news of the runaways, when, previously, it had been his first question when he arrived home on Friday evenings. Suddenly Alice knew.

"It's Evie and Giorgio," she said quietly. "You've found them. You know where they are." Edward John moved away from the mare and sat heavily on the edge of the granite drinking trough.

"Don't make me tell you, Ma. Please!"

"Why not?" his mother wanted to know. "All any of us wants to do is to help them!" It took some time for Edward John to explain the reasons for his secrecy. First there was Giorgio's fear of getting Roger Bayliss into trouble for harbouring a wanted POW who had broken the terms of his permit to remain in England, and secondly, the couple's mutual fear, not only of their rediscovery by Evie's violent husband but of being parted, possibly forever, by the military police.

"So we . . . I mean I . . . have been taking food up to them. And I told them to stay hidden until the police catch Norman. I've been trying and trying to think of a plan but they've no money and no papers — not even ration books!"

Alice had joined him in the stall and now sat beside him on the edge of the trough, putting an arm round his shoulders and pulling him towards her. Suddenly he was a twelve-year-old boy who had been lying to his mother and keeping to himself a responsibility that was too much for him. He would very much have liked to cry but managed not to. His mother, sensing this, released him.

"You don't have to tell us where they are, Edward John, I promise, but you and I do need to tell your stepfather about this. He'll have some good ideas. He'll know what's best to do." He turned and looked gravely at her. He had regained control of his feelings and was carefully considering his options. If he agreed to tell his stepfather what he knew it would have to be on his terms. But the thought of being able to share the responsibility he had carried alone this far was appealing and it would be a huge relief to no longer have to lie to his mother.

"Okay," he said, getting to his feet. Alice watched him put away the curry comb and tip oats into Tosca's manger. Then they went together into the farmhouse.

Being Sunday, it was Eileen's day off. Alice, Roger and Edward John went into the kitchen where Alice whisked up a pikelet batter, dropped each one onto the hotplate of the Aga, transferred it to a plate and spread it with clotted cream and heather honey. While they sat, relishing this delicacy, Edward John underwent something of an interrogation. His story would move forward, then Roger would stop him, go back over some of the ground and ask for details, building up a solid account of the situation of the runaways, what their chief concerns were and what was their physical condition and mental state. Edward John thought carefully before he answered this last question.

"Evie is a bit weepy sometimes. She's not getting enough sleep because Giorgio goes off at night to fetch the snared rabbits and she's scared that Norman will find him and kill him. She's fed up with being dirty and not having clean clothes, although Hester has —" He checked himself.

"Hester?" Roger Bayliss said, picking up at once on this evidence of more conspirators than his stepson had so far revealed.

"Yes," Edward John admitted. "I had to tell Dave and Hester because I couldn't get food up to the byre during the week . . . But they were sworn to secrecy, so —"

"I bet Rose knows!" Alice said, refilling their teacups.

"No, she doesn't," Edward John assured her. "They promised not to tell anyone."

"You don't have to 'tell' Rose things, darling! She just 'knows' them! But she can keep a secret better than most, as I know from personal experience. 'Nother pikelet, anyone? . . . Any ideas yet, Roger?" Her husband shook his head.

"I'll make some enquiries in the morning," he told her. "A lot of questions need answering."

"Such as?" Edward John wanted to know.

"Such as exactly how Giorgio stands with the immigration department and the Italian military police. And how culpable I am if I knowingly conceal him."

They continued to discuss the situation until it was time for Alice to drive Edward John down to Ledburton to catch the bus back to Exeter.

"Georgie had a good idea," he said as they parted. "In her letter she said Evie and Giorgio might be able to emigrate."

★　★　★

The acquisition of the car gave the Crocker family a new dimension to their lives. Apart from ferrying his mother and his wife between their two cottages, Dave found himself under pressure to venture further afield. The smallholding near the North Devon coast, where Jonas Tucker had scratched a living while he raised Hester and her brother, was within Sunday-visiting distance of Post Stone valley.

Zeke occasionally cycled over the moor to visit his sister, Hester, always bringing worse news of their father's deteriorating condition. The paralysis had tightened its grip on him and he was now confined to his bed and barely able to raise his head. He was totally dependent on his wife who cleaned him as well as she could and spooned gruel into him. When D-Day had left Hester widowed and pregnant she had been forced to leave the Land Army and had reluctantly returned to her parents. Since Thurza's birth she had married Dave Crocker. Her parents had frowned on both her marriages, having wanted her to marry within their strict faith. Consequently she was, in their judgement, damned, together with Thurza, the child of her first husband. As a result of this, when she arrived at the smallholding and led her daughter up the stairs to her father's sick room, the welcome they received was muted.

Neither grandparent had seen Thurza for several months, during which time she had ceased to be a baby and become almost a little girl. Hester was shocked to see how old and gaunt her mother had become, sitting at Jonas Tucker's bedside and, with a soiled towel, mopping the saliva that ran from the corner of his mouth.

"Say hello to Grandma," Hester urged her daughter, but there was no warmth in the older woman's face and Thurza's smile faded. Jonas refused to look at his granddaughter or even to allow Hester herself to engage his eyes, lowering his lids slowly in their sunken sockets and allowing his head to roll to one side.

"'E's not forgiven me, then, Mother," Hester said flatly.

Below, in the chill, front room, Zeke and Dave waited for the visit to be over, Dave staring out through the window at the small but well-cultivated acreage that the Tucker family owned. Much of the space was dug over now, awaiting the cartloads of manure that would replenish the soil ready for next year's sowings, but there was evidence of a good harvest of root vegetables. The chickens looked healthy, there were ducks and geese on the pond and half a dozen porkers, fattening in the pigsty.

"Looks like you'm doin' okay, Zeke," Dave said generously, knowing how hard it was for smallholders to make a living.

"'Tis touch and go most of the time," Zeke told him. "And with Father so sick and Mother taken up with looking after him . . ." Zeke had the demeanour of a man much older than his twenty-one years. His deprived childhood, followed by two years of war surviving in the Welsh coalfields as a "Bevan boy" had left him lean and wiry. Since he had been demobbed and had taken over the smallholding, his mood had been lifted by the presence in his life of Polly, a local girl. The progress of their courtship had stalled in the face of Zeke's domestic problems. Despite this, and perhaps because of it, Zeke looked healthier and more robust than when Dave had last seen him.

"Pigs look good!" Dave said, encouragingly.

"Yeah. Ready for market that lot. And there's a sow, should farrow down in a week or so. But I can't fatten 'em and turn 'em round as quick or as cheap as the big boys can. So me profit's not that good."

"You still seeing that girl over Bideford?"

"Polly. Yeah," Zeke said, dully.

"Serious, is it?" Dave asked him and saw his brother-in-law blush.

"Yeah," Zeke said, eventually.

"What you waitin' for, then?" Dave demanded, bluntly.

"There's complications."

"Nothun complicated about it, matey! You want her, you ask 'er! Simple as that!"

"Just like you and Hes, eh?" Zeke replied. "Took the pair of you almost a year to sort yourselves out, as I remember!"

"Yeah," Dave acknowledged. "But us 'ad —"

"Yeah! Complications, right?" Zeke smiled while Dave recalled how he and Hester had both struggled through a maze of feelings for one another resulting from Hester's sudden widowhood while she carried and gave birth to her GI husband's child. The fact that before she had met Reuben there had been an

128

undeclared attraction between her and Dave Crocker had triggered an overpowering sense of guilt in her when Reuben perished. Although Rose had urged her son to pursue Hester, his instinct had been to give her time and eventually, when they both understood where she was meant to be, she had come to him, with Reubens daughter in her arms.

"It bain't that I don't love Pol," Zeke said. "I'd ask her tomorrow if I'd got anything decent to offer her but — just look at this place!" The Tucker home had never been more than a roof over the family's heads, somewhere to cook their plain food, to wash, to sleep and to pray. Now, after years of struggling with poverty and with Jonas's illness, the place was a hovel. Paint was peeling, furniture was threadbare, the curtains were frayed, the windowpanes draped with cobwebs and slates were missing from the roof. Zeke watched Dave's eyes go round the miserable space. "Can't blame Mother," Zeke continued. "For years she'd helped Father on the holding but as he got worse and could do less and less, she had to do more and more. Now she'm sick too, I reckon. Or if not sick, then worn out and tired to death. And she's angry."

"Angry?" Dave asked. "Why angry?"

"With the Lord. For letting Father suffer when he were a good, God-fearing man who gave up his whole life to the Church of the Pentecostal Brethren. Preachin' on Sundays, raisin' money for new pews and that. Travellin' round the countryside, evangelisin'. Our mother says she hates God now. But she knows that's a sin she'll burn in hell for." Footsteps approached down the uncarpeted stairs and Hester appeared. She put Thurza into Dave's arms, pulled a handkerchief from a pocket, wiped her eyes and blew her nose.

"Poor Father!" she said. "Oh, poor, poor Father!"

"I'll make us a cuppa tea," Zeke said and he went into the kitchen.

It did not seem to occur to Dave Crocker that it was strange that neither Zeke nor his sister felt anything but pity for their father. Their childhood had consisted of years of extreme poverty, much of it caused by Jonas's religious obsessions. Hester must never wear a ribbon in her hair. Clothes that were pretty and colourful were sinful and forbidden, while for Zeke, kicking a football was sin. His friends were chosen for him and for both children Sundays were spent going, three times, to church, to sing hymns, kneel for hours in prayer and then, afterwards, come home to bread and milk for supper followed, until bedtime, by silent reading from the Bible. Had it not been for World War Two, when both children, on reaching the age of eighteen, were required by law to do some form of war work, they might never have broken free of their father's rigid will.

Dave, sitting with his cup of tea in his hands, observing Hester's tears and Zeke's stoic loyalty in taking on the smallholding in order to provide for his parents was, perhaps, reminded of his own Sunday School experience. "Honour thy father and thy mother," the teacher had said. She was a pretty girl who later married the verger. "Honour thy father and thy mother". And he had. And he hoped that Thurza would honour him and Hester.

130

On his next weekend at home, Edward John arrived, full of questions.

"Are they still alright? Have the police caught Norman? Did someone take food up during the week?" The answers had been "yes", "no" and "yes". Over supper Roger Bayliss gave his stepson full details of the results of the enquiries he had made during the week. It seemed that Giorgio had only to hand himself into the authorities, and now that the backlog of prisoners of war had been cleared, could be repatriated without delay to Naples where he would receive money in lieu of earnings during the years of his internment. The police search for Norman Clark had been scaled down since he did not appear to have committed any further offences, had not been reported loitering in the Post Stone neighbourhood and was therefore deemed not to be an immediate threat to either Evie or her lover. The Coventry police suspected that he was, from time to time, returning to the house of which he had tried to claim ownership. Even had he been married to Evie's mother he would have had no case because, in his will, Evie's father had named his daughter as his sole beneficiary. The few hundred pounds in her mother's post office account were also hers. More significantly, the house itself, once the probate was completed, would belong to Evie.

"So Evie's an heiress!" Edward John declared gleefully.

"Only in a very small way," Roger told him. "The house is in poor condition. It won't fetch more than a few hundred pounds."

"But better than a poke in the eye with a sharp stick?" Edward John suggested, brightly. Alice laughed. Her son's vocabulary was often a rich mix of schoolboy slang and the patois of Post Stone valley people, enlivened by the boisterous and vivid vernacular of the land girls amongst whom he had lived through two and a half formative years of his childhood — and was, in his mother's opinion, all the richer for it.

"Yes, much better!" Roger agreed. "So the situation is this," he began, going on to explain to Edward John that if Giorgio opted to stay in England and resume his work for Edwin Lucas, he could do so but would, of course, be vulnerable, should Norman come back onto the scene. "And then there's Evie," he continued. "Presumably she and Giorgio intend to marry. But she is still married to Norman and I imagine that even if we could locate him, he would resist the formalities of a divorce he didn't want and without which it could take years for Evie to get free of him."

"They'll just have to live in sin, then," Edward John announced, as though this should be a perfectly acceptable solution. Roger's opinion was that the first objective had to be to get the couple safely down off The Tops and into more practical accommodation before the winter weather set in.

"Giorgio has a job and a cottage to live in up at the Lucas farm but I doubt whether Edwin and Clarissa would be happy about the pair of them cohabiting there."

"Why not?" Edward John wanted to know. "It's not their fault they can't get married!"

"Couldn't we find somewhere for Evie here?" Alice suggested, realising, almost before Roger spoke, that there was, realistically, nowhere suitable at the higher farm now that she was using one of the main bedrooms as a design studio.

"What about the lower farm, then?" Edward John suggested. "Couldn't she live in the hostel? Hester could keep an eye on her and she could be a sort of caretaker!"

"And where would be the first place her husband would look for Evie if he did come after her again?"

"Mmm . . . Yes. Hadn't thought of that." Edward John felt suddenly frustrated and defeated by the whole situation. He yawned. He had played rugby that afternoon and was bruised and tired. His mother suggested he ran a hot bath and that the family could continue the discussion the following day.

The next morning brought disturbing news from New Zealand. Georgina's parents had received a telephone call. It was Christopher, speaking from a hospital in Dunedin. On the previous weekend he and Georgina had borrowed wet-weather gear and mountain boots and gone trekking on the lower slopes of the Southern Alps. Just above the snowline and with the spring melt at its height, the pair of them had been caught in a minor landslip. Georgina had been knocked senseless, regaining consciousness after half an hour. She was not otherwise damaged but because of the head injury, had been flown to hospital in Dunedin.

"She's perfectly okay now," Christopher assured her shocked parents. "The head injury was not serious but there was an unexpected complication. I'll give you the details later but all's well now and we'll be flying back to base in a day or so." He told them he would call them from the Forestry Commission's offices as soon as he could.

Both sets of parents were deeply concerned. John Webster tried to telephone the Forestry Commission but the time difference meant that their offices were closed.

"What do they mean by 'complications'?" Isabel repeatedly asked Alice, during several long, anxious telephone calls. "What does Christopher mean? One minute he says everything is alright and then talks about 'complications'! What complications?"

Days passed and the only news both sets of parents received was that everything was absolutely fine and no one needed to worry about a thing. Then word came that they were safely back at their home, Christopher had returned to work and the stitches had been removed from Georgina's head wound.

CHAPTER
SIX

It was several weeks later and in a letter to Alice that Georgina eventually gave the details of the complication that had kept her in hospital.

During her months in the Land Army, Georgina had confided in Alice rather than in her own mother and father, sharing with Alice the differences that emerged between her and her parents when she told them of her rejection of pacifism. She had also told Alice about her problems with Christopher's reaction to her joining the ATA and flying in conjunction with the RAF when he himself was, at that precise moment, veering strongly towards conscientious objection. She had also, later, sought Alice's opinion of her decision to end, in favour of Christopher, her brief and, at that time, unconsummated affair with Neil Fitzsimmonds.

Dazed by the fall, Georgina had been only half aware of the descent from the mountain, the sliding of the stretcher into the light aircraft, the brief and bumpy flight to Dunedin and the initial ministerings and examinations in the emergency unit of the hospital there. By that time her head ached dully and she was getting cramps in her lower abdomen. As the night passed she had been vaguely conscious of bloodstained sheets being removed from her bed and of Christopher, half asleep in a chair beside her.

Next morning she had felt surprisingly better and the pair of them were discussing how soon they would be able to return to the beach house when the young consultant in charge of Georgina's case came into the room and sat down on the end of her bed. In his hand was a clipboard with a sheaf of notes clamped to it.

"I have some difficult news," he told them, and seeing their expressions tighten with anxiety, went quickly on. "It's nothing too serious," he said, picking his words carefully, "but it may come as something of a shock. Did you know, Mrs Bayliss, that you were in the very early stages of pregnancy at the time of your accident?" Georgina's astonishment at not only the news itself but at the ramifications that immediately flooded her mind, was obvious. Her love-making with Christopher, apart from a few careless occasions before their marriage, had always been preceded by the ritual insertion of the "Dutch cap" supplied by her parents' family doctor during her engagement. The only occasion when she had not used this device was on the night she had spent in Fitzie's hotel room. "Although the foetus has been lost," the consultant continued, "the good news is that there has been absolutely no internal damage. Everything has settled down and this little mishap will not have any ill effects on future pregnancies. It might have been going to happen anyway — the miscarriage I mean. Women quite often lose babies at this very early stage and many probably don't even know it's happened. So . . ." he was smiling now, "my advice is don't dwell on it. Your head is fine. Just the small cut and a light concussion. You may get a few headaches. These will help with that." He put the bottle of tablets beside her bed. "And the stitches can come out in a day or two. So . . . lucky you, basically!"

After Christopher had thanked him copiously, the consultant left them. Christopher looked at Georgina and pulled a surprised, shocked and perhaps relieved, face.

"My God!" he said. "How did that happen? We've been so incredibly careful, haven't we!" She nodded and he looked solemnly into her eyes, unsure of her feelings. "But are you really alright, my darling? Does anything hurt?" She shook her head and managed a shaky smile.

"No." she said. "Nothing hurts except my head. I'll have one of those pills, please, and then perhaps a bit of a snooze." She watched him pour water into a tumbler, open the bottle of pills and shake one out for her.

"Dear Alice" Georgina had written as soon as they returned to what they referred to as "base". Apparently it *is* possible to be 'a little bit pregnant'!! And I was, weeks only, it seems, when I had my fall. No harm has been done so we are not going to tell my folks, who would only fuss. But I had to tell *you*.' This incomplete account of things was as far as she felt inclined to go.

Despite the distraction of the news from New Zealand the Bayliss family continued to try to devise a practical plan for the immediate future of Evie and Giorgio. It was decided that Edward John would convey to them the facts which his stepfather had established during the preceding week and while maintaining the promised secrecy regarding their hiding place, would make it clear to them that Roger Bayliss insisted that they be moved into decent, safe accommodation.

"It's not as if it was summer," Edward John told them, quoting both his mother and his stepfather as he pressed his case for them to agree to come out of hiding. "If it was, you could camp here to your heart's content! But it isn't. It's getting colder and darker." Evie and Giorgio sat side by side on the makeshift bench, a low fire smouldering at their feet, her left hand gripped in his right one and stared, silently, at Edward John. "It's dangerous up here! You could die!" he said, startling them by suddenly raising his voice. Evie began to cry, wiping her eyes on the back of a grimy hand. Edward John paused and then added more gently, "Giorgio could go back to the Lucas farm. You're still on Edwin's payroll, Giorgio. You see? Everyone wants to help! And we'll find somewhere safe for Evie. We can work this out, you know! Between us all, we can work it out! I promise!"

Edward John stayed with them for more than an hour making certain that they both understood the implications of the news Roger Bayliss had gleaned from the police, the Italian military repatriation department, and of the promise of continuing employment for Giorgio at the Lucas farm as well as a safe hiding place for Evie. He even left them with the idea that emigration might provide a long-term escape from any future threat from Norman Clark. When he was certain that they had absorbed all this information, he rode back to the higher farm.

"Just the two of us for lunch, old man," Roger Bayliss told him. "Your ma has driven over to the Websters. It seems poor old Isabel is still pretty upset about Georgina's accident. How did you manage with our runaways?"

Edward John had succeeded in making them promise not to leave their hiding place but to spend the next twenty-four hours thinking over their new options. On Sunday morning he would drive a cart up to the byre and, hopefully, bring the pair back with him to the higher farm.

"D'you think they'll keep that promise?" Roger asked. Edward John shrugged. He dreaded arriving at the byre the next day to find it abandoned, but their promise had been the best he could achieve. That afternoon he rode down to the lower farm in order to bring Hester and Dave Crocker up to date with the news. To his consternation Rose was at the cottage and he had stood in the doorway, awkwardly trying to think of an alternative reason for his visit.

"S'okay, Edward John," Dave told him, a touch guiltily. "Mum knows everything but she won't tell no one nothun'." Rose, as usual, way ahead of everyone, was sitting knitting a small, pink garment destined for Thurza who was playing at her feet.

"If Giorgio goes back to the Lucas place, Evie can come to me," she announced, her needles clicking excitedly, when the details had been explained to her. "I got me spare room. She can earn 'er keep, 'elpin' out with the bakin' and in the shop. Just while they gets things sorted, mind." She added, glancing at Edward John, "Well! That's made you smile, my lover! You like sortin' things out almost as much as I does!" Rose was fond of Edward John and had endeared herself to him on many occasions during the years at the hostel, in which he had grown from a bewildered nine-year-old, watching his mother deal with the breakdown of her marriage, to an increasingly masterful twelve-year-old.

"Us shan't be around much tomorrow," Hester warned Edward John. "We gotta go see my father, see, 'cos 'e be very poorly now."

"I'll be at my place, Edward John," Rose announced, "so you can drop Evie in to me any time after mornin' service."

It was agreed that Edward John would see that Giorgio was safely moved to the Lucas farm.

With the stitches removed from her scalp and the headaches gone, Georgina was physically fully recovered from the accident. It was probably delayed shock, she decided, that had left her feeling oddly unlike herself. She had initially decided that she would not confess to Christopher how she had come to be pregnant or whose child it was that had been lost. Her night with Neil Fitzsimmonds had been, as both he and she had described it, no more than "unfinished business", their meeting in Wellington merely a freak coincidence which had caught Georgina at a moment when her confidence in her marriage had undergone its first serious knock, a situation in which Christopher had disappointed her and which reminded her sharply of the difficulties there had been in their earlier relationship. This had left her off balance and alone with her homesickness. Her brief encounter with Fitzie had, if anything and not for the first time, clarified and intensified her feelings for Christopher. Perhaps she should have felt some sense of guilt about the "tiny fragment of tissue" that had left her body while she lay in the hospital at Dunedin but she did not. It was the doctor who had used the phrase, as he explained that a foetus, at that extremely early stage, had no feeling and no identity. She clung to this while her body adjusted to the hormonal changes the miscarriage had triggered. She longed to confide her thoughts, not to Christopher, or to her mother, but to Alice, on whom, for almost three years, she had depended, not for advice — Alice never gave advice — but for the effect her steadying influence and her sense of logic had on those who sought her help. Almost all the land girls had, on one occasion or another during their time at the hostel, confided in Alice. Annie, Hester, Gwennan, Marion, Winnie and Georgina herself had tapped on Alice's bedsitting-room door, been invited in and listened to. Often it was simply the act of putting their problem into words that suggested the solution they sought. Sometimes Alice drew attention to one fact or another that clarified things and made easier the girl's decision, or simplified her adjustment to a new and unfamiliar situation.

Georgina walked the beach below the bungalow, her sandals swinging from her hand, the sand firm and cold under the soles of her feet. The tide was low. A big surf was breaking almost a quarter of a mile away. Each wave surging in towards the beach, losing momentum, spreading, shallow and indecisive, amongst the cast-up shells, driftwood and spume. Georgina found herself visualising Alice. Conjuring her grey eyes and finding them fixed on hers, she felt suddenly calmed by the thought, almost the sensation, of Alice's mature mind infusing her own, confused consciousness. She remembered a conversation she had when, two years ago, she became certain about her feelings for Christopher and had decided to marry him. She had asked Alice whether she should tell him about her brief and at that time unconsummated relationship with Neil Fitzsimmonds.

"Confess, you mean?" Alice had asked. She was in the hostel kitchen, ironing Edward John's school shirts.

"One needs to be careful about confessions," she added and when Georgina asked why, thoughtfully explained herself. "They can be a bit of a cop-out, don't you think? It's like admitting you can't cope with something. So you want someone else to help you deal with it. You feel bad about it, so they must feel bad about it too. Or possibly worse than you do. D'you see?" Georgina had said she thought she did and Alice had elaborated. "You need to ask yourself whether you want to confess in order to make yourself feel better, when you should be concerned that there is a possibility that it might make the other person feel worse. In other words, if the problem is yours, who will benefit if you foist it onto a second party?"

"You mean, a trouble shared can be a trouble doubled"? Georgina asked and they had laughed.

Georgina's initial decision had been not to tell her husband about her recent liaison with Fitzsimmonds, which, she was now certain, had no relevance to her real feelings for Christopher or to her determination to make her marriage to him succeed. However, the unexpected revelation which had come to light after her accident had complicated things, introducing to her a sense of responsibility she was too young to have experienced before and leaving her with a sensitised conscience, in which her doubts had multiplied. Although neither she, Christopher or Fitzsimmonds had known of it, a spark of life had been created and then inadvertently extinguished by a slither of icy shale and a rolling boulder. Now, twelve thousand miles from Alice's grey eyes and sharp sensitivity, Georgina focused her mind on what she knew Alice would say to her today, as she walked this remote New Zealand beach, with seagulls wheeling and mewing overhead and the sun glittering on the snow-capped peaks of the Southern Alps.

Over the succeeding days Georgina grew stronger and was increasingly more able to rationalise her situation in a less emotional way. Neither she nor Christopher wanted a baby at this very early stage in their marriage. Christopher's look of relief when the consultant told them the foetus was lost had been palpable and had not escaped her. If the child had survived it would have been the offspring of a charming, irresponsible philanderer, forever unaware of

143

his parenthood, while she would have been committed to maintaining the lie that the child was a Bayliss, Christopher's son, Roger's grandson. Why, she wondered, did she assume it would have been a boy?

As she spent each day, walking the beach, turning over and over in her mind the difficulties and deceptions which would be involved whichever decision she took, she began to understand that the decision was already made. If there was any discomfort involved in what she had decided to do, any pangs of guilt, any future regrets, she alone would have to face them, because it was she who had caused them.

By the morning of the fifth day, with Christopher working in a nearby plantation and their temporary home cleaned and tidied, Georgina had begun to regain her confidence, her sense of well-being and of optimism.

She was comfortable, now that the decision making was over. The news of the miscarriage, which she had survived without any adverse, ongoing consequences, would, she decided, be conveyed to both sets of parents. The rest, including Neil Fitzsimmonds' involvement in it, would remain, securely, harmlessly and even comfortably, contained within Georgina's conscience.

The tide was high, the surf breaking closer to the shore. She would swim. The beach was deserted. She stepped out of her clothes, dropping them onto the powdery sand above the tideline. The water was colder than she expected as she waded in and dived under an approaching wave. She was surprised by the surge and

144

energy of the surf and then slightly alarmed to find herself out of her depth and being drawn sideways, parallel to the shore but increasingly further from it. She realised that her strong strokes were powerless against the movement of the water and a sudden fear of drowning overwhelmed her. Then she remembered the advice one of her neighbours had given her. "If you'se get caught in a rip, luv, don't try to swim against it. Swim at right angles to it and don't panic. Take your time and you'll be fine!" A quarter of a mile along the beach the surge delivered Georgina into shallow water. She felt her foot touch the sand, waded ashore and walked, shivering, breathless, dripping and naked, back to the place where she had left her clothes.

In the land girls' digs above the public saloon bar in Ledburton village, Winnie, fresh from the luxury of a hot bath and wrapped in her dressing gown, sat with one foot on her bed, applying a vivid-pink varnish to her toenails.

"You should of seen the state of her," she said to Gwennan, not for the first time. The news of the safe return to the known world of Evie and Giorgio was circulating the neighbourhood, accumulating interesting and possibly fanciful details as it went. "Filthy, she were!" Winnie continued, turning her attention to the touching up of the chipped polish on her fingertips "When they brung 'er to Mrs Crocker's place she stuck her in the bath tub straight off and scrubbed her, top to toe. Washed her hair and all. Said she'd never seen a girl in such a state and you'd think she would of done, all those years with us lot getting back to the hostel up to our necks in mud!"

"And worse," Gwennan added, briefly removing her attention from the latest copy of The Funeral Directors' Monthly. "Remember the time I had to help the vet get that still-born calf out of Mr Bayliss's favourite milkin' cow? Blood from arsehole to breakfast time there was! Had to hose me down, they did!"

"These days we don't seem to get as mucky as we used," Winnie mused.

"That's 'cos, with the blokes back from the forces, we gets 'em to do the dirty work!"

"And quite right too, I reckon!" They giggled, congratulating themselves on their crafty manipulation of the male sex. "Better get movin' if we're going down for a drink before closing time," Winnie said, screwing the top onto the bottle of varnish and admiring her restored nails.

It was Constable Twentyman who came up with a scheme designed to protect Giorgio and Evie from an unexpected attack by Norman Clark. The idea, which had to be approved, not only by the station sergeant at Ledburton police station, but by his superior in Exeter, consisted of equipping both Evie and Giorgio with high-decibel police whistles. These, threaded onto leather thongs, were to be worn round the necks of the threatened couple at all times, enabling them to attract help should Norman Clark be sighted in the neighbourhood. There was a certain amount of scoffing amongst those who always knew best but, in fact, the precaution was a sound one — a blast from the whistles carried a long way across the valley in which Giorgio would be working, and up and down the village street that passed the door of Rose Crocker's tea shop. As a result, Evie felt better about Giorgio and Giorgio felt better because she was reassured.

The couple met as frequently as their work obligations permitted. On borrowed bicycles, weather permitting, they cycled towards each other and met at several preselected rural rendezvous. When it rained there was the tea shop, where Rose would have a left-over pasty or two for Giorgio. Sometimes they met in Giorgio's cottage at the Lucas farm, where, provided the visit was not overlong, Clarissa and Edwin cast collectively blind eyes and ignored any suggestion of impropriety.

Meanwhile, when Alice was spending a week working in London, Roger applied himself with great effect to a long-term solution to the Evie-Giorgio problem. He too travelled to London, took Alice to lunch and afterwards spent a useful afternoon at New Zealand House discussing, with the appropriate official, the prospects of emigration to that country.

Roger discovered that if Giorgio allowed himself to be repatriated to his native Italy, he could apply there for an assisted passage to New Zealand, where qualified carpenters were in great demand. All he would require would be the equivalent of ten pounds sterling towards his fare and someone in New Zealand to act as a sponsor. The same principle applied to Evie, whose recent service in the Land Army, together with the

Ministry of Agriculture exams she had passed during her time at the hostel, made her, too, a desirable immigrant, as did the fact that she was a white female of marriageable age. She would have to be interviewed, pass a medical examination, produce evidence of the registration of her birth and of a reasonable standard of general education. She too would require someone in New Zealand to vouch for her. Further enquiries confirmed the fact that Christopher, currently employed by the New Zealand government, could provide sponsorship for Giorgio, while Evie's record with the WLA, plus personal references from Georgina, who would undertake to establish her in work and appropriate accommodation, would ensure her acceptance as an immigrant.

All these facts and possibilities were duly conveyed to Evie and Giorgio.

With the settlement of the legalities concerning Evie's inheritance of the house in Coventry, she would soon be free to sell it. She would also inherit the money that had been deposited in her mother's post office savings account, and these funds, together with the money due to Giorgio in lieu of earnings during his long internment as a POW, would enable the couple to establish themselves comfortably in New Zealand.

Christopher, using his new contacts in the timber trade, approached a thriving building firm in Christchurch and discovered that Lucca Angelica, the owner of the company and himself an Italian immigrant, was keen to employ experienced carpenters. Giorgio's origins, plus his pre-war work for the

Catholic church in Naples, made his employment almost guaranteed and he was invited to contact Lucca as soon as possible after his arrival in New Zealand.

"But are you sure it's what you both want?" Alice asked. The five of them, Evie, Giorgio, Alice, Roger and Edward John, were seated round the large table in the Bayliss kitchen, discussing in detail the pros and cons of the proposed emigration. "Immigrants taking advantage of the Assisted Passage scheme must stay in New Zealand for at least two years or pay back their passage money. You do understand that, don't you? It's a serious commitment. Are you certain it's what you want?"

"What we most want is that we are together, Mrs Alice," Giorgio told her, groping his way through the English words. "We no care where, so long as we together. I would like, one day, to take Evie to my home. To Napoli. To live there with my family. And maybe, after the two year, that is what we do. We shall see."

"And you, Evie?" Roger asked the girl, who was sitting, mute, her solemn eyes on Giorgio's. "What do you think about all this? It's a big decision. Twelve thousand miles from your homeland and your family." Evie shook her head.

"I don't have no family, Mr Bayliss. If there was cousins and uncles and aunts, I never saw 'em after me Dad died and I can't hardly even remember him, let alone any of them. It were just Mum and me 'til Norman come. And you know the rest. Giorgio is my family now. He's all I ever want." She became conscious of the fact that all of them were looking at her, their expressions ranging from sympathy and concern, to speculation and even doubt. She lowered her head as she felt her face redden.

"There's another thing you need to consider," Roger began, attempting to use the simplest terms in order to make it as easy as possible for Giorgio to understand him, "and that is that Evie is still married to her husband. In most cases, these days, when a marriage breaks down the couple are able to get divorced so that they can marry a new partner if they want to . . . But Evie is not free to do that. Do you understand me, Giorgio?"

"Yes, he does, Mr Bayliss," Evie said, adding her voice to Giorgio's emphatic nodding. "We have talked about it all. And how Norman wouldn't never let me go. And then there's me not being able to have no more babies. We've talked and talked about that too. All of it, truly."

"An' we no care, see?" Giorgio confirmed. "We will hope that one day we might marry but if we cannot . . . Well . . . No one cannot ever have everything you want for in your life! Of course I would like for Evie to have babies . . . but most I would like for me to have Evie . . . To have Evie like she is my wife! To take care of and love. My church does not allow divorce, but maybe, if one day we explain why we do what we have done and confess our sins to the priest, we will be forgiven and receive blessing, no?" He paused briefly and nodded, as though he wished to remove from his listeners the responsibility of having to reply. Then he continued.

150

"We go to New Zealand and we work hard for the two years we have promised and after that time, who know?" He shrugged, smiling endearingly. "We come back to Napoli? Or we not come back. We see how things are." He paused again before turning to Roger. "And please to thank you son, Mr Bayliss, for being the sponsor for me!" And then to Alice, "And you son, Mrs Alice, for how he kept his word and brought food to the byre. He most excellent boy, Mrs Alice! Most excellent boy!" It was Edward John's turn to blush.

One Sunday morning Zeke arrived at the Crocker cottage at Lower Post Stone Farm. He was driving a van which, though rusted and noisy, was proving better than towing, behind his bicycle, the wicker basket in which he had previously transported produce from the Tucker smallholding to the shopkeepers of Bideford and where, after he had disposed of it, he was in the habit of meeting Polly for a cup of tea or an ice cream.

"What I come about," he told his sister and brother-in-law when the van had been duly inspected and approved of, "is our mother. She's behavin' that funny, Hes. She sits with Father all day an' all night and don't go to bed no more! Just fetches soup and bread and milk for 'im and tries to clean 'im and that. An' all the time she's talking a load of stuff about God forsakin' her and Father. Half the time she don't seem to know me no more! Just stares at me like I'm a stranger. Proper scary it be! I reckon Father bein' so sick all this time and gettin' worse an' worse each day is doin' 'er head in! I do! I think she'm goin' balmy! An' I dunno what to do!"

They took him into their cottage, sat him at the kitchen table and gave him a cup of tea and a slice of lardy cake. This settled him down and brought the colour back to his weather-beaten, young cheeks. But it did not address the problem. It was decided that Hester would return with him to the smallholding, taking Thurza with her and staying for a few days to give what practical help she could to their mother. She would clean the place and do some washing and cooking for Zeke. Thurza's high chair and cot were loaded into the back of Zeke's van. Dave was to fend for himself and go to his mother for his dinner each evening. The afternoon was grey and a damp wind was heavy with coming rain as he watched the van lurch across the yard and vanish into the entrance to the lane.

Daylight was fading by the time the van had toiled up and over the moor. Except for the glow from the paraffin lamp in Jonas Tucker's sickroom, the cottage on the smallholding was in darkness.

It was decided that Thurza's cot would be assembled in the parlour where Hester would also sleep on a truckle bed, carried down from the attic.

Hester had brought food with her and made a meal for all of them, but when she went upstairs with a plate of boiled ham and mashed swede, her mother simply stared at her. Hester was shocked by how thin and exhausted she had become, even in the short time since she had last seen her. "Eat some supper, Mother," she had urged her. "Please eat some supper."

The next day Hester set about cleaning the cottage. She boiled the copper and worked her way through a huge accumulation of soiled bedding and a pile of Zeke's clothes. In a brisk wind she hung out line after line of washing, spread it to air on a rack above the kitchen range which Zeke kept well stoked with wood, so that by evening the cottage was warm, the floors clean enough for Thurza to crawl on them and the laundry dry enough to be folded and put away. Zeke killed a chicken which Hester stewed with onions, carrots and turnips.

Discovering that no one had used the various coupons and "points" which had been accumulating in the Tucker family's ration books, Hester persuaded Zeke to drive her into Bideford the next day, where she used this backlog of food entitlements to restock the pantry.

"I got tins of corned beef and spam and fish, Zeke," she told her brother. "All you gotta do is open one up and boil some spuds and carrots to go with it. The hens are layin' well so there's plenty of eggs. You gotta eat proper, Zeke! Promise me?" He promised. She left him with a mutton casserole and baked him a couple of apple pies and a batch of scones, but could do little to improve on the pitiful situation of their parents.

"What does the doctor say?" she had asked her brother.

"Not much," Zeke told her. "He can't do nothin' for Father and he don't seem much interested in the state our mother's in. She 'as got worse, mind, since 'e last come. He looked at Father for a while, then he said some'at about nature takin' its course. And then he left."

By ten o'clock that night Zeke was in his bed in the small, back bedroom while downstairs, in the parlour, Thurza was settled, happily enough, in her cot. The truckle bed had proved uncomfortable on the previous night, so Hester sat for some time, beside the fireplace, in the threadbare armchair that her father had used until his paralysis confined him to his bed. In the grate the embers were turning to ash. She leant forward, added the last remaining pieces of firewood and sat, watching as they caught, flamed and briefly crackled. She could hear the creak of the floorboards in the room above, where her father lay, gasping and choking. He could barely swallow now and lay, dragging the air into his struggling lungs. Why, Hester wondered, wouldn't the Good Lord, the merciful Lord, whom Jonas Tucker had worshipped all his days, let him die in peace? Why, when he had given over his entire, miserable life to praising him, could he not be compassionate now? "Let thy servant depart in peace" the Book said, didn't it? For a while Hester dozed. When she woke, the fire was out and the room was cold. She undressed, shivering, pulled on her thick, flannelette nightdress, made herself as comfortable as she could on the unyielding truckle and tried to sleep. She heard the clock strike eleven and then twelve. Still the odd creak from overhead suggested that her mother was awake, moving about the room, ministering to the husband who, through all the years of their marriage, had made her bow to his will, listen when he preached and concur when he bullied

154

his family. While he had given most of his meagre earnings to his church and his children went hungry, his wife had knelt and prayed when he told her to and never once questioned his right to rule her life and that of Hester and Zeke, imposing his uncompromising will, his deep-set, steely eyes always on them.

The yard dog broke into frenzied barking, his chain clanking as he plunged from one extreme of its length to the other. Probably a marauding fox, Hester guessed, pressing her head into the hard pillow. The barking ceased but the creak of the bedroom floorboards continued, while she lay, half asleep, longing for her own bed and for Dave, breathing and warm, beside her.

Suddenly she was wide awake. The noise from the bedroom had erupted into some sort of violence. The footfalls were loud, the bedsprings were audible, as though a struggle was taking place, things crashed and smashed. Crockery? A flagon of water? Something thudded to the floor in a splintering of glass. Hester hauled herself off the truckle bed, struggled out of a tangle of sheets and blankets and ran up the steep stairs, colliding with her brother as he almost fell out of his room. Then the pair of them, the brother and sister, Jonas Tucker's children, burst into his sickroom.

The funeral took place a week later on the western edge of the moor in a small, rank, semi-derelict chapel where the Pentecostal Brethren held their meetings. The weather was bleak. A northerly wind swept down from the moor, nipping fingertips and reddening noses.

"Well, at least 'tis dry . . ." Rose Crocker muttered, pulling at the sparse fur trim on her coat collar. She would have preferred not to have come, instead pottering in the warmth of her bakehouse. She had only herself to blame, since she could not claim that her attendance was motivated by a desire to support Hester as she mourned her father, but by the simple, unquenchable curiosity for which she was famous. Her opinion of the Pentecostal Brethren was not a high one. Who were they, these strange believers? Heathens? Pagans, even? Here was a chance for Rose to observe them at one of their rituals. Would there be incense? Incantations? The sacrifice of a live animal? A bat, perhaps, or a badger?

A leading Pentecostal preacher had arranged for the coffin to be collected from the Tucker smallholding and transported to the chapel on a farm cart. Dave drove his mother, his wife and Thurza over from Lower Post Stone and joined the small procession as it left the Tuckers' yard. First came the cart with the coffin draped in black, followed by the two cars. Zeke, his mother and Polly in one, and in the other, almost unrecognisable in the suit he had worn on the day he had married Hester, Dave Crocker. Next to him, in the passenger seat, sat Rose who had dressed for churchgoing, and behind them, Hester, wearing the same dowdy coat she had worn when she had arrived at the hostel almost three years ago. Thurza, already restless, squirmed on her mother's lap as they drove slowly behind the coffin-bearing cart, through the lanes, to the chapel.

The service had been long. Hymns, a sermon, some readings from the Bible and a dozen different prayers had been intoned in low, solemn voices while the small congregation stood and sang, knelt and prayed, stood and sang again, sat and listened, then knelt and prayed, stood and sang yet again and then finally stood and listened. Thurza had howled, been taken outside and then brought back in and then taken outside again. When the service was finally over, most of the small congregation, particularly those of another or no faith, had been reduced to an almost trance-like state of desperation and found it hard to believe that they could, at last, shuffle out into the blast of the icy wind.

As the dwindled company assembled itself in the front parlour of the Tucker cottage, Polly, seeing Zeke standing, tongue-tied, nervously asked the widow if she should make everyone a nice cup of tea. Her teeth were chattering. She had not visited the Tucker home before and was dismayed by its run-down bleakness. Polly was a quiet girl with a suggestion of guiltlessness about her which was confirmed in her wide, brown eyes, smooth hair and softly rounded face and figure. She loved Zeke and relished their weekly meetings on market day. Although patient by nature, she was becoming concerned by the slow pace of his courtship. She had found the Pentecostal Brethren funeral almost frightening in its length and intensity, and despite being dressed in the most neutral-coloured clothes she possessed and borrowing a grey felt hat from her mother, her general appearance had attracted disapproving glances from many of the attendant Brethren. At last Mrs Tucker responded to Polly's question.

"Not 'til us 'as prayed," she answered, stony-eyed. Then she dropped heavily down, her bony knees making audible contact with the stone floor, the bleak light of late afternoon deepening the lines of her gaunt face, her hands clasped and raised in a pose suggesting supplication, her lips moving silently.

The sight that had faced Hester and Zeke when they burst into their parents' bedroom on the night Jonas Tucker's soul left his body was to become a blur of sharp, shocking images which would remain with them for the rest of their lives.

The oil lamp had been knocked off the bedside table and lay on the floor, shards of broken glass glittering in a circle of burning paraffin. The bed was in chaos. Jonas's gaunt limbs, motionless now, protruded from a tangle of blankets and twisted sheets. Feathers were escaping from the ripped cover of the eiderdown. On their father's chest, astride his motionless body, their mother knelt. Her breathing was laboured. She was shaking and sweating. Hanks of her thin, greying hair hung forward, obscuring her face except for her sharp nose, from which beads of sweat, or possibly tears, dripped as she rocked, slowly now, back and forth, back and forth, a pillow pressed down and held firm, over the lower part of Jonas's face.

From that point their recollections became more practical. Zeke's priority had been to control the fire which he did swiftly and effectively, dragging the old

158

carpet over the flames, stamping them out and flinging it, smouldering, into the yard. Hester took her mother by the shoulders and eased her from the bed and lowered her into the chair in which she had sat for so long, watching as her husband's disease destroyed him. Cradling the pillow in her arms, the widow sat, only half aware, and watched her children — Zeke sweeping up the broken glass and pulling the soiled linen from the bed, Hester, straightening her father's limbs, folding his arms across his chest, wrapping his fingers round the small wooden cross he always carried and spreading a clean sheet over him, arranging it so that his blue feet and long, curled, yellowish toenails were hidden from view.

Later, after tucking blankets around their sleeping mother, they left her in her chair, went down to the kitchen and brewed a pot of tea.

"Us'll 'ave to call out the doctor," Zeke said as they sat, shuddering and sipping. It was the first of many decisions the couple were going to have to make over the coming days. Beyond the window the shapes of the smallholding, the pigpen, the henhouse and the leafless branches of the plum tree, slowly formed in the first grey light of the morning.

"Yes." Hester murmured. She was shaking, experiencing a sudden, physical reaction to the events of the night, and then slowly reacting to a sound from the next room where Thurza had begun to shake the bars of her cot and demand attention.

The doctor came in the mid afternoon. Without lifting the sheet that covered him, his pen scratching across the paper on which it was printed, he filled out Jonas Tucker's death certificate. He put his hand under the widow's chin, tilted her face into the light and scanned it, placed a bottle of tablets in Hester's hand and recommended that her mother take one, morning and evening.

"They'll calm her," he said. "Help her through her grief." He passed the death certificate to Zeke. "I'll see myself out." Stooping and holding his head sideways, he negotiated the low beam across the staircase. They had heard him start his car and then the sound of its engine, fading as it moved down the track and onto the road.

The time had come for Giorgio to leave the valley. With his papers in order and a rail pass to Southampton Dock patted into the breast pocket of the Italian army uniform he was to wear on his journey of repatriation, he carefully stowed his few belongings into his kitbag and smiled encouragingly at Evie's worried face. She was sitting on his bed in the Lucas's cottage, watching him intently as though she was trying to commit to memory every detail of his appearance. The dark, glossy hair, the velvety, attentive eyes which, when they caught hers, softened like the brown sugar melting in the fudge that Rose Crocker had taught her to make.

"Needs more sugar," she'd breathe as she forced her favourite wooden spoon through the solid mixture, "and butter instead of marge . . . but it's the best us can do these days, what with the rationing!"

160

"You no worry, *bella mia*," Giorgio whispered, reacting to Evie's anxious face. "Everything go well! I got my papers, you got yours!"

"Well, most of 'em." she said. "Not all."

"Almost all," he said. "Very soon you will have all. And then your Giorgio will be waiting for you in Napoli! And you will be standing at the rail as your ship come in and you see him and you wave at him, and —"

"But . . . Suppose I miss the ship! Or you're not there! Or Norman finds out where we've gone!"

"No one tell him where we gone! It all secret!"

"Or they won't let you go to New Zealand, after all, or —" He silenced her with a kiss. One of his afternoon kisses. Hot, Italian and insistent.

"Will be alright!" he whispered. "Everything in such order! Mr Bayliss and Christophe Bayliss, they got it all arrived!"

"Oh, Giorgio, you mean arranged," she teased him, giggling.

"*Si*. I mean arranged! Of course, arranged . . . Everyone help us! You no need worry, *bella* Eva! No worry!" His tongue was playing with her earlobe. "You stay here with me tonight, mm? Mrs Edwin not mind!"

"Mrs Edwin do mind!"

"Okay . . ." he sighed. "Then I walk you back to Signora Crocker's. We go, one last time, to the hayloft in the barn by the bridge, *si?*"

"For old time's sake, you mean?"

"Who this 'old time' ha? He some man you like before Giorgio come?"

The death of Hester's father had shocked Rose. Although she had always known that the Tucker family were regarded as peculiar, she had been unaware of the extent of this peculiarity until the day of Jonas Tucker's funeral. The dead man had been well known as a preacher in the Pentecostal Brethren sect, which local people knew was a splinter group from the better known and less fanatical Plymouth Brethren. When Hester had first arrived at the hostel, she had, in the opinion of Rose and most of the land girls, exhibited this peculiarity by wearing her pretty hair in a severe bun, black stockings, lace-up boots and long, sober skirts. Her pale skin was scrubbed and, unlike the other girls', devoid of make-up. Initially anxious to say grace before she ate her food and often shocked by the boldness of the group of young women with whom she was now forced to live and work, there had been those, Rose amongst them, who had found Hester unacceptably odd. Then, under the gentle and sometimes less than gentle, influences of hostel life, Rose Crocker and Alice Todd had watched her emerge, like a butterfly from a chrysalis, to flutter out into the world, be fallen in love with by Private Reuben Westerfeldt from North Dakota and defy her parents by marrying him. Rose too, had disapproved of the marriage but for her own reasons. She had seen her Dave, briefly home on leave from the army catering corps, fall instantly in love with Hester and had noted her initial response to him with approval. But then she had broken Dave's heart by choosing Reuben. It had been a long time after

Reuben's death on Omaha Beach before Hester and Dave recovered from the complications of that early mismatching, and an even longer time before Rose forgave Hester for hurting her boy.

The state of Jonas Tucker's cottage, his bleakly bizarre funeral and the strange demeanour of his widow had the effect of giving Rose a closer understanding of what her daughter-in-law's upbringing had been and had made her slightly ashamed of her initial hostility to this strangely raised girl. As a result of this, and in her own, reticent and grudging way, Rose had become increasingly defensive of Hester and appreciative of her excellence as mother of her granddaughter — a child who was not, in fact, her granddaughter at all, Thurza's grandmother being a woman in North Dakota who, as the result of a German bullet, had been deprived of son, daughter-in-law and grandchild.

On the day of Giorgio's departure, when Alice had driven him and Evie to Ledburton Halt, Rose had gone with them. She sat in the passenger seat, glancing occasionally, via the driving mirror, at the couple who sat silently, side by side and hand in hand in the back of the car. Alice tried a few cheerful words about how hard her husband was working to arrange it so that the ship on which Evie would be travelling to New Zealand, would be the one Giorgio would board at Naples and what a grand reunion that would be, with the whole of the rest of the exciting voyage spent on board together. She listed the ports that Christopher and Georgina's boat had called at and how much they had enjoyed Port Said and Aden and Colombo and how magnificent Sydney harbour was — but there was little response from the back seat.

The train was late and they stood on the windswept platform for long enough for Evie to start worrying about what would happen if Giorgio missed his connection and failed to reach Southampton before the sailing of the troop-carrier, which was transporting five hundred Italian POWs back to their homeland.

Then Giorgio was aboard the train, leaning out through the window and Evie was smiling into his eyes. Their adventure had begun and they would live happily ever after. They waved until the track curved, taking Giorgio's carriage out of sight.

Evie maintained her mood of optimism as she was driven back to the village.

"I'm not going to mope!" she told herself, Alice and Rose. "I shall write everyday to Giorgio in his own language! Yes! He bought me a book called *Come Parli L'italiano*. It's got all the words and the grammar and there are exercises you can do. '*Quanto costa la torta?*' means 'how much is that cake?' Evie spoke the words with an authority and inflection that exactly reproduced Giorgio's.

"But they talk English in New Zealand, don't they?" Rose wanted to know.

"Yes they do. But Giorgio and me might go to live in Italy one day."

Ten days later Evie received a blue airmail envelope from Naples where Giorgio had safely arrived to a warm welcome from his extensive family. By the same post she was informed by the Chief Migration Officer at New Zealand House that her application for an assisted passage to Wellington had been accepted. She was to sail from Tilbury in three weeks time. All she needed now was a smallpox vaccination certificate.

It had been two weeks since Theo Parker, the Bayliss's family doctor, had broken the skin on Evie's upper arm and applied the invisible vaccine. The wound had swollen and throbbed, bubbled and boiled. "Exactly as it should," he told her, smiling into her concerned eyes as he filled out the certificate, signed it and slid it across his desk to her.

"What on earth does she want to go out there for?" he asked Alice and Roger over drinks a few days later.

"It's a long story," Alice told him.

"And it's not quite over yet," Roger said, adding, "and her destination is classified information, don't forget."

"Absolutely, old man," Theo smiled. "Patient confidentiality and all that."

Although the word "marriage" was never mentioned, something of a trousseau was being put together for Evie Clark. Alice donated an exotic silk peignoir, a relic of her first marriage which she no longer cared to wear.

"It's only a hand-me-down," she confessed to Evie, who had immediately become enchanted by the lush ivory folds and wide sleeves.

"But it's beautiful," she smiled, her grey eyes wide. There was a pair of satin shoes which Winnie had worn with her bridesmaid outfit on Marion's wedding day and which pinched her feet but fitted Evie's well enough. During his first summer on the farm, Edward John had found, in a furrow in a freshly ploughed field, a small amethyst, set in seed pearls, a pendant without its chain, which had been turned up by the ploughshare. When no one claimed it, Edward John had been allowed to keep it. He liked the way the colour matched the purple of the heather on the moor and had thought, at one point, of giving it to Pamela. Now he decided to offer it to Evie as a parting present. Alice found a light silver chain she rarely wore and Edward John threaded the pendant onto it.

"To remind you of Post Stone valley" he told Evie, solemnly and blushed when she kissed him, laughing, full on the lips.

"You're going to be a proper heartbreaker one day, Edward John!" she told him blithely, laughing at his embarrassment.

CHAPTER
SEVEN

"Gee whizz!" Winnie exclaimed, a reaction perhaps to the strident American stamps on the letter that had been waiting at her digs that evening. She and Marion, born and reared within two minutes' walk of one another, had been parted when Marion met and subsequently married Sergeant Marvin Kinski, a professional US serviceman. Recently shipped over to the United States with a thousand or so other war brides, Marion had adjusted well to the life of an army wife. Now, to her delight, Marvin was soon to take up a posting in Western Germany and she was already happily planning a visit to her homeland and to her lifelong friend. Winnie turned to Gwennan who was at that moment fully occupied by a second helping of their landlady's apple crumble. "Marvin's getting posted to Germany!" she announced. "And Marion's gonna come over and visit us!" Gwennan nodded and swallowed approvingly.

"Is he now!" she managed at last, adding more custard to her half-empty plate and reloading her spoon. Winnie continued to read out her letter, her hand shaking with excitement.

"She says I better get me finger out and settle meself in me pub or she won't 'ave nowhere to stay when she comes to England 'cos she's not going to her folks! Not after them not bothering to turn up for her wedding. 'Miserable sods' she calls 'em! Anyroad, looks like there's plenty of time 'cos she says Marvin won't get no leave 'til next June."

"Well, I never . . ." Gwennan said in her clipped Welsh accent, laying her spoon on her empty plate. When she had first arrived at the hostel she had often used the phrase "indeed to goodness" but the girls soon teased her out of that. While it was true that she had no Marvin Kinski and no best friend writing to her from America, very soon now she would cease to be Gwennan Pringle, Womens' Land Army and become Miss G. Pringle. Manageress of A. D. Pringle's Funeral Parlour at Llandollery. In a few years' time, if all went well, the sign was to be altered to read "A.D. Pringle and Niece". So what did she want with best friends or a Sergeant Kinski?

Winnie and her Uncle Ted were due to take over the lease of the Red Cow early in the new year of 1946. Following the signing of contracts with the brewery and the landlord who was a local, self-made millionaire in the cotton trade, a minor refurbishment of the shabby building was being planned.

"We're keeping it traditional," Winnie had written to Marion. "I've chose a lovely ruby-red flock wallpaper for the snug and we're having a new bathroom with all tiles and that, for the commercial trade." The Red Cow, well known for its generous breakfasts and friendly bar staff, was already a favourite with travelling salesmen on the northern circuit.

Roger Bayliss would be pleased to see the back of the last two of his land girls when, by Christmas, their days in the Post Stone valley would be over. Never his favourites, it had not escaped his notice that both Winnie and Gwennan were exploiting the fact that, with two more of his labourers recently released from military service, these girls were foisting the heavier, dirtier work onto the men. Since the closing of the hostel, the cost of billeting the girls at the pub was more than Roger had bargained for.

"They do more eating than working!" he complained to Alice.

"Not as much as Mabel did!" Alice reminded him, recalling Mabel's insatiable appetite when she first arrived at the hostel. The pint-sized cockney had seemed to be making up for a lifetime of deprivation. "I'd never seen anyone eat like Mabel did!"

"So much so that no one noticed when she was with child!" Roger laughed.

"With children, you mean," Alice corrected him and they smiled as they recalled the unexpected birth of Scarlet O'Hara and Winston Ferdinand, the twins which had been proudly fathered by Ferdie Vallance, and how Roger had marched Mabel off to church, a plump infant under each arm, where Ferdie was happily waiting to make an honest woman of her.

Although Edward John was maturing fast — his increasing height balanced by strong, muscular development — a result of his fondness for rugby,

169

Pamela still outstripped him. Her figure had matured in the six months since he had first been smitten by her and now suggested womanliness rather than the delicious girlishness that had so strongly attracted him. Even when she told him that she was no longer "seeing" Mr Seale Hayne, Edward John did not experience the feeling of elation he might have expected and even found himself making unfavourable comparisons between Pamela and a girl called Daphne, whom he had recently met at the birthday party of one of his school friends.

Alice was relieved to find that Edward John had come through the recent period of tension and even depression which had, over the past few months concerned her. Uncertain of its cause she had considered that it might have been a belated reaction to her divorce or a symptom of a difficulty in his adjustment to her recent marriage to Roger Bayliss, although her instincts on the latter possibility persuaded her otherwise. Except for an initial shyness, Edward John had always approved of Roger, who had strongly encouraged his immediate and continuing interest in the land and the livestock on the two Bayliss farms. Edward John's involvement in the Giorgio and Evie situation, which had committed him to complex and sustained secrecy, had been difficult for a boy who had always found it easy to confide in his mother. Alice remembered the numerous occasions when, sensing his tension, she had asked him if he was all right, or if something was worrying him. Always she had seen the evasive eyes and the quick shake of the head and been unconvinced by his reassurance. But she trusted him and was well aware that he was approaching the time when the decisions he made would be increasingly his own. Nevertheless, when the facts became known and he was relieved of the responsibility he had taken on regarding the runaways, his mother shared that relief, and the fact that he had withstood it so well pleased her.

Letters and even the odd telegram confirmed that Georgina and Christopher had covered all the arrangements concerning Evie and Giorgio's eventual arrival in New Zealand. Roger, who had cultivated a useful relationship with various members of the immigration staff at New Zealand House, had succeeded in making it almost certain that the couple would be berthed on the same ship, though not in the same cabin, for their voyage out. Roger had even been issued with a petrol voucher which would enable him and Alice to drive Evie to Tilbury and see her safely aboard the P&O liner *Orontes* in early December. Until then, Evie would continue to live with Rose Crocker, to write almost daily — sometimes in Italian — to Giorgio who, in Naples, was putting together evidence of his education, his apprenticeships as woodturner and cabinetmaker and references from the administrators of the various Catholic churches which had employed him before the war. These, together with his war record, would not only qualify him for financial compensation for all the years of his internment but impress potential employers in his new country.

Since there was no further sign nor any news of Norman Clark, the tension inevitably eased and the valley people grew less watchful and less inquisitive. As a result there was little interest in the details of either Giorgio's departure or of Evie's plans to follow him. Some assumed that Giorgio still worked for Edwin Lucas and that Evie's residence with Rose Crocker had become permanent. Others simply did not care. Certainly the couple had ceased to be the focus of speculative interest which they had previously been. Newer, more salacious gossip, involving returning servicemen, had overtaken them. A young Fräulein from Cologne had arrived in Ledburton, with her blustering father beside her and a one-year-old and heavily freckled infant in her arms. Together they had confronted a ginger-haired cowman, recently returned to a neighbouring farm after military service in Germany, with this unwelcome evidence of his parenthood. Another unhappy family were grappling with the harsh fact that a wife had given birth during the five years her husband had spent in a Japanese internment camp and while large numbers of US servicemen had been stationed in England, training for the D-Day landings. The fact that the beautiful, black toddler had been christened Hank compounded the problem, suggesting an unrepentant attitude on the part of the erring wife. This and various other infidelities were keeping the valley gossips well occupied, and as only so much scandalised excitement could be sustained at any one time, Evie and Giorgio, conveniently became yesterday's news.

Evie's culinary skills which had hitherto been undeveloped, proved, under Rose's more experienced tuition, to be exceptional. Soon her pasties were as good, if not better than Rose's.

"Don't suppose they eat pasties in New Zealand," Rose murmured as she kneaded a lump of dough. "Or scones. Pity. You could of started up a nice little business of your own, Evie, dear."

"Georgina likes pasties," Evie told her. "So does Christopher. And there's lots of English people out there now. It says so in the book the emigration people sent."

"Is there?" Rose wanted to know. "First I heard of it. I thought they was mostly black people with bones through their noses. Anyway, they lulled Captain Cook!"

"No they didn't, Rose!"

"Well some lot down there did for him!" Rose insisted. "Speared by the blacks, he were. Our teacher told us! She showed us a picture. In grass skirts they was and carrying great long spears." Evie was not sure enough of her facts to argue with Rose, specially as she was, at that moment, a trusted and valued support. Silence fell as the two women concentrated on chopping and dicing the carrots, swedes, onions and potatoes and adding the chunks of lean beef flank for that day's batch of pasties, then forking in the sage and parsley seasoning and sprinkling on the salt and pepper. Soon the heat was rising from the ovens of Rose's little bakehouse as the ingredients melted together, the rich gravy thickened and the pastry grew

173

crisp and golden. The air became filled with a distinctive and seductive aroma which escaped from the bakehouse to waft along the village street, making every passer-by wonder how it was that he or she felt suddenly so hungry and not only hungry but possessed by an overpowering desire for something advertised on a sign over the shop door. "Try One of Rose Crocker's Famous Devon Pasties" it read. And they did.

One morning in mid November Zeke's van lumbered into the yard at the lower farm and slithered to a muddy stop. Zeke lurched out of the driver's seat and stumbled into his sister's cottage.

"Whatever's up?" Hester asked, alarmed by the state of him. "Is it Mother? Be she sick?" He was white and trembling, shaking his shaggy head and almost beyond speech.

"Sit you down!" his sister told him sharply. "And pull yourself together!" But he was beyond composure.

"No! You gotta come, Hes! Now! You gotta come cos I dunno what to do with it! Ma knew it was there! Her never said nothun but her knew! I could tell!"

"Knew what was where? What are you on about, Zeke?"

"The money!"

"What money? Whose?"

"I dunno whose! I dunno where it come from! But it's there, Hes! Loads and loads and loads of it. You gotta come! Now!"

Zeke's driving as he recrossed the moor made Hester fearful for her life and, more importantly, for Thurza's.

174

But the little girl enjoyed the rough ride and the more they swerved along the narrow lanes and swooped up, over the steep, humpbacked bridges and across the heights of the misty wilderness, the more Thurza shrieked with delight and the tighter her mother clutched her.

"Go easy, Zeke!" she pleaded. "You'll kill us all, else! Just calm down a bit and tell us what's go in' on!"

The fact that he now had the support of his sister seemed to have a steadying effect on Zeke. He slowed the car slightly and began to speak.

"Since Father was funeralled Mother won't go near their bedroom and you can see why, Hes. She knows what she done! Us all knows what she done!"

"No," Hester told him, firmly. "No one but you, me and Mother knows! And even you and me can't be certain."

"But the pilla, Hes! It were over Father's face! She'd smothered 'im!"

"No, Zeke! What we saw was Father lying dead and Mother holdin' the pilla! You don't know, and I don't know, how he'd come to be dead! She might of been plannin' on finishin' 'im but we don't know if she did! The doctor said it was natural causes killed 'im and that's good enough for me! And what's more, Ezekial Tucker, I don't want to hear another word from you about what Mother did or didn't do! 'Tis over now, whatever 'twas. And it would have bin what she thought was best for Father! She loved him, Zeke. All her life she loved him, and if at the very end, she eased his passing whatever way she saw fit, that's alright with me!"

For a while they drove in silence, leaving the moor and emerging onto farmland near the north Devon coast.

"Anyrate," Zeke said at last. "She'm behaving that odd I 'ad to get the doctor out to her. It were a different doctor as saw to Father. A younger one. Mother sits in the yard a lot these days, see, and won't come indoors. This doctor went outside and talked to her where she were. Sittin' by the henhouse she were, even though 'twas rainin' a bit. Then he come indoors and told me she be in a traumatised state. D'you know what traumatised is, Hes?" His sister shook her head. "'Tis when some'at bad's bin goin' on and it gets in your head," Zeke told her. "The doc said she's gonna have to go to Plymouth for special treatment. After that she might be better."

"Only might be?" Hester queried and then asked, "What sort of special treatment?" Zeke shrugged.

"This morning, while she were out in the yard, I thought I'd have a go at sorting out the bedroom. It's in a bit of a state as you can imagine, 'cos I haven't got round to goin' in there and seein' to it. Been puttin' it off, I daresay."

Hester looked at her brother. The familiar profile, his eyes on the road, his young face reflecting the unrelentingly bleak life his parents had inflicted on him.

"I'm sorry, Zeke!" she said. "I should of come over and stayed and helped more 'an I did! You shouldn't of'ad all this to cope with on your own! Reckon I got off light compared to you."

"I wouldn't say that, Hes. Father was pretty rough on you when you disobeyed him and married that Reuben and had to come back 'ere, on your own and pregnant. Jeez, that couldn't of bin much fun!"

"No, it weren't," Hester agreed. "But I was carryin' Thurza be then. And in a sort of way I had Dave, too . . . But after you got out the army it were back 'ere for you, with Father gettin' sicker by the day and Mother . . . Well, Mother . . ." As she spoke Zeke turned the steering wheel, pulling the van off the road and up the uneven track towards the Tucker cottage.

The widow was sitting on a wooden bench beside the front door. She had obviously been there for some time because the mist had beaded her unkempt hair and the nap of the tweed coat that hung shapelessly from her crouched shoulders. She watched as her daughter climbed out of the van, and with Thurza on her hip, approached, stooped and kissed her cold cheek. With her free hand, Hester took her mother's elbow and drew her to her feet.

"Come on, Mother. Let's get you inside."

"Zeke found the money!" she told Hester.

"Yes, Mother. Come inside. Come on now . . ."

"'Twas your father's!" her mother went on, more or less unheeded. "'Twas all earned and saved, mind! Every penny he could put aside over a lifetime of toiling and strivin'. He promised the Lord Jesus, see?"

"Yes, Mother. Come on. Out of the rain . . ."

Hester led their mother into the kitchen, and while Zeke fed the fire in the range, took off her damp coat, towelled and then brushed the tangled hair.

"'E promised to build a new chapel to the glory of God, see! On the headland, 'twas gonna be. Overlookin' the bay! Promised the Lord, he did."

"Yes, Mother . . . Hold still while I dry your 'air."

Hester hardly took in her mother's words. The widow's cold, confused condition concerned her and her attention was on the immediate task of getting her warm and dry.

"A granite chapel for the Father, the Son and the Holy Ghost, it was to be! Amen, Hester, amen!"

"Yes, Mother. Your shoes are wet. Where's your slippers to?"

"But 'e failed, see. 'E got sick and even though it weren't 'is fault, the Lord punished 'im for failin' 'im! Punished, my Jonas were — punished for getting sick! And who let 'im get sick, eh? That's what I wants to know!"

"Yes, Mother . . . Now the other foot. That's it . . ." Before long, soothed by the warmth and the ministrations of her children, the widow quietened and her eyelids drooped. Thurza too, was half asleep. Hester laid her in the little crib she had used when she had stayed, briefly, at the time of Jonas Tucker's death. Leaving the door ajar, the siblings went quietly up the stairs and into their parents' bedroom.

Here there was some evidence of Zeke's progress. All signs of the small fire caused by the broken paraffin lamp were gone and a new square of carpet replaced

178

the threadbare, scorched one. The bed was stripped and the blankets folded neatly on the stained ticking-covered mattress. The smell of sickness still hung in the stale air. But it was an open suitcase and what it contained that was the focus of attention for the brother and sister as they entered the room.

Neither Zeke nor Hester had been aware of the existence of the suitcase. In fact, Jonas had bought it in Bideford market specifically for the purpose for which it had been used for over twenty years. After the death, Zeke had pulled it out from under the bed and found it locked. On his father's watch chain there had always been a key. Neither Zeke nor Hester had ever known what it was for, nor had either of them dared to ask. Now they knew. Zeke had tried the key in the lock on the suitcase. Now it stood open, the familiar key protruding from the unfamiliar lock. Zeke watched his sister react to the sight of its contents. After a moment, her voice barely above a whisper, she asked him if he had counted it.

"On'y them notes there," he told her, pointing to a small, string-tied bundle. "And there be more'n two 'undred pounds there! And look 'ow many bundles like that there be! Must be 'undreds, Hes! Where'd 'e get it? Where could our father 'ave got 'old of money like that?" Hester was on her knees, staring into the suitcase.

"You say Mother knew it was there?" she asked. Zeke nodded.

"When I first found 'un, she were in the kitchen and I ran down and asked her. She must of expected it, sooner or later. She must of known I'd find it . . . And what I'd ask her."

"And what did she say?"

"She said it was Father's! That he'd been savin' it, all 'is life, for to build his chapel!"

"His chapel?"

"That's what Mother said. 'Twas to be to the glory of the Lord God. On the headland. You knows the place, Hes, where our land runs up to the cliff edge. And look," Zeke reached under the bundles of notes and lifted from the suitcase scrolls of paper on which were sketched various ground plans and elevations of a small, Gothic-style building, its single bell housed in a modest cupola. "See the dates on 'em drawin's, Hes? This 'un says 1925! And this 'un's 1930! We was barely born be then! All that time we was growin' up he were hoardin' this money!"

"And our mother was goin' short on food and clothes for all of us! 'Ow many times did you go to school with cardboard in the soles of your boots, Zeke? And I were dressed so odd that me classmates poked fun at me in me cut-down this and me darned that!"

"And us froze to the bone all winter 'cos he wouldn't buy no coal for the fire," Zeke said, bitterly.

"And you with your chest," his sister added. "Coughed and wheezed yourself 'alf to death, you did!"

"And this place! Fallin' down round us it be, and leakin'! And where was the money for repairs? And for our dinner? And for seed and livestock for the holding? And for fodder for the few beasts we did 'ave, eh? And corn for to keep the 'ens layin', and proper fencin' for

180

to keep the foxes off 'em? In that suitcase, Hes! That's where!"

"Just lyin' there. Locked up." Hester's voice was flat and cold. "Under their bed, while year after year us went without!"

For a long while the two of them sat, side by side on the iron bedstead, contemplating the enormity of their parents' treatment of them. Then they heard a tremulous voice from the kitchen.

"Ezekiel?" it whimpered, "Hester? Where you be to?"

CHAPTER
EIGHT

Alice, returning from another brief stint of work in London, this time designing the kitchens of a refurbished West End hotel, the details of which were still on the drawing board, relaxed in her first-class seat on the Great Western Railway train as it lumbered down the line towards Penzance, its destination. She felt, as she always felt on these occasions, a pleasing sense of fulfilment. Her design work had developed directly from the skilful, and at the time slightly desperate, way in which she had reorganised the hostel kitchen, making it possible for Rose and herself to deal as efficiently as possible with the task of cooking, within the limits of wartime food shortages, for the ten hungry land girls in her charge. This had resulted in requests for her to apply what soon became known as her "expertise" to several other local hostels, a nursing home near Tiverton and an extension to the kitchen of a nearby Fleet Air Arm base. The idea of expanding this talent into a post-war career had been encouraged by Ruth, an old school friend of Alice's, whose work brought her into contact with leading firms of London-based architects, one of whom had become the first to hire her.

Alice had been a contented, unambitious housewife until the outbreak of war gradually destroyed her world, much as it changed the lives of many of her contemporaries. First her home was wrecked by bomb damage. The rented rooms in Exeter to which her husband evacuated her proved to have been a bad choice, since that city was soon to be pointlessly and spitefully blitzed. James had never found the "safer place" he was searching for, where Alice and Edward John could live until the war was over. Instead he ended his twelve-year marriage and asked Alice to divorce him so that he would be free to marry his already pregnant girlfriend, adding that he had very little money for any of them.

Alice was a modest woman. She took little personal credit for what she had achieved since the February day in 1943, when she had first entered a damp, cold building known as Lower Post Stone farmhouse. Sometimes, on the return journey from her London work, she let her mind wander over the past years and was more than satisfied with the place to which they had delivered her. Edward John was happily working his way through his adolescence, and the feelings of admiration and deep affection she felt for Roger were a source of complete happiness to her. She had Georgina for a daughter-in-law, Christopher as a stepson and the people of the Post Stone valley seemed to her almost to be part of an extended family. She relaxed as the train rocked onwards and the twilight reduced the countryside that slid past the window to a familiar blur of trees and distant hills. Roger would meet her at

Ledburton Halt. Eileen would have prepared a casserole which would be waiting in the oven. Edward John would be home for the weekend tomorrow and, soon, Evie Clark would be safely on her way to a new life with her Giorgio. Alice dozed, waking an hour later to find the train approaching Taunton.

Later, when they had eaten their meal and caught up with one another's news, Roger expanded on his. With wartime conditions behind him he was faced with the significant changes it had wrought on the farming industry. Many discharged servicemen had picked up trades and developed skills and ambitions which, before the wartime experience, would not have seemed accessible to them. Like many of Alice's girls, the courses of their lives had been altered. It was as well, for Roger, that half his pre-war workforce, for one reason or another, failed to return to the Post Stone farms. Had they done so, he, with his increasing use of mechanisation, would not have had work for them. Of those that did return two had, in the meantime, grown from boys into men. Men with wives and, as in Ferdie Vallance's case, children. What was needed now was better accommodation for them. Roger had considered converting the lower farmhouse into two cottages but Alice had sensed in him an underlying lack of enthusiasm for this plan.

"You're hoping Christo and Georgie will come home and settle there, aren't you?" she asked him, gently. "Me too. But we shouldn't count on it, should we?" Roger had shaken his head.

184

"No. But while I'm not 'counting on it', as you put it, it seems foolish to spend money on turning the farmhouse into two dwellings when it may well be required as one. So, in view of this, I've been investigating the cost of converting the barn. We haven't used it since the fire, and even before that it was basically surplus to our requirements now that the dairy side of things is serviced by the new milking sheds up here at the higher farm. Two extra labourers' cottages would, I believe, be a good investment."

The barn fire, unnerving and spectacular as it had been, was the result of a workman having carelessly failed to properly extinguish some smouldering wood shavings, putting at risk several ponies which were temporarily stabled there and had been led to safety by Edward John and his stepfather. The blaze, which was swiftly extinguished, had been confined to a loft which was reached by two wall-mounted ladders, one at each end of the building and, midway along its length, by a flight of stone steps. At the time of the fire the loft was housing a quantity of dried hay which had produced huge amounts of choking smoke but inflicted very little damage on the heavy planks of the wooden floor or the beams and rafters above them. Although the timbers were, in one or two places, smoke-blackened and slightly scorched, they were basically sound. It was at the far end of the loft, where a wide opening, used for hauling up bales of hay and nets of mangels, gave access to it, that the fire damage was most evident. This aperture had acted as a chimney, through which the flames and smoke had been drawn. As a result, its timber lintel, framing and sill, were charred and crumbling. An ancient iron ladder which ran down the outside of the building was, in consequence, no longer solidly attached to the wall and was shunned by the farm workers who, since and because of the fire, considered it unsafe.

"Tread carefully," Roger advised his wife when, on the following morning she went with him into the Lower Post Stone barn, through its shadowy interior, up the stone steps and into the loft. "Don't touch anything," he warned her. "It's still sooty up here."

At the undamaged end of the barn, an area of the slated roof had at some time been glazed. Through the cobwebby panes the winter sun spilt in, illuminating a small section of the floorboards.

Before Alice's arrival at the farm, a partition had been erected, enclosing this area of the loft, which had been given over to Andreis Van de Loos, a Dutch refugee to whom Roger had offered shelter at the start of the war. Alice looked around the deserted space.

The bedstead on which Andreis had slept was gone, as was the table, always strewn with tubes of oil paint, palettes daubed with colour, jars of brushes and drifts of scrap paper on which he experimented, in charcoal, with the composition of the sprawling painting which was the only way he knew of expressing the torment he felt at the horrors the German occupation was inflicting on his native Holland.

"I came up a few times when Andreis was living here," Alice said quietly. "He made hundreds of sketches of Annie for his painting."

"She being the classic Jewess, of course," Roger added, quietly.

"Yes," Alice said. "She was exquisite, wasn't she."

"Wonderful eyes," Roger mused.

"I became concerned that she was spending a lot of time alone up here with him," Alice said. "I need not have been."

They stood looking at the empty space on the end wall where, on a huge wooden panel, Andreis's painting had been completed in the summer of 1943.

"Poor fellow." Roger said. "Wish I could have done more for him."

"But you were wonderful to him, darling. You helped get him out of Amsterdam and you set him up here, with somewhere to work. We fed him and he was —"

"He was still unhappy enough to shoot himself," Roger cut in, flatly, feeling the same sense of failure he had experienced when Andreis, tormented by guilt caused by what he perceived as his desertion of his family and friends when the Germans overran Holland, found himself, even when he had completed his surreal and poignant painting, unable to return, fight and almost certainly die, in his homeland. One morning he had taken the gun he used to shoot rabbits into the lower orchard, held it to his chest, misjudged the direction of the bullet and bled to death, alone, under the cider apple trees. "He wanted, so much, to be brave enough to go and fight," Roger said, gently. "But the poor bastard simply didn't have the guts."

"There are different sorts of guts, don't you think?" Alice said.

Andreis's painting, thanks to Annie and later to Hector Conway, the arts graduate who was to become her husband, was now on permanent display in Amsterdam.

"Two cottages it's gonna be!" Hester, flushed with ambition, told her husband as he wolfed his dinner that night. "With two bedrooms each and real, upstairs bathrooms with proper pull-and-let-go lavvies! None of your wash house and privvy out the back, like we got!" Dave was reading the football results in the local paper. "Thing is, Dave," Hester continued, conspiratorially, "I want one! . . . Did you hear me, Dave?" He gave her his attention at last. "I want us to 'ave one of them new cottages! You, me and our Thurza!"

"Why?" he asked, puzzled. "Us 'as already got a cottage!"

"But the new ones'll be heaps better nor this, Dave! If you was to ask Mr Bayliss, he'd let us 'ave one, wouldn't he? 'Stead of lettin' 'em out to strangers? Don't you reckon?"

"Well, he might, I s'pose," Dave said, lowering the newspaper. "But why would we want one?" His eyes moved slowly round the small space in which his dinner had been prepared and where he had eaten it and now sat, still in his work clothes, sipping the first of his after-supper cups of tea.

A kitchen was a kitchen in Dave's opinion and this one was his, just as it had been his parents' in their day and their parents before them. And theirs before that, most likely. A privvy was a privvy, wasn't it? Whether it be out in the backyard or not — and as long as you had a sink to wash your dishes in, an oven to cook your dinner in, a copper and a mangle in the scullery and a warm, dry bed at the top of your stairs, what more did you need? He pushed his empty cup across the surface of the kitchen table, towards the teapot. "This be known as Crocker's Cottage, Hes," he told his wife. "Alus 'as bin. Alus will be, s'far as I'm concerned!" Hester, hands on hips, turned to face him. Dave avoided her eyes and poured his second cup of tea himself.

Evie sat on her bed in Rose Crocker's spare bedroom. Spread out on the dressing table were all the documents necessary for her emigration. Her brand-new, unused passport had yet to be lodged with the New Zealand High Commission where it would be held until the terms of her two-year contract with the emigration department had been fulfilled. Her smallpox vaccination certificate, her education record, her birth certificate, a copy of the results of her medical examinations, confirmation of her competence in the Womens' Land Army and her National Health Service registration card, together with character references from both Roger Bayliss, as her ex-employer and Alice Todd as her then hostel warden, were all arranged neatly and were being checked and rechecked on a daily basis as the date of her embarkation approached.

Even at this point, with no sightings or news of her husband, Evie was haunted by the thought that at any moment, he might appear. Several nightmare scenarios had already occurred to her and woken her, leaving her distressed and sweating, in the long autumn nights. These incidents became increasingly alarming so that, rather than sleep, she often sat for hours, shivering, at the bedroom window, staring out into the deserted village street. Did that shadow move? Was that the shape of a man? There? In the alley opposite? But he did not come. And as day succeeded day she urged herself to be calm. To think of Giorgio. To conjure his face and his sweet smile. And to sleep, with Rose Crocker's second-best blankets pulled up, over her head, excluding the innocent sounds of the sleeping village. The rattle of a loose latch, the distant whistle of the mail train as it rocked through Ledburton Halt, a night wind, whining round Rose Crocker's chimney. She tried to focus her mind on the moment when the ship on which she was to travel would draw away from the quay, and the void between her and the grey silhouette of London became wide, then wider, then huge. Only then would the threat of Norman's sudden appearance be over.

Hester tucked Thurza into her pushchair and wheeled her up the steep lane to the higher farm. She was experiencing, that morning, a difficult mixture of guilt and determination. Her history, harsh and strange as much of it had been, had left her, at this point, in a well-balanced state. Despite the gruesome details of her father's death and the difficult moral issues raised by the discovery of his hoard of money, Hester's life was more serene and secure than it had ever been. It might have been expected that she would relish that serenity and that security, but the same instinct for survival that had delivered her to this point had made her ambitious. What she had achieved was good and pleasing. But there was more. More for her. For Thurza and for Dave, although, being set in his ways, he was not aware of it. It was not simply because she loved him that she would not allow herself to push him into things, it was because she understood that pushing him would not achieve the result she intended. If she wanted to succeed she would have to be cleverer and more subtle than that. Initially she would consult Roger Bayliss. As her husband's boss and their landlord, he was, without doubt, the most powerful influence on their lives, and regarded by the valley people as master of his farms and the hundreds of acres that surrounded them. The walk up the steep lane took the edge off her tension, made her reduce her stride, breathe more deeply and think more calmly. By the time she reached the kitchen of the higher farm, put her head round the half-open door and called out to see if Eileen was about, she was her normal, smiling, bonny self.

"Boss about?" she asked.

"What d'you want with 'im, my lover?" Eileen asked, slicing carrots.

"Just need to ask 'im some'at," Hester told her.

"He's a busy man these days, Hester. What with 'im being a magistrate and that, on top of all this fuss with Evie Clark. You'll not be wastin' 'is time, will you? What's it you want to see 'im about?" There was a pause. Eileen peeled an onion, wiped her eyes and turned them, watering, on Hester. "Mmm?" It was a question to which Eileen definitely needed an answer. And which, when it came down to it, Hester needed to ask. Unable to seek advice from her own mother and disinclined to involve Dave's, because Rose would, inevitably, take her son's side in any discussion, she was instinctively turning to the next best thing which, in this instance, was Eileen, whose reputation for good, solid, common sense was widely respected in the Post Stone valley.

"'Tis they cottages," Hester began. Leaving Thurza asleep in her buggy, she sidled onto one of the chairs set around the kitchen table on which Eileen was preparing tonight's dinner and began by describing the plans for the new cottages at the lower farm in precise and glowing detail, emphasising the perfection of the modern bathrooms and how the kitchens were to be personally designed by Mrs Bayliss herself, who was, as Eileen already knew, an expert on such things. Eileen put down her sharp knife, transferred some cubed parsnips into the casserole dish and met Hester's eyes.

"And you and Dave wants one of 'em, is that it?"

"Yes." Hester said, and then hesitated. You had to be honest with Eileen, otherwise, what was the point. "Well, *I* does," she admitted.

"And Dave don't. Right?" Eileen asked. Hester nodded.

"'E don't even want me to ask," she whined. "Says that our cottage has alus been good enough for 'im and all the Crockers before 'im and what am I on about!"

"Well, what *are* you on about Hester, my dear?" was Eileen's disappointing response. "You was happy enough to move into that cottage a few months back, weren't you! You and a child that isn't even Dave's?" Hester winced. "Seems to me you want to learn to count your blessings, Missie!"

"I do count 'em, Eileen! Every day! Honest. It's just —"

"It's just 'much wants more'! Yes, lovey, I knows what it is, alright!" Eileen chopped vigorously and the moments passed. "The Crocker cottage is as old as this valley, Hester. They do say 'twas there even before either of the farmhouses was built. To be honest with you, 'tis a bit of a wreck, no one could deny that. But 'tis Dave's wreck, Hester. 'Tis where 'e were born and raised. 'Twas what 'e come home to, when 'e got 'imself half killed in the war. You remember that? A great lump of shrapnel in 'is leg, he 'ad. You was one of they land girls then. You needs to think about all that afore you goes to the boss and starts stirrin' things up! You gotta sort things out with your Dave afore you does that, my dear. Know what I'd do?" Hester shook her head. "I'd get off home and I'd cook him 'is favourite grub for 'is dinner. That's what I'd do." And she did.

CHAPTER
NINE

Zeke stood and stared at the pile of loose limestone. It had been there for as long as he could remember, although, now, it was more or less completely hidden by brambles, ivies and straggles of old mans beard. A small quarry, long since abandoned, formed a craggy background, a place to which, on the rare occasions when he could elude his father, the young Zeke had escaped to play alone with his limited imagination. One summer he had built a fort of stone blocks and made it weatherproof by roofing part of it with slates supported on a frame of saplings. In one corner he constructed a basic fireplace where he roasted the odd rabbit, filched from his father's traps. It was his refuge. His sanctuary. No one knew of it. Not even his little sister who would attempt to follow him until the stinging nettles and the brambles proved too much for her bare legs.

"No, you can't come, Hes! 'Tis a boys' place I goes to. It bain't for girls. Go 'ome." Hester had whined and sulked but knew better than to follow him. One day he had found his sanctuary destroyed, its roof pulled down, its firestones scattered. That night, as the family sat, as usual, in silence, consuming a thin, mutton stew,

Jonas told his wife and children that there was a vagrant in the neighbourhood.

"Bin campin' up near the old quarry, the thievin' varmint. You're to tell me the instant you sees or hears any one prowlin' about and I'll take me shotgun to 'un! D'you 'ear me?"

"Yes, Father."

"Yes, Father."

"Yes, Jonas."

Today, after assessing the quality and quantity of the quarried stone, Zeke moved on, up onto the bald headland where Jonas Tucker had dreamt of building his chapel. Zeke found an area where several wooden pegs, driven into the hard earth, indicated that this was the chosen place. If there were ghosts, Zeke thought, standing near the cliff edge, looking out along the wild, empty North Devon coastline, this was surely the place where Jonas Tucker's soul would linger.

With his mother safely in a convalescent home, following radical treatment for what the specialist had described to Zeke as "a mental condition causing extreme depression", he found himself alone in the Tucker cottage for the first time in his life. Without his mother's baleful, watchful eyes on him, he wandered freely through the cottage and its ancient outbuildings, making his own objective assessment of their condition, deciding firstly what might be done and secondly, what would have to be done in order to turn the place into a decent home for himself and Polly.

The face of the cottage was a shabbily built, Victorian facade, a clumsy attempt to modernise what had once been an ancient stone structure. Jonas had acquired it, together with five acres of land, when the owner became insolvent in the late twenties. Behind the cottage were several solid outbuildings which Zeke now saw as potential extensions to the existing accommodation. Each day, having completed his work on the holding, he circled these outbuildings with a measuring rod in his hands and aspirations in his head.

There had been a little over two thousand pounds in Jonas Tucker's trunk and a few hundred more in the bank account he had used to buy seed and stock for the holding. This, taking into account the strange circumstances of the Tucker family, Hester and Zeke, after considerable thought, proposed to divide as they saw fit. The Pentecostal Brethren would receive five hundred pounds in memory of their father. Hester's share, as a married woman with a husband to provide for her, would also be five hundred, while Zeke, whose work on the holding had achieved its present, modest solvency and who would be responsible for their mother over her declining years, needed funds with which to repair the cottage and make it acceptable for this purpose and to the girl he hoped to marry. For this his share was to be the remaining thousand pounds plus the business account in the bank.

"No one knows about this money," Zeke reminded his sister, "and no one needs to know, right?"

"'Cept Dave," Hester said. "I 'aven't said nothin' to 'im yet, but I got to, Zeke. I don't like keepin' things from 'im."

196

"But 'e'll tell 'is ma and you know what Rose Crocker be like! 'Twill be all over the valley in no time flat!" Hester knew this was true. She hesitated and then shook her head.

"No, Zeke. If I takes it, I gotta tell my Dave." They sat, eyes locked.

"Yeah," Zeke sighed, eventually. 'Course you 'ave to, Hes. Course you does . . . After some further thought his face lit. "Tell you what, though! Tell you what we could do! We could make your share over to Thurza!"

"Thurza?"

"Yeah! A legacy from 'er grandad! Us'll start up a post office account for her! You needn't come into it! I'll open it and I'll tell Dave it were our father's wish! Which it should of bin in the Tightness of things. Anyroad, 'twill be on my conscience, not yourn! 'Ow about that, then? Eh?"

And so it happened that Thurza Alice (daughter of Hester née Tucker, widow of the late Private Reuben Westerfeldt, 29th Division, US Army and subsequently adopted by her new husband David William Crocker, cowman, of Lower Post Stone Farm, Ledburton), became, at the age of almost twelve months, a person of means.

The clouds were low on the morning of Evie's departure. A strong south-westerly wind was driving squalls of rain up the valley. By eight o'clock, breakfasted and with their overnight bags beside the front door, the petrol tank of their car filled to capacity by courtesy of an emigration officer at New Zealand

House, Roger and Alice Bayliss were on schedule. Alice was about to drive down to the village to collect Evie, while Roger spent the twenty minutes this would take in the farm office, briefing his labourers on their duties for the rest of that day and the morning of the following one. Dave and Ferdie were to spend the time removing hay and mangels from the loft of the barn at the lower farm so that the builders could get better access to it when they arrived to start work on the two cottages. Taking Dave aside, Roger told him what he had already guessed. It had been decided that precise knowledge of the details of Evie's departure should be restricted to as few people as possible, her ultimate destination being already classified as secret.

"This time tomorrow she'll be halfway down the Bay of Biscay," Roger told him, quietly, adding, "We should be back by early afternoon. No one must know that she's gone and certainly not where she's going, understood?"

"Understood, sir!" Dave's ruddy face flushed with excitement. "And good luck to the pair of 'em, I say!"

Even Rose Crocker had not known for sure that the day of departure had arrived until the evening before it, when after taking a bath and washing her hair, Evie checked her documents for one last time before carefully stowing them in the leather handbag that Alice had given her as a parting present.

"You best 'ave an early night, my lover," Rose advised, solemnly, on learning that Alice would be collecting Evie at precisely ten minutes past eight next morning. Evie had nodded, compliantly.

198

"The London docks is a long way off, Mr Bayliss says, and he wants to get an early start 'cos you never knows with the weather this time of year." Evie and Rose sat over the fire, for the last time sipping their customary bedtime cocoa, although it was barely half past eight.

Alice drove carefully down the lane towards the narrow bridge that crossed the stream. A squall of wind-driven rain lashed the car, almost blotting out the landscape below her. She peered ahead while her windscreen wipers noisily did their best to prevent her vision being seriously blurred, adjusted her speed and moved slowly on. As the rain lessened, she smiled ruefully. Was there to be no end to her responsibilities for her land girls? Even now, with all but three of them gone from the valley — all but two by tonight, when Evie's ship would have sailed — she had risen at six-thirty in order to prepare for the long drive to London and through it to Tilbury Docks. Later she and Roger would spend a difficult evening with her friend Ruth, who made no secret of her dislike of Roger. On the following morning they would make the journey home again. Then and only then, would Alice feel that she had properly discharged her responsibility for Evie. But now there was Georgina, whom Alice had felt able to tick off her list of worries when she had made her decision to marry Christopher. However, some of Georgina's recent letters had seemed to Alice to be a little odd. Was she as happy as she repeatedly insisted? Had the recent miscarriage upset her more than she was admitting?

And why had she chosen, initially at any rate, to keep the news from her parents? Alice sighed. It was, she decided, rather like having ten daughters. Always one or another of them giving her cause for concern. Like poor Mrs Bennett.

The rain increased again as she negotiated the narrow, ivy-covered bridge, just beyond which the lane divided, the right fork running parallel to the stream before reaching the lower farm, the right continuing up, over the hill before dropping down into the village.

As Alice engaged second gear, ready to begin the steep climb up, from the valley floor, she saw the figure of a man in the centre of the lane. He was moving away from her, plodding heavily towards the fork in the lane. Hearing the car he slowed, stopped and turned to face it. The narrowness of the lane, its steep banks overgrown with tangled autumn vegetation, made it impossible for Alice to drive safely past him unless he stood aside. She hesitated and then, in order to draw his attention to the situation, politely sounded her horn. Instead of letting her pass he came towards her until he was standing directly in front of the car, peering at her windscreen which was obscured not only by the heavy rain but by the brisk movement of the wipers. Alice lowered her window, winding it down until she could lean out enough to call out to him.

"Would you stand aside, please!" It was as he came towards her, rounding the car's offside wing, that she recognised him. Even with his face half obscured by an upturned collar and a rain-sodden cloth cap, Norman Clark's features were unmistakable. For a second she froze, her mind grappling with a sequence of half-developed scenarios. She knew she should react while she had the momentary advantage of surprise, because there was a possibility that, being unfamiliar with the Bayliss car, Norman Clark had not yet identified her. They had, after all, met only once and briefly, when he had arrived unexpectedly and removed Evie from the hostel. Alice with her left hand on the gear lever and her foot on the clutch, revved the engine. In that split second Norman Clark reached the partially open window and thrust his face so close to Alice's that she could smell his sour breath.

If he had not recognised her before, he did now. With her way no longer impeded, Alice was about to release the clutch when Clark reached in through the lowered window and seized her right wrist. She struggled, unable to shake him off or to fully close the window.

"Tell me where she is!" he bawled. "Tell me! I'll stop at nothing 'til I gets it out of yer! Don't think I don't mean it!" His spittle and his anger exploded into her face.

"Where who is?" she demanded, struggling to inch the window up, trapping his forearm but unable to release his grip and feeling her bones creak under the pressure of his huge fist.

"My wife!" he bawled. "Evie! That's who! As if you didn't know!"

"Your wife? How should I know where she is?" Alice shouted desperately. "You took her home to Coventry!" He twisted her wrist until it felt as though the skin was being stripped from it. The pain was so acute that Alice howled through gritted teeth. It was not so much a cry of pain as of fury. The open section of the window was small but it was enough, blocked now by his intruding arm and the grip from which she could not free herself. She began to yell at him. Using words and phrases she had learnt during the most extreme and fortunately rare disputes between one or other of the most volatile of her land girls, she delivered herself of every foul expletive she could lay her tongue to — some of which she barely knew the meaning of — before reverting to the more elegant but equally vehement vocabulary which was her own. "Let go of me NOW, you filthy, bullying oaf! You half-witted lout! You moron!"

Clark shook his head as though to rid his ears of the surprising tirade of abuse. His grip on her wrist slackened slightly as he pressed his face against the opening in the window.

"Reckon you got her hid in that hostel of yours!" he hissed, horribly close to her ear. "She's there, isn't she? Eh? . . . Eh?"

"Why would she be there?" Alice countered, pulling desperately away from him. "The place has been boarded up for months!" She gritted her teeth and then with a sudden, brutal wrench, twisted her wrist from his grasp and rolled up the window, briefly trapping his grimy fingers. "Get away from my car!" She yelled, slamming the engine into gear and noisily releasing the clutch. His fingers were dragged free as the tyres skidded and then gripped in the mud. As the car lurched forward Norman's face briefly struck the glass beside Alice and she flinched away from the open pores in the greasy skin that was so close to hers. At that moment Alice became convinced that he was going out of his mind.

"So you can go to the police station, I s'pose!" he roared at her as the car heaved forward.

"If you've any sense you won't be here when they come for you!" she yelled back.

Accelerating up the incline she found him in her rear-view mirror, an abject, solitary figure, half hidden by wind-driven rain, standing, flat-footed in the middle of the narrow lane. He looked trapped, Alice thought. And perhaps he was. By the miserable mess his life had become. There had been a time, when Alice was told of Norman Clark's deprived childhood, how he had been reared by irresponsible relatives, foster homes and then an orphanage, that she had felt a concern for the unwanted, unloved boy. But the fact was that he had grown into a violent and abusive man whose treatment of Evie, and the sight of the injury to her own wrist, which was reddening, purpling and throbbing as she gripped the wheel, focused her on the absolute necessity of removing Evie from the threat of his violence.

While she covered the short distance from the bridge, over the hill and then down into the village street, Alice formulated a plan of action for her return journey to the farm. First she slowed the car, pulled the cuff of her gloves up and the sleeve of her coat down, so that her injured wrist was invisible. Then, telling Evie and Rose that Mr Bayliss was anxious to begin the drive to London as soon as possible, Alice cut short their farewells and soon had Evie safely beside her, with her suitcase in the boot and a travelling rug over her knees.

"I don't need this, Mrs Bayliss," Evie said. "It's not that cold."

"Just leave it there, Evie," Alice said firmly, taking the car rapidly down the street. "And wave goodbye to Mrs Crocker, there's a good girl." Picking up on Alice's tension, Evie did as she was told.

Alice's plan, should she encounter Norman Clark in the lane, was to make Evie conceal herself under the rug and to take the car, fast, and hopefully without killing him, past him. If he was not in the lane she would continue up to the higher farm and insist that Evie moved into the back seat and waited while she fetched her husband and the journey to London could begin. She considered it essential that, if possible, the fact of Norman Clark's reappearance and his physical attack on herself, should be kept from Evie until the day's mission had been accomplished.

As she entered the higher farmhouse Alice made sure that her injured wrist was concealed. Despite this, it was immediately obvious to Roger that something was distressing her. His first instinct on hearing her brief account of the incident was to cancel the trip to London. Alice emphatically opposed this, insisting that too many arrangements, here, in Naples and even in New Zealand, depended on it. Instead they would notify the police, and telephone the lower farm where Ferdie Vallance and Dave Crocker would by now have arrived. Edwin Lucas would also be warned, but as

204

Clark did not know that Evie had been living at Rose Crocker's tea shop, she herself was not in any danger.

Within five minutes the calls were made and the car left the yard, turning north into the lane which would take it eventually to the London road.

Evie, in the back seat, sat regarding Alice's profile.

"There's something up, isn't there, Mrs Bayliss?" She announced, solemnly. She was not insensitive to the small signs of anxiety she had seen that morning. There was a brief silence while the car puttered on, along the lane which, at this point, was hardly more than a cart track. They were now beyond the point that Norman Clark could possibly have reached had he headed uphill, past the higher farm, and there had been no sign of him. Alice turned round in her seat and smiled.

"There certainly is 'something up', Evie," she said, as brightly as she could. "Somebody we know is going to make a long sea voyage and meet a tall, handsome man!" Evie smiled. Roger and Alice managed to laugh briefly, before settling down for the long hours of driving that lay ahead.

After Roger's call, Edwin Lucas telephoned Ledburton police station and informed Constable Twentyman that Norman Clark had been seen in the area and had caused an affray involving Mrs Bayliss. Twentyman undertook to contact his superiors and asked Edwin to report any new sightings or incidents. When, an hour later, Norman appeared in the Lucas yard, demanding to know where "the Eyerie POW" was, Edwin told him,

205

perfectly truthfully, that Giorgio had been repatriated weeks ago, along with the last of the Italian prisoners. Norman had stood, swaying slightly, glaring at Edwin, blinking his small eyes, his powerful arms hanging at his sides, clenching and unclenching his huge fists. Then he made a strange sound that Edwin Lucas later described to his wife as something between a threat and a moan. Or possibly a sob and a blasphemy, he wasn't sure. He had watched Norman turn on his heel and stumble off, through the veils of rain. Then he dialled Twentyman's number and reported the new sighting.

"Where's he heading?" Twentyman wanted to know.

"Couldn't say, Constable," Edwin had replied. "Looked to me like he hardly knew himself."

In the barn of the lower farm Dave Crocker had taken Roger's call, warning him that Clark had been seen in the lanes between the village and the farms, how he had threatened Alice Bayliss and that she was concerned by his overexcited and violent state.

Hanging the police whistle round Hester's neck, Dave told her to keep an eye on the lane and the yard and to blow the whistle, loud and long, if she saw any sign of Clark. Its piercing sound would be easily audible to him and Ferdie in the barn where they would be working, he in the loft and Ferdie in the yard below him, where he was loading the mangels onto a cart, neither man more than fifty yards from the Crocker cottage.

Norman Clark was wet, tired and hungry. He had been living from hand to mouth for some weeks, earning a few pounds here and there in Coventry and sometimes sleeping in the sad little house he had once shared with Evie and her mother. Returning to it several nights previously, he had found the locks changed and an estate agent's sign on the gate advertising the fact that the property was for sale. He had broken in, smashing the glass in the kitchen window and slept, one last night, in the bed he had shared with Evie and in which his infant son had been stillborn. Next morning he had stuffed his few remaining belongings, including a wallet containing a snapshot of Evie and her mother, taken on Blackpool seafront, into his knapsack. He retraced his footsteps, the soles of his boots crackling across the splinters of glass on the kitchen floor and eased himself out through the narrow window. Leaving the gate swinging behind him he slouched, without looking back, down the street.

It had taken him two days of hitch-hiking to reach the Post Stone valley. By the morning of his encounter with Alice he was not only light-headed with hunger but stiff and cold following a night spent in the musty lee of a damp hayrick. He watched her car vanish into the tunnel-like entrance to the lane where it rose steeply away from him. His decision to search for Evie at the Lucas farm was based on the fact that he knew it was where Giorgio had once worked. Persuaded by Edwin Lucas, and in no uncertain terms, that Giorgio was long gone, he allowed gravity to return him to the valley floor and to the bridge where he had encountered the warden. Here he hauled himself over the parapet, and dropping down into the shallow river bed, followed it, half a mile further upstream, to where, at Lower Post Stone Farm, it was spanned by the next, small, humpbacked bridge.

Breathing hard, wet, cold and hungry, he crept in, under the arch of the bridge. The shallow stream was already discolouring as storm water made its way down the valley. Needing to rest, he hauled himself up onto a ledge inside the apex of the arch and ate the last of a packet of ginger biscuits which was all that remained of a small selection of edibles that he had pilfered from a grocery shop in Tiverton on the previous day. The food soothed him but he was almost overcome with exhaustion. Wedging his knapsack under his head and stretching his aching legs along the length of the ledge he slid into a light sleep.

The frustrations and deprivations of Norman Clark's life had reduced him to a point where he had relinquished all of his ambitions but one. One, which was arguably more an obsession than an ambition. On this single objective he focused what was left of himself. Both emotionally and physically, he was driven beyond reason by his overwhelming determination to find and take possession of Evie. Quite why she had come to represent this sole, remaining objective was hard to define. Theirs had never been a love story. As she had grown from child to adolescent it had been her mother who had insisted on regularising the relationship between her daughter and her lodger. The papers had been signed and Evie had become Norman's wife. He had reacted to the loss of his son with a bitter, accusative anger, blaming Evie for it and treating her with increasing hostility. His war, most of which had been spent in an internment camp in northern Germany, had been, for him, an isolating experience. He shunned the camaraderie which kept most of his fellow prisoners as occupied and as high-spirited as was possible. Instead, confining himself to a solitary regime of physical exercises, which, despite the limited amount of food available to him, had transformed his bulk into muscles and earned him the nickname "Tarzan". His ponderous brawn had protected him from any confrontation which, triggered by his malevolence, might have resulted in physical violence. Perhaps, if when he had been discharged from the army and made his way back to the little house in Coventry, he had found Evie waiting for him, docile and compliant, he might have recovered himself and resumed a life similar to his pre-war existence, an outcome which would have been happier for him than for her. Instead he had found Evie gone, working as a land girl, two hundred miles away.

"She'll not come back," his mother-in-law had told him, tersely. Enid sat wheezing, her head over a bowl of steaming water laced with Friar's Balsam. "I wrote her a letter when I heard you was comin' 'ome. All I got was a postcard of Exeter cathedral saying she's stoppin' where she is 'cos she likes it there. 'Spose she might of got herself a bloke after all this time. She never did 'ave much time for you, Norman." She bent closer to the bowl, draped a towel over her head to keep in the steam and began to cough.

It had been on the following day that Norman Clark had caught a train to Ledburton Halt, found his way to Higher Post Stone Farm and, brandishing his marriage certificate, forced Roger Bayliss to tell him where he would find his wife. Then he had almost forcibly removed her from the hostel at the lower farm and taken her with him, back to Coventry.

The rain clouds had lifted revealing a watery sky. Two hours had passed since the news that Norman Clark had been seen near the village had reached Dave Crocker at the lower farm. Hester looked at her clock. It was time for elevenses and needing the reassurance of a chat with her husband and Ferdie Vallance, she decided to take cups of tea across the yard to them, together with a couple of her mother-in-law's currant buns. While she buttered the buns, set out the mugs, brewed and poured the tea, added milk and stirred in the sugar, she stooped, every so often, to check the view from her low window for any sign of Norman Clark. She had anticipated that if he approached at all it would be via the lane, so was taken aback to see a figure, which she instantly recognised as his, haul itself up, over the low wall that separated the water meadow from the yard. Locking her door and with Thurza under one arm, Hester ran up her narrow stairs, opened her bedroom window, took a deep breath and expelled every vestige of it into the police whistle. The sound reverberated weirdly round the yard, bouncing off one surface, slamming into another, echoing and rebounding, so that, combined with the noise of the wind and

210

rain and the cackle of alarmed jackdaws, it was impossible to identify its source. Hester, realising this, withdrew slightly and watched the yard as the jackdaws flapped into the sky above the farmhouse chimneys.

Norman Clark's only reaction to the sound of the whistle was to stand, motionless. Whatever part the sound of the whistle was to play in ensuing events, he needed to get his bearings. The yard was familiar to him. He had been here twice before — once in high summer, to fetch Evie home, and later, after she had escaped from the house in Coventry, in his first, abortive, attempt to find her.

The lower windows of the deserted farmhouse were shuttered now and the roses and creepers that covered the porch had not been pruned since summer and now hung in great swags across the door, adding to the overall impression of desertion. Then, through a veil of rain, Norman saw, near the entrance to the barn, the half-loaded cart and Ferdie Vallance, shovel in hand, standing, open-mouthed beside it.

Seeing Norman stumbling towards him, head down, shoulders hunched, fists clenched and gaining momentum with each heavy step he took, Ferdie threw aside his shovel, grabbed a long-handled, two-pronged hayfork, faced the intruder and assumed a defiant and threatening stance. Dave Crocker, who had been working in the loft when the first whistle blast had penetrated the noise of the gale, shinned down an interior ladder and unarmed and breathless, took his place solidly beside Ferdie.

Hester, for good measure, supplied a second, even more emphatic blast from the police whistle that had waited so long to be useful and now fully vindicated those who had, all those weeks ago, suggested its use for this specific purpose.

Norman rolled up to Dave Crocker with the kinetic energy of a Sherman tank, took him by his shirt front, slammed him against the barn wall and all but knocked the breath out of him before being caught, more by chance than judgement, by a wild swing from Dave. This split the skin above Norman's right eye. Blood ran, unnoticed, down his cheek and dripped from his jaw as the two men, fists raised, circled each other like a couple of bare-knuckle fighters.

Hester, trapped in her cottage and unable to reach the yard phone, dumped Thurza into her playpen and hesitated, just inside her door, her heart thumping, watching the scene and then wincing when it developed into a full-scale brawl involving all three men. Dave and Norman, almost equally matched, ran at each other like stags in the rutting season while Ferdie, half their size but nimble and fearless, leapt and nipped, tripped and grabbed, using all the methods of attack that his injured leg had forced him to employ as he had grown from boy to man.

Later, remembering the scene, Hester was to compare Norman with the enraged and cornered bull she had recently watched in a film about matadors. She had "never seen anything like it, not in the yard of the lower farm!" Blood had coursed down his face. He snorted and ranted and pawed the ground, howling like a wild animal and making unintelligible sounds. The only word Hester had been able to distinguish had been his wife's name. "Evie!" he had bellowed. "Tell me where Evie is!" The three men rolled on the ground, sprawling one moment and then staggering to their feet, slipping in the mud, throwing punches and grabbing each other in unlikely headlocks. Ferdie Vallance persistently tackled Norman by launching himself at the huge man's ankles, once succeeding in bringing him down like a felled tree.

At one point, using the hayfork as a bayonet, Ferdie made a run at Norman who seized the shaft of the fork and, with frightening ease, flung both it and Ferdie aside. This gave Dave an opportunity to arm himself with the shovel, but it was becoming obvious that Norman's anger and almost superhuman strength were superior to the combined efforts of Dave Crocker and Ferdie Vallance's to overpower him.

While Norman and Dave were briefly locked together, Ferdie lurched into the barn and tried to reach the wall-mounted telephone. Norman misread his movement, and because he was so intent on discovering Evie's whereabouts, concluded that it was somewhere inside the barn that he would find her. Shoving Dave aside, he plunged past him, jerked the telephone from Ferdie's hand and hauled on the wires until they ripped free from the wall and trailed uselessly across the cobbled floor. Then he ran the length of the row of disused stalls, peering into each one and shouting Evie's name.

"I knows you're in here!" he bawled, his voice breaking with emotion. "I'll find you wherever you are! Come out, Evie! Do as I tell you! I'm your husband! You gotta do as I say, d'you hear me? Wherever you're hiding you come out! Now, woman! Now!"

Dave and Ferdie stood gasping with exhaustion, watching Norman's fruitless search.

Finding nothing, Norman reached the far end of the barn where one of two wall-mounted iron ladders ran up to a square hole in the loft and gave access to it. Summoning what was left of his strength, he hauled himself up, hand over hand and disappeared into the loft, still bellowing his wife's name.

Ferdie and Dave could hear him moving about, searching the loft's dark corners and the spaces behind the bales of straw which, in places, were piled as high as the rafters. The impact of his boots, despite being muffled by scattered straw, made the wooden structure creak and reverberate as his considerable weight ranged back and forth. After one significant thud, he cried out. This was followed by silence in which only the sound of the gale was audible. Dave and Ferdie stood, listening. Perhaps exhaustion had overtaken Clark? Or was he lurking, ready to surprise them? In fact, in the semi-darkness, he had struck his head on a beam, knocking himself almost senseless.

Against the sounds of the rising storm, Dave and Ferdie attempted to form some sort of plan of action. "Us needs to get 'im down and tie 'im up," Dave whispered. "We needs rope . . ." Ferdie cast about him for a suitable length of anything strong enough. He

214

finally twisted half a dozen yards of binding twine into a workable length and coiled it up. Dave looped it over his shoulder, lifted a warped and rusted sickle from a nail on the barn wall where it had hung for years, and flexing his fingers round its worn handle, made his way to where a flight of stone steps ran up to the loft. Ferdie followed, his heart in his mouth and his hayfork in his hand.

There were four means of access to the loft. In addition to two, wall-mounted iron ladders and the flight of stone steps, a third iron ladder, attached to the exterior wall at the far end of the barn, ran thirty feet down to the yard below. This ladder was no longer in use since the fire had damaged the heavy wooden sill to which it was attached.

There was very little light in the loft and what there was lay at its extreme ends. At one, a patch of diffused daylight penetrated the glazed portion of the roof where Andreis had made his painting and at the other there was a tall, narrow aperture, open to the weather, through which bales of hay and nets of crops such as swedes and mangels could be winched up from the yard. This too, admitted a limited amount of daylight.

As silently as possible Dave and Ferdie climbed the stone steps, slowly raising their heads above the floor level of the loft and then stepping cautiously out onto the wide, rough-hewn planks that floored it. Here they paused, listening for any sound that might reveal the whereabouts of Norman Clark and preparing to devise a feasible course of action should they locate him.

Although they listened intently, the wind, moving through and round the barn, was causing the old structure to groan and creak, masking any slight sounds Norman Clark may have made. It was a stalemate.

It would take at least twenty minutes for either Dave or Ferdie to drive the horse-drawn cart up to the higher farm to raise the alarm. Twenty minutes, during which, whoever remained behind, would be left to single-handedly protect Hester and Thurza, should Norman resume his search and possibly find and threaten them. Eventually it was decided that Ferdie would go for help, taking Hester and Thurza with him, while Dave did his best to avoid a confrontation with Norman until reinforcements arrived. Neither of them was confident that this plan was a good one but, with no telephone and both Hester and Thurza, as well as themselves, vulnerable to the violence of a man whom their combined efforts had failed to overpower, their options were limited.

Ferdie was just about to descend the steps when they both heard a small sound, something between a snore and a groan. This led them to Norman Clark. He lay on his back. On his forehead was evidence of a severe impact with a low beam that spanned the loft a few feet above him. He seemed semi-conscious; nevertheless, as they assessed the situation, they kept a safe distance between themselves and the sprawling man. Blood oozed from the abrasion on his head and there was already an increasing area of swelling. As they watched, he inhaled, moaned and appeared to be slowly coming to his senses.

216

From the door of her cottage Hester had watched the fight until the three men lurched into the interior of the barn and become lost in its shadows. At first she could hear Norman Clark shouting for his wife. Then silence had fallen. Baffled and increasingly anxious, Hester considered crossing the yard and attempting to use the telephone to call for help. But Dave had told her to stay inside her locked door. So she waited. The cups of tea she had made for her menfolk growing slowly cold. Thurza sat solidly in her playpen, her thumb in her mouth, and watched her mother.

After five minutes of silence, Hester felt a sense of acute alarm hollowing her stomach. If Dave and Ferdie had succeeded in overpowering Norman, why hadn't one or the other of them emerged from the barn to tell her so? If they had managed to use the telephone, why could she not hear the bell on the police car as it sped through the lanes towards the lower farm? What if both men were dead? Could Norman have taken Dave by surprise and impaled him on a hayfork? And then throttled Ferdie with his huge hands? And if so, where was he? Was he about to emerge from the barn and begin a systematic search of the lower farm buildings? A search that would inevitably lead him to her cottage, to herself and to Thurza? Should she approach the barn, and if there was no sign of the men, use the telephone to raise the alarm? Thurza, her arms around her golliwog, was nodding off, half asleep amongst her blankets. The wind had risen and the rain was now torrential, filling the yard puddles and clouding the rising water in the stream. Hester stepped into her rubber boots, thrust her arms into her muddy, waterproof coat, and pulling its hood up over her head, leant into the weather and covered the distance between her and the entrance to the barn at a fast, slithering run. She approached the telephone and saw at once the severed wires and the dangling mouthpiece. She stared around, her eyes adjusting slowly to the shadowy space where gloom became near darkness behind the high wooden structures of the stalls. But where was Dave? Where was Ferdie? And where, in heaven's name, was Norman Clark?

Above her and in concentrated silence, Dave and Ferdie were struggling to secure Norman, initially, by tying his feet together with the skein of binding twine. Fumbling in their haste, they were aware that he was regaining consciousness, moving his limbs, rolling his head and mumbling disconnected words. The twine was hard to control, slipping and unravelling as Ferdie tried to wind it round the huge man's ankles. Dave found a piece of rope which would have proved to be too short even if Norman's lids were not flickering and then, his eyes barely focusing, opening. He hauled himself into a sitting position and stared round in confusion. It could only be seconds before he became fully aware of his situation.

Below, at the entrance to the barn, Hester could hear nothing above the drumming and gurgling of the torrential rain and the gusts of wind which rattled everything that was hinged or latched or bolted, every loose slate or swinging gate or unsecured window or door. Hester's instinct tempted her to climb the steps into the loft but her reason reminded her that all three men were somewhere in the barn, either amongst the stalls or in the loft overhead. If Norman Clark had managed to elude or overpower Ferdie and Dave, he could have climbed down from the loft and be hiding somewhere close to her. Possibly watching her. She dared not move further into the barn or climb the steps to the loft as this would cut off her only means of escape. If she became trapped, Thurza would be defenceless in the cottage.

She left the barn and in the teeth of the gale rounded it until she stood under the end wall, where the iron ladder ran up to the charred sill, thirty feet above her. She raised her head and shouted her husband's name. But the wind snatched the sound and bore it away. Picking up a bent and discarded bucket, she slammed it against the ladder. The sound of metal on metal was significant even within the noise of the gale. She struck the ladder again and then again.

In the loft the sound seemed to rouse Norman Clark to full consciousness. He lurched to his feet and in one surge of power, seized a bolt of wood, caught Ferdie a glancing blow to the side of the head which sent him sprawling, and butted Dave in the face with his forehead, knocking him, briefly, off his feet.

Hester had stepped back and was several feet from the base of the barn wall and looking up towards the opening above her. The wind took the pale hair that escaped from the hood of her waterproof and whipped it across her eyes which were already half blinded by the stinging rain. Squinting upwards she saw the figure of a man clinging to the charred frame of the opening in the wall.

Dave, once more on his feet, blood streaming from his nose, saw that Ferdie still lay where he had fallen but was already stirring while Norman, having reached the aperture, was staring dizzily down at a figure far below him.

Through the rain and the blood which was seeping from his wounded forehead and eye, Norman saw the shape of the girl. The damp hair blowing, the smudged, white face, lifted, the lips moving soundlessly.

"Dave!" Hester shouted desperately. "Ferdie! Where you be to?" The gale carried the words away.

Norman Clark could barely see. Objects were haloed. His vision doubled and there were two girls below him, looking up at him, shouting to him. Two girls, where there should have been only one. Then the two girls blurred together and he saw her. Evie! He dropped to his knees on the edge of the sill and leant precariously out into space. He shouted her name, his voice a hoarse whimper.

Hester looked up at the contorted face peering down at her. She saw the wild eyes, the blanched skin and the blood. Recognising Norman Clark and seeing no sign of either Dave or Ferdie Vallance, it seemed logical to Hester that both had been overpowered. That they were either dead or unable to defend themselves or her and that she was alone, facing a madman who believed she was his missing wife. Then she saw Dave. Standing behind the kneeling man, Dave stooped, got an arm round Norman's thick neck, hauled him to his feet and

220

away from the edge of the drop. For a moment and before Norman began to struggle, Dave caught sight of Hester.

"Get away!" he shouted to her. "Get home and bar the door!" For a moment Hester hesitated but Norman was still bawling Evie's, name, still convinced in his deranged and damaged mind, that it was Evie, thirty feet below him. Evie — her face half hidden by blowing hair and the hood of her mackintosh — who was staring up at him. She was about to turn and run when Norman, summoning all of his remaining strength, snatched up the bolt of timber he had used to strike Ferdie and was standing, confronting Dave, his arm raised to strike, his back to the aperture. In the seconds it took for Dave to reel back, Norman had flung his weapon aside, stooped, grasped the highest rung of the iron ladder and swung his weight out, over the lip of the sill.

At that moment, with her hood blown back from her face, her hair plastered to her skull and Norman Clark's voice calling her Evie and commanding her to stop, Hester began to run. Her boots slithered as she stumbled and splashed through the storm water that was flooding across the yard. A freak gust of wind caught Norman's words and to Hester it seemed that he had reached the ground and was closing in on her. He was angry now. His voice an hysterical shriek, his abusive words threatening violence. Reaching the corner of the barn, she stopped, flattened herself against the streaming wall and looked back.

Norman was a yard from the top of the ladder. His fingers groping and slipping, his feet struggled for purchase on the worn rungs. Above him, braced against the edge of the aperture, Dave and Ferdie peered down.

If Norman did not know why they made no attempt to reach him or dislodge him, they knew. Hester too. She moved forward a few steps and stood, stock-still in the lashing wind and rain, watching, hypnotised, as Norman continued his slow, precarious descent.

CHAPTER
TEN

Roger Bayliss checked his watch when, on the left-hand side of the road, the looming shapes of Stonehenge solidified in the murk. He had planned to reach the henge by eleven-thirty and was gratified that he had made it, almost precisely on time. He selected a place where the short grass that bordered the roadway was level with it, eased his onside wheels onto it and applied his handbrake.

"Coffee?" he suggested to Alice. Eileen had prepared two meals for this journey. Flapjacks, shortbread and a flask of coffee were designed to keep the travellers fed until lunchtime when a substantial hamper would be broached.

"Know what that is, Evie?" Roger asked when the coffee was poured and the food distributed.

"Some rocks?" Evie answered, biting into a piece of the shortbread and without much apparent interest in the majestic standing stones.

"Yes. But they are very old rocks," Roger told her.

"I thought all rocks were very old," Evie said.

Alice laughed.

"But these are very, very old rocks, Evie," she said, "and very special ones. Don't you think they look a bit special?" When Evie agreed, Roger embarked on a short lecture expounding most of the known facts about the history of the henge. The words, "burial-mounds", "rituals", "Beaker folk", "solstices", "pagans" and "druids" were introduced, defined and hopefully became part of Evie's vocabulary. To make the place come alive for the politely listening girl he described how Thomas Hardy had used the henge as the location of the arrest of Tess, the heroine of one of his most famous novels. But as Evie had not read the book or ever heard of Tess Durbeyfield, the connection between the unfamiliar place and the unread novel meant little to her. Although she nodded and smiled vaguely at Roger she was more interested in the road ahead as they pulled out onto it and resumed their journey. Roger Bayliss was disappointed by this. He smiled at Alice when she leant across and patted his knee as he changed gear, accelerated and gave the great, grey stones a last glance.

Their route through London avoided the well-known landmarks. Evie, who had been hoping to catch a glimpse of Big Ben and Buckingham Palace, was disappointed. Roger became concerned that this part of the journey was taking them much longer than he had anticipated. It was decided that they would not stop for lunch until they arrived at Tilbury.

The gale that was lashing the West Country had veered north, leaving London grey and cold as the December afternoon approached.

"A good day to be leaving England," Alice said as they threaded their way into the docks where there was still plenty of evidence of wartime bomb damage. Rows of fragile warehouses stood, skeletal and precarious, amongst warped and twisted cranes and hoists. The scene was a monochrome of greys and sepias until they saw the ship.

The *Orontes*, in common with her sister ships, was painted a curious shade of muted, pinkish gold. Set in those murky surroundings, she glowed like a harvest moon at twilight, then, when a brief break in the cloud flooded the scene with wintery sunshine, blushed like an opal. Or a pumpkin in a pantomime.

"Is that my ship?" Evie breathed. "Is it? Is it mine?"

By now the vessel loomed over them, its gangways busy with people and porters pushing trolleys laden with luggage ranging from cabin trunks to hatboxes.

"Yes," Alice said. "It's yours. There's the name on the stern. You see?" Evie had not imagined that her ship, indeed, any ship, could be so large. She stood, her face expressing her awe, astonishment and an underlying, overwhelming excitement. Probably because all these were feelings she associated with Giorgio, when she exclaimed *"Mama mia!"* her Italian accent was perfect.

Two hours remained before Evie had to make herself known to the emigration officer. They parked the car, and although Eileen's lunch was excellent, they barely noticed it, eating quickly and hungrily. After Evie's papers had been checked, her case labelled "wanted on the voyage" and wheeled away, there was a delay before the boarding passes would be handed out.

225

There seemed to be nothing left to say. They smiled awkwardly and found a draughty cafe where Roger bought them mugs of tea.

"What have you done to your wrist, Mrs Bayliss?" Evie asked suddenly, taking Alice by surprise. From time to time on the journey, when they ate their lunch and now, as Alice sipped her tea, Evie had caught glimpses of the bruises and contused flesh just visible between the sleeve of her coat and her glove. Alice blushed, and pulling her cuff down over the injury, made a confused and unconvincing attempt to explain it. Evie shook her head.

"Something happened this morning, didn't it?" she persisted: "Was it when you came to fetch me from Rose Crocker's?"

"It doesn't matter now," Alice said, "Really it doesn't, Evie. Let's not spoil our last —"

"It was Norman, wasn't it? He came looking for me again! I knew it! I just knew he would!"

"But he didn't find you, Evie! And he never will! In a couple of hours you'll be —"

"Safe? Will I be? Will I ever be? And he hurt you, Mrs Bayliss! And what about the others?"

"The others?"

"The others in the valley! Hester and Dave and their Thurza! And Ferdie and Edward John! Mrs Crocker and everyone else who helped me!"

"That's all been taken care of, Evie." Roger spoke calmly and with more confidence than he felt. "Everybody was warned. The police were called. Norman Clark has no idea where you are or where you

226

are going and no one who does know will tell him. He has broken his bail and will be in custody by now. Drink your tea and let's get you aboard."

Evie found a place on the rail and waved and blew kisses until her face and their faces blurred into unrecognisable shapes.

"She's got a point, you know," Roger said, allowing himself to relax the forced smile he had kept in place for the past hour. "I think we should get home, Alice."

"Tonight?"

"Yes. If you feel up to it. I'm a bit concerned about our people. There's probably nothing to worry about and they're all absolutely fine, but . . . What do you think?"

"I think we should go."

The pumpkin ship was by now a diminishing blob of colour as daylight faded over the grey Thames. If Evie was still waving, they could not distinguish her from the other figures leaning on the rail. While Roger bought petrol Alice telephoned Ruth and cancelled the arrangements they had made for that evening.

"Oh . . . But —" Ruth protested. She was a woman unused to having her plans cancelled.

"No 'buts', Ruth," Alice told her, firmly. "I do apologise, my dear. Can't explain now. I'll write. Byeeee."

It was after midnight when they arrived home. There had been drifts of leaves and even fallen branches in the lanes after they left the main road but the air was still when they pulled into the yard of the higher farm. As Roger extinguished the headlights the total, familiar darkness of the countryside enveloped them. No lights showed in the farmhouse windows or in the cottage occupied by Ferdie and Mabel and their family. As their night vision began to reveal the familiar shapes of the yard they looked down into the valley where the lower farmhouse was, as usual, in darkness. Nor were any lights showing in the windows of the Crocker cottage. The distant stream was in spate. In the near silence they could hear it making its noisy way along the valley floor. The owls in the woods that rose up behind the farmhouse towards The Tops sounded drowsy. Roger heaved a sigh, part relief, part exhaustion.

"Long day," he said, putting an arm around Alice.

They were both suddenly desperately tired. In silence they went indoors, carried mugs of hot milk upstairs and were in their bed within half an hour.

Roger woke early and as Alice made her way sleepily to the bathroom, he dressed hurriedly in his farming clothes. In the yard he encountered Ferdie who had just delivered the dairy cows to Mabel for the early morning milking.

"Everything alright here?" Roger asked.

"Yessuh. Why wouldn't it be? Wasn't expectin' you home this early though, sir. Young Evie get on her way okay, did she?"

"What? Oh, yes. She did. It all went according to plan."

"That's good, sir. Oh, there was one thing, sir."

"What's that?"

"Daphne, sir."

"Who?"

"The cow my Mabel calls Daphne. The one with the crushed horn?"

"Oh. Yes. Calls her Daphne, does she . . ."

"She do, sir, yes. You knows what my Mabel's like when it comes to cows."

"Well? What about . . . Daphne?"

"She started calvin' late yesterday. Don't seem to be doin' too well. May be nothin' but we reckons you should take a peek at 'er."

"Yes. I will. Thanks, Ferdie."

"Pleasure sir."

"Um, Ferdie . . .?"

"Sir?"

"No sign of Corporal Clark?"

"No, sir, no. Dave got your message about 'im bein' seen hereabouts, and later on Edwin Lucas phoned the lower farm to say as he'd bin 'angin round 'is place and 'e'd told 'im to push off and that 'e was calling the police."

"No sign of him at the lower farm, then?"

"No. No sign of 'im there."

Roger re-entered the farmhouse where he encountered Eileen.

"Wasn't expectin' you 'ome for hours," she announced testily. "Thought we'd got burglars, I did, when I 'eard madam moving about upstairs. And I haven't even started on your breakfasts, not knowing as you'd be wantin' any!"

"Sorry, Eileen. Very sorry. Thoughtless of us . . ."

He left her, pink with righteous indignation and joined his wife in their bedroom.

Alice was sitting at the dressing table wrapped in a white towelling bathrobe and brushing her hair. She met his eyes via the mirror.

"Absolutely had to have a bath," she smiled. "Essential, after yesterday." The bruises on her wrist were still livid. "Now, tell me. Is everyone alright? Did anything happen?" Roger sat heavily in the small upholstered chair that his first wife had used when she did her sewing, a fact which Roger had long since forgotten — and looked appreciatively at Alice.

"Absolutely nothing, as far as I can make out!"

"Really? But —"

"What, exactly, did you say to Clark in the lane yesterday?"

"Heavens! I don't know! Everything I could think of as far as I can remember. All the foul language I learnt from my girls! And then some of my own! I don't know, Roger! Why d'you ask? Has someone complained?" Roger smiled, the anxieties of the recent days, beginning to ease.

"Apparently not, and whatever it was it seems to have done the trick!"

"What 'trick'?" Alice asked. "I did say I'd call the police but considering the state he was in I doubt if that would have discouraged him. Did it?"

"Not completely, it seems. Ferdie says he went up to the Lucas farm, assuming Giorgio was still working there, I suppose. Edwin put him right on that, gave him

230

his marching orders and said he was calling the police and . . ."

"And?"

"And that, according to Ferdie Vallance, was the last anyone saw of him. When I've had some breakfast I'll go down to the lower farm and have a word with Dave Crocker. The weather was pretty wild here yesterday. No one got much work done and there's been some storm damage, apparently."

The damage Ferdie Vallance had referred to had not been caused directly by the storm, which had no more than slightly worsened the condition of the charred sill to which the iron ladder had been fixed. The reason the metal attachments had pulled free, causing the ladder to hesitate, tip backwards and then crash down onto the derelict cattle pens underneath it, had been the sudden weight of Norman Clark as he lowered himself over the sill and, half blinded by rain and the blood flowing from his injured head, began to descend it.

Hester, fearing that when he reached the ground and still under the illusion that she was his wife, Norman would pursue her, had fled and then stopped in her tracks when she grasped the situation and, just as Ferdie and Dave had done, foresaw what was about to happen. All three of them watched speechlessly, Dave and Ferdie crouching, leaning out, through the aperture in the barn wall and Hester from across the yard, as the ladder, bearing Norman Clark's huge weight, came slowly away from the wall, pieces of splintered wood falling past him as he clung helplessly

231

to it. Then, as it swayed outwards, the lower attachments had pulled out of the ancient mortar and it swung back, further and faster from the wall as the force of gravity took it. Peering down at the falling man, his fingers white on the rungs of the ladder, Ferdie and Dave saw the look of terror on his face and heard him cry out as he groped with one hand towards them. Then came the sound none of the watchers would ever forget, as Norman Clark's skull made noisy contact with the edge of a granite water trough.

The three of them had gathered round, oblivious of the wind and rain, staring at what was left of Norman Clark. He lay, spreadeagled on his back, like an over-stuffed rag doll. His head, draining of blood, had cracked open like a raw egg on impact with the edge of the trough. Hester turned away and retched.

"Go to Thurza," Dave told her but she shook her head.

"What'll us do?" she said. And then louder and more desperately, "What'll us do, Dave?"

The prospect of the situation falling into the hands of the judiciary was not an option for these three, whose experience of life had taught them that "the law" was something to be avoided at all costs. It was the law that threatened you if you trespassed, poached game or pilfered apples. It dragged people off with their hands behind their backs and threw them into cells, flogged them, hanged them or sent them to the colonies. During their years at the village school, each class had been addressed by a senior police officer from Exeter, and although he had removed his helmet, smiled at them and even attempted a joke or two, he had gravely lectured them on the absolute necessity of avoiding a life of crime — with all its inevitable unpleasantness — and had vividly described the misery of being sentenced to life behind bars. Witness boxes, warrants, oaths, juries, prison officers, policemen, executioners and especially judges were all "the law".

So "What'll us do?" Hester repeated, tearfully. "We killed 'im!"

"No we didn't," Dave told her. "Fallin' off the ladder killed him." Dave's nose, where Norman Clark had struck it with his forehead, had stopped bleeding but was swelling visibly.

"S'pose we could of warned 'im," Ferdie said, uncertain where self-defence ended and guilt began.

"'E wouldn't 'ave listened," Dave said, sounding as though he had a clothes peg on his nose, "'cos he thought it were Evie down 'ere and that we was just tryin' to stop 'im gettin' at 'er." There was a pause while their brains grappled with their situation. "Who knows 'e come 'ere?" Dave said at last, almost to himself.

"No one," Hester said. "No one but us three. Mr Bayliss phoned to say as he'd been seen near the village and then —"

"Then Edwin Lucas rang and said he'd turned up at his place . . ." Ferdie added.

"But no one knows he come down 'ere," Dave said. "'Cept us."

Ferdie, eyes and mouth gaping, looked from Hester to Dave and then back again. If any ideas were going to come, they would be from one or the other of them, because his mind had, for the moment at any rate, been shut down by the horror of what had just happened. The rain fell solidly, blotting out everything beyond the wreckage that was all that remained of Norman Clark. They stepped back, into the shelter of the cart shed and stood, huddled, dripping, breathing unevenly in great shuddering gasps. With shaking hands Dave rolled a cigarette, the damp paper sticking to his fingers.

"Can't say 'e didn't 'ave it comin'," he mumbled, holding a match to his roll-up. "Can't say the bastard didn't deserve it!"

"He were gonna kill Dave and me!" Ferdie said, slightly restored by the fact that they were sheltered now and Dave was drawing on his roll-up in a positive, familiar way. "If 'e 'adn't seen you, Hes, thought you was Evie and tried to get down to you — 'e would of done for Dave and me and no mistake! We was no match for him with that temper on 'im!" He paused, his eyes on a veil of wind-driven rain as it swept away up the valley. "Us gotta get rid of 'im!" he concluded. "That's what us gotta do."

"And how d'you reckon we do that, eh?" Dave asked, hopelessly, dragging on his cigarette. There was a pause.

"Easy," Ferdie said, surprisingly. A thought had swum suddenly into a head that was still fuddled by the blow Norman Clark had struck him. "Slurry pit," he said. Dave and Hester looked at him incredulously. "'T' wouldn't be the first time," Ferdie added, almost defensively, in response to their shocked reaction.

"Though I reckon there's not too many alive now as remembers it. I weren't no more'n a nipper when I 'eard of it and you was most prob'ly not even born, Dave, so . . ."

"Remembers what?" Dave demanded.

"Story went that six lads from the village all marched off together to World War One and on'y three come back. 'Kitchener wants you' the posters said so off they went. Left right. But out in them trenches two of those boys got so's they couldn't take it no more — the shellin' and the dead and the blood and the mud . . . Threw down their rifles, they did, and hid in a ditch. And this bloke, Horace something he were called, told the MPs where they was to. Charged 'em with desertion, the army did! Stood 'em up against a wall." Ferdie raised and then slowly lowered an imaginary rifle. "And shot 'em dead by firin' squad! Hardly out of school, they was, those lads." There was a shocked pause.

"Well, go on, then," Dave said soberly. "What's that got to do with Norman Clark?"

"Well, the word got out, see," Ferdie went on. "And when this Horace come back here . . . well . . . folk . . . sorted 'im out."

"Sorted him . . . ?" Dave asked.

"Sorted . . . ?" Hester echoed.

"Yeah," Ferdie continued, becoming more confident as he retold the story. "Sorted 'im proper, they did. First off, no one was to speak to 'im, see, an' 'e were cold-shouldered in the Maltsters! 'E couldn't get work nor no thin'. Took to doin' 'is drinkin' miles off, where no one knew 'im. Took their time over 'im, they did, the Ledburton folk. Then he just . . . wasn't about no more. Last time anyone recalled seein' 'im was in the Crown, over to Aunebridge. Locals reckoned as a bunch of Ledburton blokes waylaid 'im on 'is way 'ome and did for him. Never seen again, 'e wasn't. Folk came up with lots of notions 'bout where he could of bin dumped. Some said the Exe, or the bottom of that ole mineshaft over Brewer's way. Or in a slurry pit. I reckon 'twas a slurry pit, meself. Everyone had a slurry pit in them days." Ferdie's eyes had moved past Hester and Dave and settled beyond the lowest extremity of the yard where, below the newly repaired wall, lay what remained of the Lower Post Stone slurry pit. Less used now, since the dairy herd had been moved up to the higher farm, it lay, putrid and stinking. Deep beneath its crusty surface and rendered down by acrid gases and toxic fluids, were broken farm implements and a tangle of disintegrated bones. Over many decades, long before regulations said otherwise, deformed calves, dead sheep, the carcasses of foxes, the odd badger and whole litters of feral kittens had been slung into the rank sludge. At least one overzealous foxhound that had mistaken the surface for a short cut back to the pack had been drawn down to an ugly death.

Apart from a few dead branches in the lane, none of which was too large to be shattered by the wheels of Roger Bayliss's tractor, he could see very little storm damage to the farm buildings of Lower Post Stone. Hester called to him from the door of her cottage and

236

enquired after Evie's departure. He told her all had gone well and asked where Dave was.

"Round be'ind the barn, sir," she told him. "Where the storm damage be."

The iron ladder, fractured and warped, had been pulled away from the trough across which it had fallen and laid, horizontally, against the foot of the barn wall.

"What happened to your nose?" Roger wanted to know.

"'Tis nothin', sir," Dave told him. "Just a scratch and a bit of a bruise from when the ladder come down. 'E was swingin' loose, see, from where 'e broke away from the sill. 'Tis rotten as a pear up there, sir, since the fire."

"Lucky no one was hurt," Roger said.

"Yessuh, very lucky indeed . . . Wasn't expectin' you and Mrs Alice back so soon, sir?"

"No. We changed our plans after my wife saw Norman Clark in the lane yesterday. We wanted to be sure there hadn't been any trouble. See any sign of him down here?"

"Not down 'ere sir, no. Though he were up by Mr Lucas's place."

"I warned Lucas he might be," Roger said.

"And he warned me, sir. On the yard telephone but . . ."

"But no sign of him, eh?"

"No, sir. No sign."

"Right," Roger said. "Any other damage, d'you reckon?"

"Not as far as I can see, sir, no."

Satisfied that Norman Clark's assault on Alice, resulting in her damaged wrist, appeared to be his only crime on the previous day, Roger found himself focusing on that. In a terse conversation with Constable Twentyman's immediate superior, he registered the assault and was asked for the names of any witnesses. When it transpired that the only other person who could confirm Clark's presence in the valley was Edwin Lucas, who had sent him on his way, the police seemed to lose interest.

Roger drove Alice to Theo Parker's consulting room where her injury was examined. Although no bones were broken there was considerable damage to the tendons and soft tissue of the hand and lower forearm. Parker strapped the wrist and advised Alice to wear it in a sling for a couple of days and then resume as much movement as she felt comfortable with. He sat at his desk to write an account of the injury and of his treatment of it.

"The police will need that," he told Roger, sliding his report into an envelope.

"Such a fuss!" Alice said, almost apologetically.

"Not at all," Parker told her. "It wouldn't have taken much more pressure to break a bone or two. Added to which, you were in charge of a moving vehicle at the time. So, a serious assault, I would say. The law will probably need a formal statement from you when they charge him."

"If they catch him," Roger added. "They don't seem to be having much success with that."

It had taken Rose very little time to sense the tension in the Crocker cottage.

"What's up with your nose, son?" she demanded. "If you was going to tell me you walked into a door, don't bother yourself 'cos we Crockers don't walk into no doors!"

"It's like I told Mr Bayliss, Ma. It were the ladder done it, when I were sortin' out the storm damage."

"I see," Rose responded tartly. "And that's 'storm damage' on the knuckles of your right hand, is it? Mabel told Eileen as Ferdie Vallance has got a lump the size of a mangel on the side of 'is head! That's 'storm damage' too, I daresay? Some'at's goin' on, Dave, and don't you deny it!" Her sharp eyes flicked between Dave's and Hester's. "Just look at the pair of you! Two more guiltier faces I never did see! And there's Alice Todd — I mean Bayliss, with her arm in a sling! It were Norman Clark done that, I knows that much! So you might as well tell me the rest of it, Dave! You knows full well I'll get it out of you in the end!" This being true, he told her.

She made him begin at the beginning, at the point when Hester, seeing Clark enter the yard, blew the police whistle as a warning to her husband, through to the moment when Norman Clark lay dead, the heavy rain washing away the blood that had ceased pouring from his shattered skull. Rose narrowed her eyes.

"And then?" she prompted. Hester sat, cradling Thurza, her eyes downcast. "What did you do then, son?" Rose repeated. Dave gulped, gathered himself and in a low voice described to his mother how he and Ferdie, using a length of chain, had weighted the body by lashing it to a disused harrow. Using the remaining chain, they had hauled the harrow over the deepest part of the pit, released it and thrown the chain in after it.

Rose, better than any of them, knew the history of the pit. How, for centuries, seething and putrid, it had absorbed the run-off from the cattle stalls, bubbling like a witches' caldron under the summer suns and only rarely, in the time of floods, overspilling its fetid banks where nothing grew or had grown, either within or before living memory. Even in the coldest winter its surface seldom froze over. It was as though the fires of Hades fed it, so that in the season of frosts it lay suppurating, under a pale vapour, a blot on the snowy innocence of the surrounding landscape.

Rose sat, blinking slowly like a wise owl, breathing audibly as she concentrated on this awkward set of facts, concerned first with its immediate effect on her family and then, if that effect represented a serious threat, how that threat could be dealt with by whatever means were necessary to demolish it.

Born in the last years of Queen Victoria's reign and raised in the tough environment of rural Devonshire, where, in the village school she had learnt her ABC and done her sums on a slate, Rose had endured poverty and witnessed sickness, deprivation and death. She was familiar with the harshness and often the injustice of the law which she regarded with a sullen blend of distrust and contempt. Country people of her generation survived, as their antecedents had done, by

240

luck, hard work and a certain amount of animal cunning. An approach which she now prepared to apply to her son's predicament.

"Well," she began, in a low, controlled voice, engaging and holding Dave's eyes. "Seems to me that although he deserved to die, 'twasn't you as killed him."

"No," Dave said in the same level tone that his mother was using. "'Twas the fall as killed him." Hester nodded, affirming Dave's innocence. "I tried to stop 'im usin' that ladder, Ma, honest I did. But he come at me with the same hunk of wood he'd used to clout Ferdie!"

"So," Rose concluded, "it were an accident, pure and simple. Or self-defence. Whichever. Either way 'twas not your doing. Not your doing, Dave. Right?"

"Should us 'ave told the police, though?" Hester asked, uncertainly.

"There'll be some as'll reckon us should of," Rose said. "But you can't trust the law. All that lot does is make matters worse, I reckon. Make up their minds to suit theirselves, they do, and never let no one speak. They close their ears to anything they don't want to 'ear, truth or not. I've seen 'em make too many mistakes in my lifetime — too many jailings and unwarranted punishings not to keep well away from 'em. It's not like there's any doubt what Norman Clark done. Us all saw the state young Evie was in when she got away from 'im. And 'ow he 'alf killed Ferdie when 'e turned up 'ere, lookin' for 'er. Anyway . . ." she paused. "'Tis too late now! With 'im chained to that 'arrow and under six foot of sludge . . . No. What's done is done. Just you remember this, none but us knows and none but us need ever know. Right?"

"Ferdie knows," Hester said, plaintively. "And 'is Mabel's gonna ask how 'e hurt 'is 'ead."

"Storm damage, Hester," Rose said firmly. "Ferdie Vallance is no fool when it comes down to it and his Mabel certainly isn't. Sharp as a tack, Mabel be!" Rose took Hester's worried face gently between her rough hands. "There's plenty of secrets in this valley, Hester, dear. Allus has bin. Allus will be. Now, pull yourself together, dearie, and make us a nice cuppa tea, eh?"

For some days Hester and Dave were, to varying degrees, uncomfortably cognisant of their involvement in this monstrous thing that had happened. A man, however flawed and dangerous, had died, possibly deservedly, certainly horribly and they had disposed of his corpse as if he were a tainted animal. But as time passed, rationality began to diminish any recurring feelings of guilt. After the heavy rain, the slurry pit soon resumed its normal level, its surface blooming with familiar areas of thickening, crusty scum. The crumbling masonry above the aperture in the end wall of the barn was repaired and a new pulley installed in preparation for the building of the two cottages, on which work was scheduled to begin in the New Year.

At the higher farm, both Alice and Roger remained concerned by the lack or resolution to the Norman Clark situation. Alice worried that some loose-tongued local gossip could have let slip that Evie had emigrated

242

to New Zealand, as a result of which Clark might try to follow her there. Roger doubted this.

"We played the New Zealand part of the plan pretty close to our chests and those who did know of it —"

"Were not exactly sworn to secrecy, though, were they?" Alice interrupted.

"No," Roger admitted, "because, if you remember, we decided against that on the grounds that it would have drawn unwanted attention to the situation."

"Mmm. But, Rose, Roger. She's a notorious gossip!"

"True. But she's also canny. Secrecy is part of Rose's currency and she'll use it effectively. She wants a happy outcome to this and her family kept well out of things. She'll make sure those who know, don't tell. Evie had no police record, therefore the only official evidence of her departure is held, in confidence, by the New Zealand authorities. The proceeds of her legacy will be deposited in the bank account which I helped her set up, using this address as hers. No. I really don't believe there are any loose ends, my love, and I think we can assume that we have seen the last of Norman Clark hereabouts."

"Let's hope so," Alice sighed. "But he was in a very strange state when I encountered him. Quite deranged, in fact. I honestly think he would have killed me if he'd managed to drag me out of the car and I refused to tell him where Evie was hidden."

The police filed Alice's account of the assault. Norman Clark was still on their wanted list and would be charged when apprehended.

"It's almost Christmas," Alice realised, a few days later. Apart from her first Christmas in the valley, when a snow storm had cancelled the trains and marooned the girls in the lower farmhouse, Alice and Edward John had celebrated virtually alone. On that snowy occasion a contingent of GIs had arrived at the hostel with Christmas dinner cooked in the camp and a very good time had been had by all.

This year, Winnie and Gwennan, the last of the land girls still working on the Bayliss farm, were due to leave it on Christmas Eve and Rose Crocker had suggested a party in her tea shop as a farewell to them. She, Alice and Eileen were to provide cakes and Roger's contribution would be beer, a bottle of gin and some soft drinks.

"It's funny, isn't it . . ." Winnie said, with her eyebrow tweezers poised, examining her reflection in the dressing table mirror she shared with Gwennan in their noisy digs above the public bar, "How Evie — little, mousie Evie, who no one hardly even noticed, goes off to live happily-ever-after with her handsome Italian lover! Just like at the pictures! Things don't come more romantic than that, do they!"

"I don't reckon being married to that Norman Clark was very romantic!" Gwennan said. "Draggin' her off by the scruff of her neck like he did. Disgraceful, it was!"

"Yeah . . . But Evie, Gwennan! Our funny little Evie, eh?"

With her suitcases already half packed, Gwennan had begun to realise that she might miss the company of

Winnie much as she now missed the rest of the land girls who had already left the Post Stone farms. When she had first arrived at the hostel she had regarded herself as superior to the other girls but, over the years, her association with them had changed her and softened her. From being scornful of it, she now enjoyed flicking through the pages of *Women's Own* and was increasingly interested in vanishing creams, brands of shampoo and skirt lengths. Sensing that the girls had initially disliked her critical attitude, she had worsened the situation by being waspish and even spiteful. Only slowly had she responded to the atmosphere of warmth created by the relationships of one girl to another and their respect and even affection for their warden.

"Not long now, Gwennan!" Alice called to her one morning across the yard of the upper farm.

"D'you know, Mrs Todd," Gwennan said, forgetting to use Alice's new name, her Welsh accent as clipped and prim as ever, "I'd always thought I'd be pleased when the time came for me to leave here and go home to Wales. But now I reckon I'll miss it! It's the company, see, I liked the company of the girls — once I got used to them, that is. To their bad behaviour and so on." Alice smiled. "And you, Mrs . . . um . . . Bayliss. Ever so nice to me you've been. I reckon you done a first-class job here, you know. A really first-class job!"

"Well, thank you, Gwennan, it's very kind of you to say so!" They exchanged smiles, expressing more genuine warmth than they had felt for one another over all the months since the war had first thrown them together.

Higher Post Stone Farm

Dearest Georgina,
Great excitement here. At last Evie is safely on her
way and the even better news is that Giorgio has a
berth on the same ship to New Zealand, he, of
course, boarding at Naples. I'd love to witness that
reunion, wouldn't you? Things went smoothly at
this end except that as we left to drive Evie to
Tilbury her husband turned up here and there was
some unpleasantness. He did not find her, there
has been no sign of him since, thank goodness,
and he has no idea where she is going and we shall
keep it that way! We are leaving it to you and
Christo to contact the shipping company and
arrange things at your end.

Your last letter was so full of the joys of the
South Island and your lovely summer weather, just
when things are getting foul here. We are quite
envious!

Edward John is very full of himself as he is now
captain of his house's rugby team. He is coming
with us to lunch with your parents on Boxing Day
where, no doubt, you two will be much missed. We
shall all raise our glasses in your direction.

Your father-in-law is in good fettle and joins me
in sending you both our very best love . . .
Alice.

P.S. Thank you for the snapshots. You look so
well and happy. xx

Edward John arrived home for the weekend eager for details of Evie's departure and was then consumed with curiosity and concern regarding Norman Clark's brief reappearance in the valley. He became frustrated on hearing of the police's apparent lack of attention to the assault on his mother, despite her assurances that it was all over now and that no real harm had been done.

"But that's three people he's attacked, Mum! You, Evie and Ferdie Vallance!"

"Four," Roger corrected him. "Evie saw him hit Giorgio over the head with a piece of lead piping when he went to look for her in Coventry."

"I'd forgotten that," Edward John said. "Giorgio had to keep quiet about it because he'd broken his parole, poor fellow. So Norman Clark is still on the loose after injuring four people! And the police are doing nothing?"

"They're watching the railway stations and the main roads and all the local bobbies are on the lookout for him," Alice told him. "But there have been no confirmed reports of any sighting since he left the Lucas farm on the morning we drove Evie to Tilbury."

"But he must be somewhere!"

"We're hoping we can assume he is finally convinced that Evie is not here," Roger said but Edward John was not prepared to let the subject rest.

"So he's allowed to roam free, is he? A violent criminal wandering about the countryside? It's ridiculous! I'm going to find him!" he announced vehemently. "I'm going to make a citizen's arrest!"

"No you're not, darling," his mother said. "You are going to leave that task to the authorities. Your school breaks up soon and after that we'll all have a thoroughly nice Christmas!" Her boy smiled reluctantly.

There had been a time, when Roger Bayliss was becoming first attracted and then attached to Alice Todd, that he had begun to appreciate what a thoroughly nice child her son was. He tried and found it difficult to recall his own son's personality at the ages of ten, eleven and twelve, which had been Edward John's ages since he began spending his weekends and school holidays at the hostel. He remembered the boy being initially reserved and very slightly hostile to him, wary of his treatment of his mother when she, damaged by the failure of her marriage, had first taken on the daunting role of hostel warden, a position which, initially, had almost overwhelmed her. Roger's son, at that age, had probably been more affected by his own mother's recent death than his father had appreciated at the time.

Although Frances and Roger had been a fond couple, she was never the robust, gentleman-farmer's wife that he had needed and even before her early death, Roger, at barely thirty, and with his own parents dead and gone, was struggling not only with the management of the two farms but also with the responsibility of raising, virtually single-handed, his only child. He had found it impossible to talk to Christopher about their loss and this distance between them had continued through Christopher's schooling and into his training and service in the RAF. Although

Roger feared for his son's life and was concerned that he should not experience the trauma he himself had suffered as a result of his own early experience of war, it had been Alice who, to a large extent, had eventually resolved the breach between father and son.

It was possibly the fact that he had no direct responsibility for Edward John that made Roger's relationship with him an easier one than he had experienced with Christopher. In addition to this, Edward John's instant and enduring interest in the farms, something which his own son, at that age, had not exhibited, appealed to Roger, who soon came to value the boy's keen powers of observation. More than once he had averted disaster by spotting a sick beast, a breached hedgerow or a blocked drain before serious harm could be done.

It seemed likely that Edward John's interest in the farms might, if Christopher declined it, provide Roger with an heir to his acres. But the boy's headmaster spoke highly of his intelligence and both Roger and Alice understood that his ambitions were not yet formed and might lead him in other directions, possibly into medicine or the law.

Roger was unaware that Christopher had always assumed that he would step up to the Post Stone farms when his father felt inclined to step down. Had the war not intervened, Christopher would have progressed from public school to Seale Hayne Agricultural College before joining his father on their land. His catastrophic breakdown, after three years in the RAF, had been followed by what he regarded as his banishment to the woodman's cottage in the Bayliss forest. Here, after slowly recovering, both physically and emotionally, he had studied arboriculture, distanced himself from his father and the Post Stone farms and finally decided on a change of direction in his damaged life. Marrying Georgina and accepting the New Zealand contract had achieved this. Now, fully occupied by his marriage and his work, he was living in the present, optimistic about his future and happier than he had ever been.

"Dear Pa," he had written, recently.

"We are going camping over Christmas (mid summer here!). We have borrowed a tent and intend to drive a couple of hundred miles up the west coast into the Mount Cook ranges.

Evie and Giorgio will get a ferry south, when they disembark in Wellington, and we shall meet them and help them settle in. We've arranged government assistance regarding accommodation while Giorgio finds work, etc.

You'll most probably get another letter (or even a card!) before Christmas — the post is pretty erratic in these parts! But if not, have a happy one!

Much love from us both . . .

Christo

Edward John, pulling the hood of his duffel coat over his head, went out into the bitter cold of an east wind. As usual at midday on a Saturday, Dave was turning the two carthorses out into the paddock where they would crop the short grass and munch the remaining windfalls of the cider crop until their work began again on Monday. He saw Edward John approaching him, grinning broadly.

"Success!" Edward John had shouted, brandishing a clenched fist. For a moment Dave looked baffled. "This time next week Evie will be in Naples! With Giorgio! So we did it! Hooray for us, Dave!" he finished, jubilantly.

Dave's involvement in the whole sequence of events, from the discovery of Evie hiding in the hostel, through to her concealment in the byre on The Tops, to her departure from the Post Stone valley, had been replaced in his mind by more recent events of which Edward John was unaware.

"Yeah," he said. "Mission accomplished alright."

"Could have gone horribly wrong," Edward John said, "him turning up here the other day!"

"Yeah. Could of," Dave agreed, heavily.

"Pretty odd, though," Edward John continued, "the way he took off like that, after he had a go at my poor mother."

"He went up Lucas's place," Dave said, hoping this would conclude the exchange. But the boy fell into step with him as he walked the horses on, towards the paddock gate.

"So I hear," he persisted and then paused. "We know he went there . . . But where did he go after that?" Dave shook his head and fidgeted with the leading reins in his hand. The horses, impatient for freedom, tossed their heads.

"Reckon he buggered off," Dave shrugged, unlatching the gate. "'Cos no one's seen 'im since."

251

"You'd think he'd have gone on looking for Evie, though, wouldn't you?" Edward John said thoughtfully. "My mother says that when she saw him he was very worked up about things and absolutely determined to find her."

"Reckon 'e must of 'ad enough," Dave said, vaguely, slipping the bridles from the horses' heavy heads. "Decided to give up on 'er, I shouldn't wonder." He slapped Prince's rounded rump, murmuring, "Go on, git on there." The horses needed no encouragement and pushed through the gate, ambling off, almost coltishly relishing their liberation.

CHAPTER
ELEVEN

As Dave eased his car up the bumpy track to the Tucker smallholding he slowed and sat, the engine idling, Hester beside him, and stared through his windscreen. Although structurally unchanged, a coat of whitewash had transformed the face of the cottage.

"You am't seen nothun yet!" Zeke proudly told them, emerging from the newly painted front door and followed closely by Polly who led them into the parlour, which was also freshly painted and refurnished with a new sofa and two armchairs. "Polly's folks give 'em us," Zeke told them.

"And Zeke give me this," Polly beamed, extending her left hand and spreading her fingers to show off the small gold and garnet ring on her wedding finger.

"And you still am't seen nothun yet!" Zeke insisted. The accommodation inside the cottage had been improved by an ambitious extension that extended into what had been the backyard. On ground level this formed a large farmhouse kitchen, a pantry, a scullery and a laundry which incorporated the old bathroom. Leading out of this was a space furnished for Jonas Tucker's widow, whose mental illness had, the specialists assured her children, responded well to treatment and in which she now lived.

Zeke and Hester found their mother quiet and strangely detached, treating them and Thurza almost as strangers. But she was calm. The look of anxiety which had left her narrow, furrowed face, was now replaced by a bland indifference.

"How are you today, Mother?" Hester asked her, kneeling in front of her and taking her empty hands in hers. After a while the widow assured them that she was quite alright. She thanked Hester for asking and gently withdrew her hands from her daughter's. They left her sitting quietly in her room and climbed the stairs to inspect the new bedroom and bathroom.

"Us 'as used up almost all the money we found under the bed," Zeke quietly told his sister. "Most of the stone come from the outbuildin's we knocked down and a bit from the old quarry. Polly's dad and one of her brothers gave us a hand with the heavy stuff and Polly done most of the inside paintin' 'erself."

"We're gettin' wed soon as it's finished!" Polly told them. "The banns is called and I've got me dress and everything!" Hester had gazed wistfully at the white porcelain fittings in the gleaming bathroom.

"Oh, Polly! It's just like in the magazines!"

"I know!" Polly agreed, happily.

"That's what we could have, Dave!" Hester sighed, as they drove home across the moor, where a light snowfall was settling on the highest ground. "A bathroom with an indoor pull-and-let-go and a big

254

shiny bath tub! If only you'd ask Mr Bayliss to give us one of them new cottages 'e's buildin'." Dave leant forward, his concentration focused on the narrow road, watching for the wandering sheep and moorland ponies that were likely to stray, suddenly, into his headlights.

Hester pressed on, opening the next stage in what she expected would be a serious and if necessary, lengthy discussion, with the word "and". "*And*," she said. "And . . . I want to learn to drive our motor."

"Drive? You? What for?" Dave asked, not unpleasantly but with a slight hint of amusement in his voice. "I drives the motor, Hes. What would you want to drive the motor for?"

"So's I can take Thurzie to school and that."

"But she won't be goin' to school for four years yet!"

"Kindergarten! She could go to kindergarten, Dave. Lots of the little ones do, nowadays . . . And I could go visit your mum in the week when you're at work. She's allus on about how she don't see enough of Thurzie an' me. What d'you reckon, eh?"

Dave meticulously double-declutched as he changed into first gear and began the slow, steep descent into one of the valleys on the south side of the moor.

"I dunno . . . I never thought of you drivin', Hes. I can't imagine it."

"Why not? Because I'm a woman? Mrs Bayliss drives and she's a woman!"

"Yeah . . . But you'm not so much a woman as all that, Hes, are you. I mean you'm more of a girl. My girl." She had to smile. They crossed the narrow bridge

255

at the bottom of the valley and began the long climb up towards higher ground.

"But the Princess Elizabeth drives," Hester continued, inspired by photographs she had seen in *Picture Post*. "She drove great army lorries for the war effort. I seen the pictures. And she's a girl, in't she? So. What d'you think Dave, eh?"

"I dunno what I think, Hester. All this about new cottages and bathrooms and that. And now drivin'. Its just one bloomin' thing after another with you lately." Hester leant towards him and stroked his firm thigh.

"Yeah," she whispered, sympathetically. "But that's life, i'n't it Dave — one bloomin' thing after another."

"Just like a picture postcard!" the passengers exclaimed to one another, leaning on the rail of the *SS Orontes* as she altered course and the expanding vista of the Bay of Naples was slowly revealed to them.

The ship had rolled its way uncomfortably across the Mediterranean through wintery headwinds but today was still, the sea like blue silk under a cloudless sky. Evie lifted her face to the Italian sun which, even in mid December, felt pleasantly warm on her skin. The bay was alive with shipping, from small fishing craft to cargo boats, all moving at various speeds and in different directions, some heading out to sea, others homing in on the port itself where cranes, wharfs and warehouses were beginning to become discernible as the *Orontes* made her measured approach.

Across the bay Mount Vesuvius shimmered, lavender blue against the sky, its iconic shape recognised even by those who had never seen it before.

A stout, ageing man, immaculate in a white suit and a panama hat, who had boarded the ship in Tilbury, had this morning ventured down from the fist-class decks to mingle with the hoi polloi. Doffing his hat to Evie he smiled, his white teeth contrasting strongly with the neatly waxed moustache. "*Vedi Napoli e poi muori!*" he said. Evie looked blank, so he tried again in excellent English with an Italian accent. "See Napoli and die! Mm? You have heard these words?"

"Yes," Evie told him.

"And you understand what they means? Mm?" Evie smiled vaguely. "No? Well then I shall tell you. Some people attribute the phrase to the Bourbons. Mm? Others say it came from the great Goethe himself. But . . ." he shrugged, "who knows! To those of us who love this place it has an altogether simpler meaning. You wish to hear that?" Evie nodded. "Napoli is most beautiful, as you see." He waved his arms to encompass the panorama before them. "So beautiful, in fact, that once you have seen it, your pleasure in life is complete! *Capice?* Ah! I see that you understand! *Arrivederci*, my dear young lady . . . *Arrivederci!*" He lifted his hat again, gave a little bow and bounced on his tiny feet in their highly polished shoes. Then he was gone, swallowed up in the crowd of passengers who were massing along the rail, excited by the prospect of setting foot in a foreign country. Gibraltar, their first port of call, being a British colony, hadn't quite qualified as "foreign".

Two tugboats had the *Orontes* now and were edging her slowly closer to the wharf, which was already alive with taxis, cars and lorries bringing the provisions which would be loaded aboard during the few hours the ship would remain alongside.

Evie scanned the hundreds of upturned faces. How would she identify Giorgio in such a crowd? How would he distinguish her from the dozens of passengers jostling along the rail above him?

Giorgio squinted up into the low morning sun, the pink ship towering over him as it edged closer to the dockside.

Was that her, in a hat? Or there, with a scarf tied under her chin? Was she somewhere amidships? Towards the bow? Or way back on the stern deck? Was she there at all? Or had she not been brave enough or sufficiently in love with him to leave her native country?

Her eyes raked the crowd below her and with every passing second her anxiety increased. Why wasn't he there? Had the ship arrived too early or too late? Had he been persuaded by his family not to leave them? Had he met some local girl who had loved him all her life and was now claiming him? What would she do if he wasn't there? Leave the ship and search for him? Or sail on to New Zealand alone? One of the women with whom she shared a cabin, and to whom she had confided her situation, pushed through the crowd of passengers and joined her at the rail.

"Spotted your fella yet?" she asked, and at that moment one of the faces on the wharf became Giorgio's face. He had already seen Evie and was waving both his arms to attract her attention. Beside him was his brother, Salvo, with one of his children on his shoulders and the other in the arms of his wife.

"Yes!" Evie said, tears blurring her eyes. "Yes, he's there! You see? You see?" She stood, blowing kisses with both hands while the mooring lines were attached, the gangways lowered and the passengers began to spill down them onto the quay. Then, Evie's arms were round Giorgio's neck, his lips were on hers and he had lifted her feet from the ground, and while Salvo and his family cheered, swung her round and round. "Ah! *Bravo*, Giorgio! *Bravo*, Eva!"

It was raining in the Post Stone valley. Not a soft, mild, westerly drizzle but steady, cold and from the north-east. Edward John had saddled up Tosca, borrowed his stepfather's full-length, waterproof hunting coat, found a wide-brimmed felt hat in the tackle room and was riding down, through the fields, to Lower Post Stone. But he was not Edward John Todd. He was Randolph Scott in *The Desperadoes*, Gary Cooper in *The Westerner*. Or possibly Henry Fonda or Dana Andrews in *The Ox-bow Incident*. Tempted to say "Howdee, pardner" when he encountered Ferdie Vallance in the yard of the lower farm, he was glad he hadn't when Ferdie asked him why he was dressed up like a scarecrow.

Edward John, being an only child until, aged nine, he had been forced to share his mother with ten, almost fully grown young women, had learnt to amuse himself, using his well-stimulated imagination to provide him with the scenarios of adventures, plots, plans and theories which made him independent of other children. Although he was sociable enough and mixed well with his peers, he was undaunted when left to his own devices.

While he was satisfied by the news that Evie was safely aboard the ship which would, any day now, unite her with Giorgio, he had found himself repeatedly drawn to the mystery of Norman Clark's disappearance.

On the first and second occasions of Clark's attempts to repossess his wife, his departures from the valley had been witnessed. The first, by Roger Bayliss himself, who had put the unhappy couple on a train at Ledburton Halt and the second, after Clark's assault on Ferdie Vallance, by the stationmaster who had seen him board a train travelling north. But any evidence of his third departure ended abruptly, when he had been ordered off Edwin Lucas's land and had slouched, despondently away, into the rainy landscape. Alice Todd's description of his state of mind suggested to Edward John that the man might have been sufficiently deranged to be suicidal. But no body had been discovered swinging from a tree, floating face down in the river Exe or mutilated on a railway line.

Edward John slid from Tosca's saddle and tethered her to a hitching post in the yard of the lower farm.

Timber, for the conversion of the barn into two cottages, had already been delivered and stacked out of the weather. Having inspected this he made his way round to the rear of the barn where Dave Crocker and Ferdie Vallance were demolishing a redundant pigpen.

"Any news of young Evie?" Ferdie wanted to know. Edward John confirmed that the ship was due in Naples any day now but that it would be some time before the couple were reunited.

"That's Egypt, innit?" Dave asked. "All camels and that!"

"Yes," Edward John said, vaguely. "All camels and that." He was squinting up at the damaged sill of the aperture in the end wall of the barn, his eye caught by the marks where the iron nails and bolts that had attached the ladder had pulled away from the rotten wood and further down the wall, from the crumbling mortar.

"It's hard to see how a gale could have caused that," he said. Dave and Ferdie exchanged glances. "It looks to me as if someone, who didn't know about the fire damage, had tried to use the ladder." Ferdie, loading a barrow with stones from the pigpen, took its weight and trundled out of sight. Edward John stood, waiting for Dave to answer him.

"Could of," Dave said, shrugging. "Ferdie and I was working round t'other side of the barn that day. Loadin' mangels, we was. Like I told Mr Bayliss, the next mornin' us found the ladder down on the ground." This partially accurate account of things so nearly matched the truth that Dave almost believed it himself. Edward John pulled a face which implied his scepticism. Ferdie rejoined them and began loading the empty barrow.

"But what sort of gale blows an iron ladder off a wall?" Edward John persisted.

"Reckon the rain 'ad softened the charred sill and the ladder worked loose," Dave said firmly. Edward John nodded.

"And what do you reckon, Ferdie?" he asked. Ferdie, taken aback and off guard, mumbled something Edward John couldn't hear. "What?" he persisted.

"I reckon that those who asks no questions gets told no lies!" Ferdie repeated. Then he stood, head lowered, fixing Edward John with a harsh, defensive stare, his hands flexing and unflexing on the shaft of the pickaxe he was using to break up the stones. Then he dropped his eyes, swung the pick and dislodged a hefty piece of slate. Edward John glanced at Dave who was smiling indulgently.

"Reckon our Ferdie got out of his bed on the wrong side this mornin!" he said, his grin so broad that Edward John found himself smiling too. Then both the men bent their backs over the pile of masonry, heaving the blocks onto the barrow. Edward John watched them for a few moments and then left them. When he was out of their sight, Dave straightened and turned furiously on Ferdie.

"What in the name of flamin' heck did you have to go and say that for, you brainless bugger!"

"All I said was 'them that —'"

"'Asks no questions gets told no lies.' Yeah, I heard what you said, alright! You'm a nit-brain, Ferdie Vallance! A nit-brain! Edward John may on'y be a kid but 'e's a smart one! When that lad puts two and two together, 'e makes four! Sure as eggs is eggs, 'e'll reckon some'at's gone on and it'll not take long for 'im to work out what!" Ferdie sulkily considered this.

"P'raps us should tell 'im," he suggested.

"Tell 'im? Tell Edward John? Not likely! Least people know 'bout this the better!"

"Lots know already, though. What with my Mabel and your Hester and your Mum!"

"But all of them knows better than to let it go no further!" Dave insisted. "Edward John would tell his ma, most likely, and she'd tell the boss and the boss be a magistrate now! We'd have the law down on us in no time!"

Dave sat down heavily on the low wall, rested his forearms on his knees, his big hands hanging loosely between them.

"That's where us got it wrong, though, Ferdie. Us should of called the law instead of chuckin' 'im in the slurry. We 'adn't done nothing wrong 'til then. What happened with the ladder were an accident, pure and simple. There was plenty of witnesses to the GBH what Clark 'ad done to Evie. Then the Eyetie. Then you. And Mrs Bayliss. Then the pair of us. 'E'd 've gone down for all that, for sure, and we'd of bin in the clear!" He looked up at the damaged wall and then at the buckled metal of the ladder. Ferdie was doubtfully shaking his head.

"You reckon the law would 'ave believed us? They got a nasty way of twistin' things, that lot, Dave. Imagine what the newspapers would say!" Dave acknowledged the truth of this with a sigh.

"Yeah . . ." he said. "You can just see the 'eadlines, can't you. 'Locals murder returned soldier over two-timin' land girl'."

"But it weren't murder," Ferdie said. "It were an accident."

"Try provin' that, when the bastard's body be under six foot of sludge and weighted down be 'alf an 'arrow."

They were right about Edward John. He had put two and two together and although he had not made four, he was closer to it than he was to three, or even five.

His first theory was that Norman Clark had found his way down from the Lucas farm to Lower Post Stone where he still hoped to find Evie. Instead he had been discovered by Dave and Ferdie who set on him in an attempt to run him off the property. The ensuing fight, which had resulted in the bruises and cuts which both Dave and Ferdie later claimed to have been caused by the storm, could have been both violent and protracted, ending in Clark making his escape, as he had after the earlier incident, across the fields. This hypothesis raised the question of how, given that the local constabulary had been, by then, alerted to Clark's presence in the area and were actively searching for him, no one had seen any sign of him. And, more inexplicably, why, if Clark had arrived at the lower farm, neither Dave, Ferdie or even Hester, had not immediately contacted the police? Edward John at that point knew nothing of

264

the disconnected telephone or how Dave had subsequently replaced the damaged wiring.

As each of his theories raised more questions than it answered Edward John allowed himself to be distracted by the complex question of his own future. He would be leaving his prep school at the end of the next summer term. In line with tradition and in common with all the boys in his year, he had recently spent half an hour with his headmaster, discussing his ambitions.

Geoffrey Turbot, known affectionately if not respectfully as "Fishy", offered Edward John a ginger biscuit from the tin on his desk and then continued his scrutiny of his pupil's end-of-term report. It was obvious to Edward John that the biscuit was intended to put him at his ease, but as he already knew his report was a good one and consequently was not at all ill at ease, he simply sat enjoying the biscuit and watching Fishy's spectacles slide down his long, bony nose.

"Well, young man?" Turbot asked, removing the spectacles, closing the report and clasping his hands on the inky blotter in front of him. "What's it to be? Agriculture or medicine?" Geoffrey Turbot was familiar with Edward John's history, his parents' broken marriage, his charming and resourceful mother and his warm relationship with his recently acquired stepfather.

"Farming, probably," Edward John told him and then, reacting to his headmaster's slightly quizzical expression, added, "There's a lot to it, you know, and my stepfather is very good at it. I like the Post Stone valley. And the people. And the animals. So I'll probably try for Seale Hayne and then . . ." Edward

John was picking up the distinct impression that Fishy was not entirely happy with his answer. The headmaster helped himself to a biscuit and pushed the tin towards Edward John.

"You used the word 'probably' twice, young man."

"Did I?" Edward John said.

The discussion that followed was not an unfamiliar one to the headmaster. Boys leaving prep school were almost always in a vulnerable state when it came to making decisions about their ambitions. Some evaded the issue altogether, leaving it, in the short term at any rate, to their teachers to suggest the subjects best suited to equip them for modest success in a respectable profession, or for the long term, to parental ambition which often resulted in disappointment.

In Turbot's experience, only a very few boys at twelve years plus a few months felt confident enough to resist outside pressures from whichever direction they came. Often this led to false starts or, more sadly, to whole lives being blighted by wistful reflection. "What I always wanted to do." "Who I always wanted to be" . . .

The headmaster watched his pupil eat the second biscuit. On the boy's face was a slight frown, his eyes were fixed on some distant prospect. Or perhaps on nothing at all. He swallowed the last of the biscuit, and after a moment, almost apologetically engaged the headmaster's eyes.

"Sorry, sir," he said. "I was just thinking . . ."

"You go ahead," Turbot said, groping amongst the clutter on his desk for pipe, tobacco pouch and matches. "Have a good think. No hurry. No hurry at all." He thumbed golden shreds of Barney's Full Strength down into the bowl of his pipe, drew the match flame into it and had been pulling and puffing gently for some time before Edward John spoke.

"I had thought," he said, "at one time, that I might like to be a vet, but . . ."

"But what?" Turbot said, through teeth clamped round the stem of his pipe.

"But . . . it takes such ages to qualify. It's a massive subject. All the different species, you see. Not like being an ordinary doctor and only having to study humans."

"And that seemed a bit daunting, did it?" Turbot asked.

"A bit. And then I thought about being a brain surgeon or something. A haematologist, perhaps. They study —"

"The blood. Yes. That sounds quite challenging. Your results for science, biology and physics indicate that you have capabilities in that direction. You'd need to keep up your Latin, of course, and your maths but —"

"But then I rather went off medicine," Edward John said, apologetically, adding, "Because I really would hate to have to live in a city, you see, and brain surgeons and haematologists more or less have to because it's where the big hospitals are and where the groundbreaking research goes on."

"Mmm," Turbot said. "Groundbreaking research, eh. Well, yes, I suppose it does. It's a dilemma, isn't it."

"Yes, it is a bit." Edward John watched Turbot knock the ashes from the bowl of his pipe.

"The thing is, old chap," the headmaster said, "that you really don't have to make any big decisions at this stage of things."

"Don't I?" Edward John asked. "I sort of thought I did. Don't I have to tell my housemaster at Wellington which subjects I'm going to study for School Cert. and Matric. and everything?"

"True. You do. But the clever thing is to cover all your bases. Concentrate on subjects that not only interest you but have a link to any of the careers you are considering and just give the others a bit of a nod from time to time, to keep everyone happy. See what I mean?" Edward John clearly did see and said so. "Now scram," Turbot said. "Poor old Harrison Minor has been kicking his heels outside my door for far too long. Tell him to come in, will you?"

"Yes, sir. And thank you very much, sir."

Harrison Minor was propping up a wall in the corridor. "In you go, Harri Mi," Edward John called to him, feeling oddly relieved and rather pleased with himself. But as he walked down the long corridor that would take him back to his classroom, his mind busy with his headmaster's words, he found himself faced with the inevitable scene in which he would have to tell Roger Bayliss that however much he loved the Post Stone valley, together with the processes of farming it and the beasts and the people involved, he did not want to make it the hub of his life. Although he knew that Roger was proud of his scholastic achievements, he also knew that he hoped, in view of the unlikelihood of his

268

own son taking over the farms, that Alice's son would do so.

The Christmas festivities were to begin on December the twenty-third with Rose's tea party, celebrating the departure, on the following day, of the last two of the Post Stone land girls.

Winnie and Gwennan had contrived to avoid much that could be described as manual work during their final weeks on the farms, and as a result, Roger Bayliss resented having to pay their virtually unearned wages plus their board and lodging at the pub.

"Think of it as a Christmas bonus, darling," Alice coaxed him. "A thank you for their hard work over all these years." When Roger responded with a sound which closely resembled a "bah humbug", she accused him of behaving like Scrooge. Roger, without lowering his copy of *The Times*, told her that he had always sympathised strongly with Ebenezer Scrooge.

"One of my literary heroes," he said. "The poor fellow, left to his own devices, would obviously have much preferred to spend Christmas in his own company rather than with that ghastly family of his, ghosts or no ghosts. Rather feeble of him to let himself get talked into it, I've always thought!" Alice laughed at him.

"Just try to keep your miserable feelings to yourself this afternoon, there's a dear — and don't forget to compliment Eileen on her trifle."

Eileen had not had a lot to do with the land girls, who had been housed in the lower farmhouse, but had earned herself an invitation to the party by producing a huge bowl foaming with whipped cream and garnished with preserved summer fruits, all of this topping a layer of buttery sponge, drowning in custard and half a bottle of Roger Bayliss's best sherry.

Winnie and Gwennan were quite overcome by the number of people who had gathered in Rose's tea room. The Crocker family were joined by Hester's brother Zeke and Polly, his bride. Ferdie and Mabel Vallance had brought their twins, Scarlet O'Hara and Winston, nimble two-year-olds, who mislaid themselves under the tables and amongst the chair legs, while Thurza Crocker, already exhibiting a strong sense of independence, waved her arms, flexed her cherubic legs and demanded to be allowed to join them.

"Just look at you all!" Gwennan exclaimed, confronted by the noisy roomful.

"I'll most likely cry before I'm done!" Winnie warned them as a cheer went up when she and Gwennan made their entrance.

Winnie was wearing one of the outfits she had assembled for her new role as landlady of the refurbished public house "with accommodation for travelling gentlemen" of which she and her Uncle Ted were now co-licensees. Her ruby-red velvet frock showed off a figure which was just beginning to show the first signs of maturity. Her hair was tightly and permanently waved, its colour a harder, darker chestnut than usual, while her make-up suggested that it would survive long evenings spent supervising her saloon bar, her public bar and her snug.

270

Gwennan too had completed her transformation from sober land girl to sober manageress of a funeral parlour and had purchased her charcoal-grey, worsted suit from a superior ladies' outfitter in Exeter. The narrow skirt and fitted, shoulder-padded jacket made her slightly gawky figure appear almost elegant and very similar to the model in the copy of *Vogue* which she had borrowed from Alice Bayliss. The neat white blouse, with its modest, lace-trimmed collar, softened the bleak bones of her face, while her unremarkable hair remained unremarkable.

"Very businesslike, Gwennan," Alice told her, knowing that this was precisely the effect intended. She was rewarded by one of Gwennan's rare smiles.

A picture postcard had arrived that morning at the higher farm, bearing an Italian stamp and a message to "dear all". It showed a panoramic view of the Bay of Naples with the ubiquitous Mount Vesuvius prominently featured. The message confirmed that the lovers were safely reunited, that the ship would sail that evening, that they both sent their love to everyone and would write soon. The card was circulated from hand to sticky hand and only narrowly missed a serious chewing when Hester eased it from between her daughter's newly acquired milk teeth.

When the trifle bowl had been scraped clean and everyone had worked their way through the less spectacular contributions of food, the children had spilt the lemonade, the men had downed the beer, the ladies the gin and oranges and were now sipping tea, Roger Bayliss tapped his glass with his trifle spoon and made a slightly formal speech in which the valuable contribution that Winnie and Gwennan had made to the war effort was mentioned. He then adopted a heavily Teutonic accent in order to tell a joke about German soldiers in North Africa, which posed the question "why in the desert do you not hungry go?" the answer having something to do with it being "because of the sand which in the desert is!" No one quite understood it but everyone laughed and applauded because they felt happy and the boss was "a good ol' boy" of whom they all approved.

"'Nother cup of tea, Mr Bayliss, sir?" Rose asked, appearing suddenly beside him. When he politely declined Rose gave him one of what Alice had always described as "her Rose looks". This "look" was a blend of concern, sympathy and curiosity. Alice had learnt to treat these looks warily because the next stage was very often a question that fell into the category of prying, or, to put it even less kindly, though more honestly, of downright nosiness. "I bet you're missing your Christopher, aren't you," she told him, nodding in agreement with herself and continuing before he could respond, with, "It's times like these when you feel it most, I daresay." Roger shook his head vaguely and looked for Alice, hoping he could signal to her for immediate help. But Alice was deep in conversation with Polly and Zeke. "That New Zealand place is such a long way off," Rose continued, shaking her head as though it was at least as far off as the moon, and then delivering her knockout blow. "I don't suppose they'll ever come back, do you? People never do. And there you were, Mr Bayliss, planning for him to take over the farms from you one day! What's that saying — something to do with mice? I can never remember it proper. Scottish it is . . . But you know what I mean, I'm sure. Such a shame. You certain you don't want more tea?" Roger again refused the proffered pot and Rose retreated, tut-tutting as she went.

Roger had, that morning received another letter from his son which, coming so soon after the previous one, alerted him to the fact that it might contain important information.

"Hi Pa," he read.

"We have just received some exciting news. I've been offered a promotion which, after discussing things with Georgie, I'm going to accept. They are putting me in charge of all the plantation projects on the eastern side of South Island. It will mean moving to Dunedin where the forestry commission HQ is. We get a splendid old house to live in, and although we both love it here on our beach, we think it will be better for Georgie — she sometimes feels a bit isolated. She will almost certainly be offered work — if she wants it — with the Min. of Ag. (based on her Land Army experience and all those exams she took when she was one of Alice's girls).

Things won't happen until next March when it will be autumn here, which suits us, as this place is heaven at this time of the year. It means my contract will be extended but I have stipulated that

273

three years is the absolute max that Georgie and I will spend out here.

Much as we both love it, the call of home and family is strong and I don't much fancy life without our farmland, Pa. So . . . your prodigal son looks like lobbing back into the Post Stone valley in a couple years' time!

If that's okay with you?

Everything organised at this end for Evie and Giorgio. Will update you soonest.

Happy Christmas (again!)

And love to you both from us both . . .

Christo and Georgie.

XX

Alice joined Roger and they smiled over his description of his rather one-sided conversation with Rose.

"You should have told her Christo's news," she said. "It would have cheered her up."

"No," Roger said. "It wasn't 'cheering up' she was after. I think she was enjoying her role as comforter of the abandoned parent. Ouch!" he exclaimed, as Scarlet O'Hara, in full cry and wielding the heavy serving spoon from the trifle bowl, struck him hard on his shin bone and then smiled up into his face and asked, "'Poon hurt?"

"Bad girl!" Mabel admonished, with a touch of pride, as she hauled her daughter away from her wincing boss.

"Can we leave now? Please!" Roger asked his wife, rubbing his shin.

274

Day had followed day and any local curiosity there had been concerning Norman Clark's recent reappearance in the valley and his abrupt departure from it, seemed to have dissipated, much like the thick mists or sharp frosts that occurred on most days at this time of the year and were usually gone by mid morning.

Life moved on in the valley. It was as though the winter storm that had struck on the day of the incident and roared through the Bayliss woods, up and over the bleak grassland of The Tops and on, across the moor, had taken with it, into oblivion, Norman Clark's violence and any evidence of the gory accident that had ended his sad story. Despite this, Dave and Hester, Ferdie, Mabel and Rose, had found themselves drawn together at the party, standing in a group, sipping, biting into cake and smiling awkwardly, like the conspirators they had become while concealing and supporting Evie and Giorgio and, since the incident that had ended Norman Clark's life, carefully guarding their secret. Edward John, finding it difficult to accept the possibility that Clark had simply conceded defeat, continued to explore his own theories regarding the man's disappearance.

"Orright?" Dave, his mouth full of cake, had asked Edward John. Edward John nodded and moved away from the group. When he was out of earshot Rose spoke in a low voice.

"No one said nothun to no one, then?" she wanted to know, and when this was confirmed by all of them she added, "And no one's not ever goin' to say nothin', neither. Ever. Right?" They all concurred. It was at this point that Roger Bayliss had tapped his glass and embarked on his speech. By the time it was concluded, the group had drifted apart.

Since the successful removal of Evie from the dangerous domination imposed by her husband and the news of her happy reunion with Giorgio Zingaretti, Edward John had begun to be concerned by the fact that whatever the facts of Norman Clark's disappearance, the pair would be unable to marry without proof of his death. And since, were he still alive, he would be unlikely to agree to a divorce, it seemed that a legal marriage was going to remain unattainable for them.

"Penny for them?" Roger asked his stepson later that evening. Edward John, deep in thought, started almost guiltily. His hardening suspicions regarding Norman Clark's disappearance made him guarded and cautious.

"Nothing, really . . ." he said absently.

"No?" Roger persisted. "I thought you were looking distinctly wistful."

"I was thinking about Evie and Giorgio," Edward John admitted, truthfully.

"It's all good news there, surely?" Roger enquired.

"Except that they can't ever get married, can they? Not with Norman alive, I mean."

"Well, certainly not for awhile," Roger told him, surprising Edward John.

"But I thought unless he divorced her it would be bigamy or something."

"As the law stands," Roger told him, "if, after seven years have passed, Clark can't be found and has made no attempt to contact Evie, the marriage can be annulled." Edward John knew what annulled meant and his face briefly reflected the impact of this information.

"So . . . She'd be free to remarry?" he queried.

"Yes. Why d'you ask?" Roger wanted to know. Edward John shrugged.

Later in the evening, sitting with Roger, one on each side of their fire, Alice reread Christopher's letter.

"Does Edward John know about this?" she asked her husband.

"Not yet," he told her.

"Why?"

"Because I'm not sure how he'll take it," Roger said. "It's pretty clear from what Christo says that he sees himself eventually taking over from me here. But ever since Edward John set foot on the farms it's been obvious he fancies farming, and when Christo seemed to have lost interest, Edward John might have thought . . ." He paused, scanning Alice's face and thinking how like an angel she looked, lit by the blending of lamplight with firelight.

"You used the word 'thought' ," Alice said and saw Roger's attention refocus on the subject under discussion. "I think you're right about what he 'thought', but I'm not so sure it's what he thinks now."

"Really?" Roger asked in surprise. "You think he's losing interest in the farms?"

"No," she said, "I don't think he'll ever do that but . . ."

"But?"

"Well, when he was nine years old Edward John wanted to be a vet. But he didn't think he was clever enough. Now his schoolmasters seem to think he is clever enough. You've said yourself he is exceptional. 'A highly developed intellect for a twelve-year-old', you once said."

"You're right," Roger smiled. "I did say that and it's true. So . . . you think he may be looking at broader horizons than my modest acres could offer him, do you?"

"I think it would ease his mind enormously if he thought that choosing something other than farming would not disappoint you or hurt your feelings — he's very fond of you, you know. And now that we know that Christo is planning to return to the valley you wouldn't be disappointed, would you? And that is why, darling, I think you should give my boy an early Christmas present by letting him read Christo's letter . . . Mmm?"

"Oh, wise and most exquisite of women," Roger murmured, getting to his feet. "I think a small brandy is called for, no? Just to settle our stomachs, after Eileen's prodigious trifle."

Alice had volunteered to drive Winnie and Gwennan to the station. She saw this as discharging a final and affectionate duty to the last of the land girls to whom she had been warden. From ten girls at the start, down to half a dozen when the end of the war was celebrated, to two with the closing of the hostel. These two, ultimate departures, had a special importance to Alice. It would be the final scene of a significant episode in her life and she was very aware of the journey she had made. She was conscious not only of the effect of the war years on herself but on her son and on the young women who had come and gone from the hostel, some briefly, others, like Georgina, who had become a member of her family, and Hester Tucker and Mabel Hodges, who had married into the local community. Evie was undoubtedly the girl whose life had been most radically altered by the chance that had delivered her to Lower Post Stone Farm. Altered more radically even, than Alice was aware.

The storm which the war had created had stranded all of them in unfamiliar territory and then, as the turmoil receded, they had, one by one, moved on and away, taking what they could, as well as what they could not avoid, from the chances and the experiences they had been given.

Winnie and Gwennan were standing outside the pub with their various suitcases and carry-alls clustered round their ankles. The wearing of Land Army issue hats had always been a bone of contention. The girls had unanimously shunned them and had only ever worn them under duress for occasional church parades and, once, for a funeral. Today, as a sort of prank and looking totally inappropriate with their civilian clothes, both girls were sporting the wide-brimmed, khaki felt hats as they stood giggling and waving to Alice as she brought the car to a standstill beside them.

"Very suitable!" she called to them, playing up to their joke. "Put your cases in the boot and let's get on our way or we shall miss your train!"

279

The locomotive was already puffing up the incline towards Ledburton Halt as they hauled their luggage across the platform. As it stood, blowing and hissing, they heaved their cases into a carriage and up onto the rack above the seats. Before any serious leave-taking could get underway the stationmaster was blowing his whistle and slamming doors. There was no time for tears. Just swift, warm hugs, before Alice was alone on the platform and Winnie and Gwennan were two heads, leaning, one above the other, out of the window, shouting goodbye and blowing kisses. Just before reaching the curve in the track which would take them out of sight the girls removed their hats and shied them into the air with whoops of delight. Alice whooped back. Then the carriage had rounded the curve and they were gone, leaving the two hats skimming through the air, out into a field in which a couple of milking cows paused in the chewing of cud and eyed them suspiciously as they landed amongst the tufts of wintery grass.

Epilogue

Lower Post Stone Farm
Summer 1957

A mud-splattered Land Rover pulls up in the lane outside Lower Post Stone farmhouse from which Kiwi Bayliss runs, reaches the open window of the Land Rover and turns a bewitching, ten-year-old's smile on its driver. She is, he realises, at that wonderful stage in her life when everything has the potential to be an adventure.

"Have you come to see the photo?" she asks and when he nods, smiling back at her, adds, "The parents think they know who it is but I'm not allowed to tell you! Come on!" She runs ahead of him up the path and into the farmhouse. "Edward John's here!" she yells "Oh, where is everyone? And where is the photo?"

Seated at the farmhouse kitchen table with the family clustered round him, Edward John examines the snapshot. All he has been told is that the picture has just been found. He doesn't know where or in what circumstances. Christopher, Georgina, Kiwi and Pom stand stock-still, barely breathing, expectant, the children suppressing giggles. Then Edward John speaks.

"Evie," he says. "It's definitely Evie. Where . . . ?"

His question is cut by a burst of laughter, everyone is speaking at once so that Edward John can't hear anyone. Smiling, he puts his hands over his ears.

"Shut up, everyone!" Georgina orders.

"One at a time!" Christopher says.

"Me, then!" says Pom. "Me first! Because I'm the one who found it!" He meets his sister's scowl and she turns sulkily away.

"Where?" Edward John asks again.

"Under the bridge," Pom tells him. He is leaning on the table, turned, so that he can see Edward John's reaction. "There's a sort of ledge that sticks out . . ."

"Near the roof. Yes, I remember it." Edward John had explored the farm as thoroughly in the forties as Pom is in the process of doing, now, in the fifties. "But how can it have survived this long? It must have been inside something?"

"It was," Kiwi interrupts. "It was in a sort of leathery wallet thing . . ."

"Which was inside another sort of bag . . ."

"A kind of kitbag," Kiwi adds.

"A kitbag?" Edward John asks sharply, suddenly more serious. "What sort of —"

"It was all mouldy and falling to bits," Kiwi says, waving her hands, miming the disintegration.

"And you dropped it in the stream and it got washed away!" her brother chips in, accusingly.

"It wasn't my fault!" she protests. "And, anyway, there was nothing in it except some sodden rags. It all just fell to bits in the water."

Edward John turns the snapshot in his hands. Nothing on the back. Only the smudged image on the front. Evie. Younger than when she arrived at the hostel. But definitely Evie.

"The leather wallet that this was inside," he asks Pom, "— was there nothing else in it? No papers of any sort?" The boy shakes his head.

"Nope. There could once have been some but they were all wet and mushy and coming in bits," he says.

"Even the snapshot was pretty far gone when the kids first brought it in," Georgina adds. "We dried it carefully and then you could just about see what it was."

"And then who it was," Christopher adds.

Hours later, when the children are in bed and Georgina, Christopher and Edward John have dawdled over the food Georgina has cooked for them and are finishing the bottle of Macon that had been Edward John's contribution, they speak again about the long-lost snapshot which Pom has taken to his room and pinned onto his noticeboard.

There are lengthy pauses in the conversation, as Georgina and Christopher pick over the facts that emerge as Edward John answers their questions. Slowly, they both begin to sense in Edward John a reluctance to explore or endorse the various theories or explanations that they themselves offer for the discovery of the photograph. As they continue to ply him with queries, his evasiveness increases.

"So . . . presumably, Norman Clark put it there," Christopher says. "Hides it, you think? Along with a kitbag containing what were once items of clothing?" Edward John shrugs and pours the last of the wine into his glass.

"Well, who else would have done?" Georgina wants to know. No one answers her.

"But why would he?" Christopher asks.

"And when would he?" Georgina persists. "He came down here twice, looking for Evie, right? Once to fetch her from the hostel and take her home to Coventry, then, after that, he came again. She wasn't here, there was a scuffle and Ferdie, Dave and Hester saw him leave the valley. So, both times there were witnesses to the fact that he left the area. Roger the first time, when he drove Clark and Evie to the station and put them on the Birmingham train, and the second time, by the stationmaster himself, did you say?" Edward John nods. "But the third time he came — the day Evie sailed from Tilbury — all we know is that he vanished off the face of the earth after Edwin Lucas sent him packing. Is that right?" Edward John nods again. "So when is he supposed to have left the kitbag with the photograph in it, under the bridge? And how come no one knows what happened to him after he left Lucas's yard? And why, if he was still so obsessive about finding Evie, did no one see him afterwards — or since?"

There is a long pause. Edward John gives a shaky sigh. He looks at Georgina and then at Christopher, swallows the last of his wine and says, "You'd better brace yourselves, you two."

284

He still has mixed feelings about telling them. For twelve years the knowledge has been confined to himself, the Crockers and the Vallances. The sleeping dogs have lain undisturbed for all that time and could have continued to do so. But now, this photograph, this small, damp shadow of the past, has fallen into the hands of two inquisitive children. "The reason no one has seen him since," he tells them, "is because he's dead."

It is midnight before Edward John has laid all the facts before them, describing how, his suspicions once roused led him on to discover what happened on that stormy December morning. Georgina has brewed a second pot of tea. The night has turned cold and Christopher has laid and lit the open fire.

"So what made you suspicious?" Christopher asks and Edward John explains again how the account given by Ferdie and Dave of the damaged ladder, their own injuries, plus the disappearance of a broken harrow which Roger Bayliss had decided to get repaired rather than replaced, had finally given him a scenario which proved to be very close to the truth.

"At one point I honestly believed they'd killed him," he tells them. "That was the worst time for me because it looked like being murder. But after I confronted them, I became convinced that it was an accident. It was all so horribly plausible. The mistake they made was not to go straight to the police."

"Why on earth didn't they?" Georgina wants to know.

"Hester would have phoned them from the barn but Clark had pulled the wires off the wall." He pauses, watching their faces as they receive and then react to each piece of the jigsaw. "And" — he hesitates — "Well . . . The thing I think we all accept and mustn't forget is the fact that the valley people have a deep, inbred distrust of the law. Farm labourers were hanged for snaring rabbits and women deported for stealing a loaf of bread — almost within living memory, you know! 'One law for the rich and another for the poor'. Oh, they've moved on a bit since Victorian times, but more slowly here, in the back of beyond, than in the cities. Generations of hardship have taught them basic survival tactics and I reckon there are worse secrets in these parts than this one." He pauses, watching them.

"It's true," Christopher muses. "Pa told me a few things when I was a kid. About country people taking the law into their own hands. Old women burnt as witches when someone's kid had a fever or a horse went lame. That sort of thing. Mysterious deaths. Unexplained disappearances and so on. I wouldn't put it past our Rose to have cast a spell or two in her day . . ."

"Shush!" Georgina says, laughing and briefly easing the tension.

"There was such a pile of evidence against Clark," Edward John says, "including his attack on my mother on the morning of the incident that killed him, that Dave and Ferdie probably wouldn't have been charged. Their disposal of the corpse is what would have told against them." Georgina shudders. Edward John's description of the weighting of the body and the image of the crusty surface of the slurry pit closing over it will haunt her. "That was why I decided to keep quiet," Edward John continues and then, looking at them both, sighs. "And now I've spread the responsibility to you two. Sorry! One of the disadvantages, perhaps, of having two bright kids! If they hadn't found that snapshot . . ." He sighs again. "It's a huge relief to have told you. Although, in a way, a bit of a risk. You might feel obliged to . . . I don't know . . . to take a more responsible view?" Georgina shakes her head and puts her hand on Edward John's.

"I'm with you," she says. "Absolutely with you. There's no doubt that Clark deserved what he got, 'accident' or not."

"And it was an accident, Georgie! I couldn't be more certain of it. I have spoken to all of them, together and separately and listened, over and over to each account. I saw the ladder and the wall weeks before I put the whole thing together. That ladder had been pulled away from the wall when someone heavy tried to use it. Everyone on the farm knew it was unsafe. No one had used it since the fire. Both Ferdie and Dave had splinters of wood in the wounds they tried to claim were 'storm damage'. Splinters from the bolt of timber Clark used to lay Ferdie out and then whacked Dave with. The telephone wires *had* been pulled out. I saw evidence of the repair. And another thing we know now, since the photograph turned up, fits with Hester's account of seeing Clark climb up over the parapet of the bridge, and that he was not carrying the knapsack he had with him when he attacked my mother and when he encountered Edwin Lucas. I could go on. D'you want me to?"

Christopher shakes his head and sits for some time considering the various aspects of the dilemma. The effect of a police investigation of this kind on his father and stepmother and on the lives of those members of the farms' workforce who would be directly and possibly destructively involved in it, deserved consideration.

"No," he says at last. "What would be the point of digging over all that? And after all this time. Who would gain?"

"No one, now," Edward John says. "Evie would have, back then, because she would have been able to marry Giorgio without waiting seven years until her marriage to Norman could be annulled." They sit for a while, sipping cups of tea from the second pot, considering the conclusion they have come to and adjusting to its implications.

A night wind is pressing on the old farmhouse which is responding with a series of soft creaks. Georgina cocks her head and smiles. Edward John understands the smile.

"Sounds familiar, doesn't it?" he asks her. She nods and he turns to Christopher. "In the war, when this room was my mother's bedsitting room and I slept here when I was off school, I used to love the creaking of this building."

"Me too," Georgina says. "I persuaded Alice to let me sleep in the little room over the porch — the one Kiwi has now. Very draughty it was then — but I loved it. All the other land girls had to share. I was a bit of a spoilt brat, I'm afraid!"

"Clearly!" Christopher laughs, and then adds, "Those were the days! . . . But come on. No more reminiscing about the dear old war. Have we decided what to do with this unfortunate information?"

"Yes, we have," Georgina says, without hesitation. "We do nothing. It's none of our business. Okay, it would probably have been wiser for Ferdie and Dave to have fessed up at the time but . . ."

"But they didn't because that's how they think and the way they are and we have to respect that," Edward John says, aware that Christopher still seems unconvinced by this argument.

"But don't you think someone might —"

"Spill the beans?" Edward John says, interrupting him. "Who would do that?"

"And why?" Georgina wants to know. "After all this time?"

A log shifts in the fireplace. Christopher frowns and runs his fingers through his hair.

"But what about our kids?" he asks Georgina. "They could see we were pretty intrigued by that photograph. Won't they want to know more? Won't they tell people about it? Alice and my pa for instance? If *they* became inquisitive — the whole balloon could go up!"

"We'll play it down," Georgina says. "If the children ask any more questions about it I'll tell them that the snapshot was interesting because it was obviously left here when the war ended and the land girls all went home. Then it can get mislaid, then lost, then forgotten.

I'll deal with that." Christopher is still not entirely convinced. "You're tired, sweetheart," Georgina says. "You've got milking in four hours' time. You need sleep. We don't have to decide anything tonight if you don't want to. But just think of the consequences if we don't keep quiet." Edward John gets to his feet, stretches his long limbs and yawns.

"Better get off," he says. It is a forty-minute drive to his digs in Dorchester where he has recently accepted a junior partnership in an expanding, large-animal veterinarian practice.

"There's always the sofa," Georgina suggests. "I'll fetch some blankets and pillows."

A few hours later Edward John and Christopher drive up to the higher farm where Ferdie Vallance and Mabel are already herding the dairy cows into the milking shed.

"See you soon, matey," Edward John shouts to Christopher as their ways part. "Give my love to my mama, will you? Tell her I've got next Monday off so I'll see her on Sunday night. Plus laundry!"

"Oh, she'll love that!" Christopher laughs.

"She will, actually!" Edward John calls, almost adding "you know what mother's are" and then remembering that, in fact, Christopher does not know.

He takes the Land Rover up through the lanes and out of the valley. The sun is already high and the familiar landscape brilliant with the flora of full summer. Foxgloves, honeysuckle and tall grasses flick past his open window. Buttercups and Schiaparelli-pink campions blaze amongst the frothing meadowsweet that fills the cab with its scent. The happiness that his mother has found with Roger Bayliss pleases Edward John, as does the practical solidity and warmth of Georgina and Christopher's marriage. He is careful with his own emotions, conscious of the damage irresponsibility can cause, but "one day he'll find her, moonlight behind her". In the meantime there is an intriguing girl on one of the farms he regularly visits in the course of his work.

At Lower Post Stone Georgina enters her son's bedroom. He is still sleeping, one arm flung across his pillow, an unravelling Piglet, knitted by Rose Crocker, is propped, as usual, against his bedhead. On his pinboard, amongst pictures of cricketers, footballers, several horses and a springer spaniel named Jim, is the snapshot of Evie.

Since Christopher has brought his wife and children back from New Zealand to occupy Lower Post Stone Farm, news of Evie and Giorgio, married at last and settled in his native Italy, has become infrequent, confined, as the years have passed, to a Christmas letter to Alice Bayliss. One of Giorgio's younger brothers has been widowed, leaving two motherless babies whom Evie has lovingly absorbed into her life and is happily raising, within the heart of the huge, chaotic Zingaretti family. Alice has shown Georgina the latest photographs of what Evie calls "*meie bambini*," the small, dark-eyed boy and girl who sit, one on each of Evie's knees, smiling into the camera lens while Giorgio looks on, approvingly. "Uncle", they call him, "*Zio Giorgio*" and Evie is "*Zia Eva*", their aunt.

Georgina removes the snapshot of the twelve-year-old Evie from the board. Is it her imagination, or is it fading almost visibly as she holds it carefully in her hands? Is it possible, even probable, now that it is exposed again to air, light and changing temperatures, that it will become brittle? Crumble into nothing? Cease to exist? It has already outlived its relevance. Its survival over the past twelve years, has depended, almost freakishly, on circumstances that have resulted in its preservation in a rotting leather wallet, inside Norman Clark's mouldering, military kitbag, abandoned in the apex of an arched bridge across this tributary of the river Exe.

Georgina considers her options, trusting the same instincts and logic that have influenced all her decisions, to clarify and resolve this one.

She makes her way quietly through the familiar farmhouse, conscious of its echoes and of the shadows of those who have peopled it. She crosses the yard, the low sun warm on her skin.

Sitting on the parapet of the bridge, with the familiar, morning sounds reaching her from the yard and the valley beyond it, she accepts that this decision is not hers to make but simply to recognise. She will let the ceaseless passage of the stream, as it moves noisily away, along the valley floor, resolve this story. She looks for a while at the smudged blur that was, once upon a time, Evie. The quiet one. The one no one noticed.

The farmhouse is awake now. Pom emerges and makes for the barn, an egg basket in his hand. Jim, the springer, follows him, sees Georgina, stops, stretches

292

elaborately, fore and aft and comes, wagging towards her. She hears the sound of the Land Rover approaching from the higher farm. Christo, arriving back for his breakfast.

Georgina leans out, over the low parapet of the bridge, the snapshot between finger and thumb. And lets it drop. Watching as it slides down the air, reaches the moving water, hesitates for a moment, like a fallen leaf, on the surface, before the current takes it, turns it, twists it briefly and then draws it down into deeper, fast-flowing water, where it will swiftly disintegrate amongst the river stones.

Muddy Boots and Silk Stockings

Julia Stoneham

It's 1943 and the country is at war. Yet on one remote Devonshire farm the days are not so dark. An unlikely group of land girls are finding out about life, love and loss, forming surprising friendships along the way.

When Alice Todd's husband runs off with another woman, she is forced to find a means to provide for herself and her young son. Accepting a position as a hostel warden at an old Devonshire farmhouse, Alice finds herself looking after a group of ten volunteer land girls.

The job is not as easy as it first seems. Not only does Alice have to deal with the uncompromising farm owner and her resentful and unhelpful assistant Rose, but as her young charges arrive at the farm, she discovers every girl has a story — and some have rather dark secrets.

ISBN 978-0-7531-8186-7 (hb)
ISBN 978-0-7531-8187-4 (pb)

The Girl at the Farmhouse Gate

Julia Stoneham

An evocative story of love, loss and the tragedy of war

It is early spring in 1944 and Allied troops will soon invade northern France. Alice Todd is beginning her second year as warden of a Land Army hostel located in the wilds of Devonshire. Here she has won the affection and confidence of the girls in her charge and found herself caught up in lives which are complex, humorous and sometimes tragic.

ISBN 978-0-7531-8616-9 (hb)
ISBN 978-0-7531-8617-6 (pb)

Alice's Girls

Julia Stoneham

In the last months of World War II, ten Land Girls are serving at Post Stone Farm, under the watchful eye of their warden, Alice Todd. The local Land Army representative had at first been reluctant to give Alice the warden's job, and Roger Bayliss, the farm's owner seemed not to have any confidence in her at all. But she proved herself more than capable of the job and she has won the girls' admiration.

But Alice privately admits that one of the reasons she is so involved with the lives of her girls is that she has worries of her own. Recently divorced and with a ten-year-old son to bring up, she fears for the future. When peace is finally declared, and all Alice's girls make plans for their lives after the Land Army, she too has a decision to make.

ISBN 978-0-7531-8836-1 (hb)
ISBN 978-0-7531-8837-8 (pb)

Divided Loyalty

Roberta Grieve

Forbidden by her father to work alongside him on their Sussex farm, Celia Raines takes a job at the local printing works. When war comes, the farmhands join the forces and Celia hopes to achieve her ambition of being a farmer. But it is too late. Her boss has taken on sensitive work for the Ministry of Information and Celia is forced to stay at her job. Romance blossoms between Celia and Matthew Dangerfield, an RAF friend of her brother Edgar. Both men are engaged on bombing missions but Edgar is beginning to have doubts. Celia and Matt quarrel when he confides in her his concerns about the effect Edgar is having on morale. When Matt's plane is shot down while returning from a bombing mission, Celia knows they may never get the chance to resolve their differences and find happiness.

ISBN 978-0-7531-5388-8 (hb)
ISBN 978-0-7531-5389-5 (pb)